ABSINTHE MINDED

KATHRYN M. HEARST

Cover Artist Dar Albert, Wicked Smart Designs

Editor Holly Atkinson

Proofreader Book Nook Nuts Proofreading

❀ Created with Vellum

ABSINTHE
Minded

For the hottest bartender in New Orleans...
You know who you are.

Gabe

"This has to be a mistake."

I reread the results of the paternity test and glanced from the newborn to the apparent mother of my child. Sure, I'd gone with her to do a cheek swab a few weeks back, but I never thought anything would come of it.

In the time it took me to open my front door and scan the page, my swanky French Quarter townhouse had become the set of the Maury Povich Show—*Gabe Marchionni. You are the father.*

I'd always wanted kids, but not like this, not now, and not with... Let's just say, I'd always imagined I'd have them with Maggie, the one who got away.

"Everything you need is in the bag." Chantal tossed her hair over her shoulder. "Bye, Gabe. Have a nice life."

"That's it? You're leaving?" I motioned to the sleeping infant. "She's too young. She needs a mom. I have no idea what to do with an infant."

"Take her to your parents. They'll be thrilled." The woman I'd dated a few times, almost a year ago, turned on her stilettos. "I have to be at the cruise terminal in fifteen minutes."

"Chantal, wait. You can't be serious." I stalked after her but remembered the baby on my doorstep. Unlike my *ex-whatever-the-hell-she-was*, I wouldn't leave a child alone. "At least stay long enough to tell me how to take care of her."

"I wrote instructions." She waved without bothering to turn her head.

My every instinct screamed for me to go after her. Chantal had abandoned her child, our child, *my child*. What the hell was I going to do with an infant?

I sank to the top step and sat beside the sleeping baby. Head in my hands, I ran through my options and came up empty. One thing was clear. I needed help and I'd need more than books with titles like *Diaper Changing 101* and *Infant Care for Morons*.

"God help you. Looks like you're stuck with me." She was a cute little thing all bundled up in pink blankets. Hints of dark hair peeked out from beneath her baby-beanie, and the cool, New Orleans winter, air had turned her cheeks and button nose rosy. "What's your name?"

The baby didn't reply.

I pulled an envelope from the diaper bag. Chantal had, in fact, left instructions. *Feed and change her when she cries.* That's all she'd written. I resisted the urge to shout obscenities and scanned the birth certificate. My throat tightened. "She named you after me?"

Looking back, I never should have dated Chantal. She was mixed up in a business deal gone wrong with my father.

Our *relationship* had much more to do with physical attraction and my need to rebel than real feelings.

I'd ended things when she'd tripped my *crazy-girl-warning-system*, but nothing could prepare me for this. Not only had she hidden her pregnancy, she'd named our daughter after me. Gabriella Antoinette DuBois.

"How about we call you Ella?" I brushed my fingertips over her head, and my heart rate increased to an allegro. *I'm a father. Mother Mary, give me strength.*

My thoughts drifted to a woman I hadn't seen in over a year and hadn't kissed in four. A woman whose heart I'd broken. Sure, I'd had my reasons, and yes, I'd behaved like a jackass, but I'd always believed we'd end up together.

What would Maggie think about Ella?

I ran my finger over the baby's cheek. She turned her head and opened her mouth as if to nurse. "I bet she'd love you. Does she love me? Not so much."

Five minutes later, I put an end to my wallowing and got my ass in gear. I knew what I had to do, even if it cost me more than my pride. I grabbed my keys and my kid and strapped the car seat into the back of my Porsche. "Ready to meet your grandparents?"

Ella stared at me with a stoic expression that reminded me of my father. If she grew up to be half as much of a pain in the ass as my old man, I was in serious trouble.

"You have nothing to worry about. They'll love you. It's me they're going to kill." I tugged at her seatbelt to make sure it'd locked and slid into the driver's seat.

I could only guess how my parents would react, though I doubted they'd throw me a party. My father had given me and my brother the same lecture a hundred times. *We're*

Catholic. No sex before marriage, but boys will be boys. You screw up and make a kid, you man up and get married.

Hell, my mother hated my brother Joe's girlfriend, an Irish girl from the wrong side of town. But she'd planned the wedding after he'd knocked Rebecca up.

Good thing Chantal left town. I shuddered at the thought of spending the rest of my life with a woman like her.

I drummed a beat on the steering wheel and considered the best way to approach my folks with the news. They'd never turn away their own flesh and blood, but that didn't mean they wouldn't make my life a living hell—and they had the means to do it.

Despite the fact I'd recently celebrated my thirtieth birthday, my parents had me by the short and curlies. They were old-school Sicilian, which meant they controlled nearly every aspect of mine and my brothers' lives, either by guilt or their tight hold on the purse strings. It also meant that the family business went the way of the Capones and Gambinos.

Shocking to most, but I'd grown up in it. Yep, my surprise baby was a mafia princess.

"You okay back there?" I glanced in the rearview to make sure the car seat/carrier hadn't fallen over. *Not for nothing, but rear-facing car seats suck. How am I supposed to know if she turns blue or something if I can't see her?*

With the French Quarter behind me, I turned on St. Charles Street and headed for the Garden District. Driving up Chestnut Street gave me the same sinking feeling as climbing the first hill on a roller coaster. Once I turned into Casa de Marchionni, my stomach would be in my throat until the ride ended—only this would last the rest of my freaking life.

How in the hell did I knock her up? I replayed mine and Chantal's sexcapades. The woman was wild, too wild for me to have risked going in bare. Nope. I was sure I'd suited up, but then how had I won the *less-than-one-percent-condom-failure* lottery?

I parked and hurried to the passenger's side of the Porsche. With the front seat moved as far forward as it would go, I squeezed my upper body into the tight space, but couldn't quite reach the release button. I lifted to the balls of my feet and attempted to close the distance.

My foot slipped and all hell broke loose. I fell. The hard-plastic handle on the car seat hit me in the solar plexus. The baby wailed. And for some ungodly reason the antitheft alarm went off.

Ella's carrier laced over one arm and the diaper bag on my shoulder, I limped through the front door into the pristine white marble of my childhood. "Ma?" I called from the foyer. "Pops? Anyone home?"

Footsteps approached from the direction of the kitchen, too quick to be my mother.

I turned and smiled at Hildie, the woman who had raised me and my five brothers.

"Miss Hildie." I drew her frail body into a half embrace. "Still as pretty as ever."

She arched a brow at the screaming infant. "I never thought I'd see the day when you'd be looking after a baby, and a loud one at that. Where are her parents?"

"She's mine."

White showed all the way around her eyes. "Lord have mercy, your mama didn't tell me you had a daughter."

I leaned closer to keep my voice down. "She doesn't know."

"I'll go get her for you. Go into the parlor and wait." The woman gave the baby one last longing look and hurried out of the room. I knew self-preservation when I saw it. Miss Hildie would keep her distance until the fireworks ended.

I crouched and attempted to free Ella from the straps and buckles of her carrier. Tried and failed. *Seriously, who the hell makes these things? Houdini?*

Evelyn Marchionni stood in the entryway of the parlor dressed in white capris and a matching sweater. She looked as magazine-perfect as the rest of the house.

I forced a smile, but she stared at the baby and made the sign of the cross—a hell of a thing to do after laying eyes on her granddaughter for the first time.

"Hi, Ma. This is Gabriella Antoinette." I stood and motioned to the baby. "Ella, this is your grandmother."

Evelyn took a quick step back, as if trying to keep herself from toppling over.

I resisted the urge to roll my eyes. No need to add more fuel to the fire. Instead, I grinned and waited for her to finish with the dramatics.

"Give me that baby." She held her arms out and tapped her foot.

"I would, but I can't get her out of this thing."

Evelyn sighed the sigh mothers have used to condemn their children since Eve gave birth to Cain and Abel. She shook her head, knelt beside the carrier, and extracted my daughter. The baby on her shoulder, she smacked the back of my head.

"Ow. Jesus."

"And he takes the Lord's name in vain!" Evelyn's Italian accent thickened her words and ruined the illusion of a dainty southern belle. "She's at least a month old and you just now bring her to me? Are you nuts? Is she yours?"

"Yeah, she's mine. I only found out about her an hour ago."

"Of course, she's yours. Look at those eyes. She looks like you." Cooing over the baby, she reached over and smacked me again. "Where's her mother?"

"She's gone. Left Ella with me and took off." I sighed and sat on one of the stiff loveseats.

Evelyn glared until I squirmed. "I take it you two aren't close?"

I shook my head.

"This is going to kill your father, you know." Her voice cracked, but it had nothing to do with the melodrama she'd dished out until then. This was real concern for her husband.

I dreaded the day when my father left this earth. For the usual reasons, of course, but also how my life would change. "How's he doing? What are the docs saying?"

"The same. He refused the chemo." She waved her hand. "This girl you impregnated... Dare I ask if she's Catholic?"

"Atheist."

After whispering a slew of curses in Italian, she turned her face toward the ceiling and prayed—also in Italian. "You will come here and live with us. You're a good boy, but you're like your father...you can't keep it in your pants. You can't raise a child—not a little angel like this one."

"I got it covered, Ma. I just need a little help getting going."

"No way will I let a grandbaby of mine grow up in a bachelor's pad." She lowered her voice as if we were in mixed company. "It's bad enough that Guthrie girl is raising your niece and nephews."

Maggie Guthrie, my brother's sister-in-law, my ex, and the love of my life.

My chest tightened. I hadn't seen her since Joe and Rebecca's funerals, but I'd thought about her every damned day.

Maggie

I ADJUSTED MY BLACK JACKET AND FLUFFED MY HAIR one last time before I pressed the *enter conference* button. Within a couple of seconds, four faces, including my boss, stared back at me from the monitor and then it went blank.

"No, no, no." Panic wrapped its cold hard fingers around my throat. I pressed various keys in rapid succession, checked the connection to the power cord on the laptop and the wall. Nothing. On hands and knees, I crawled under the dining room table and groaned. Someone had almost chewed the cord in half, and I knew who.

I glared at the dog. "Cocoa! What did you do?"

The chocolate lab lifted her head, snorted, and went back to sleep.

Grabbing my phone, I dialed Marlena's cell.

No answer.

I tried again. "Come on, Marlena."

On the verge of a meltdown, I called the office on my way to the garage. "Hello, this is Maggie Guthrie. I have a conference call with Marlena Dupree. I'm having technical difficulties. May I speak to her?"

"One moment, please," the disembodied voice replied.

The duct tape sat on the shelf where I'd left it. Hurrying back to the computer, I stubbed my toe on the chair and had to bite back a groan when the receptionist came back on the line.

"Ms. Dupree isn't in her office. Would you like to leave a message?"

"No. I know. I mean. We were on a conference call."

"Do you know which room she's in?"

"No. Can you find her? She's not answering her cell."

"Of course." Hold music replaced the impatient voice as I dove under the table and wrapped a long strip of tape around the mangled cord. Praying to anyone who would listen, I poked my head out from beneath the table to check the monitor.

Nothing.

"Oh, come on." I pinched the tape tighter, and the screen came to life. I banged my forehead on the table but managed to type my password into the welcome screen. What felt like an eternity later the machine booted up, and I re-entered the virtual conference call.

Four faces stared with varying degrees of concern. Marlena, my boss, spoke first, "Good morning, Maggie. Thank you for joining us. Is everything all right, dear?"

"Yes. Sorry about that, technical difficulties." I smiled at the screen and turned my cell phone to silent beneath the table.

"Very well. Let's start, shall we."

Ignoring the bead of sweat running down my forehead, I squared my shoulders and waited for Marlena to speak.

"Maggie, as you know, the mission of *NOLA Society News* is to inform residents and visitors of the cultural side of New Orleans." Marlena paused to allow the others on the call to nod. "We loved your work when you first joined us..."

Loved? My throat tightened, but my plastic smile remained in place. "Thank you. I love my job."

"Our heart goes out to you, taking on your sister's children. However, your change in circumstances has impacted your columns." Marlena sighed.

"Our readership isn't interested in local family-friendly events," Ted Denning, Director of Marketing, added.

"I've been thinking the same thing. In fact, I have an idea for a new piece." I lied through my teeth.

My life had gone to complete shit in the previous three days. Not only had Ryan, the youngest of my deceased sister's children, come down with an ear infection, I'd received a court summons for yet another custody hearing. Not to mention, my late rent payments and a second notice on the power bill. I desperately needed this job.

I'd figure it out. There was no sense in feeling sorry for myself or asking how this had become my life. Shit happens, even batshit crazy stuff like my sister and her husband dying and leaving me custody of their kids.

Marlena's voice drew my attention back to the monitor. "Maggie, at this point—"

"Nouveau Orleans." I blurted out the first words that tumbled through my head.

"Excuse me?" Ted narrowed his eyes.

I swallowed hard. "The name of my new article, Nouveau Orleans. For years the magazine has covered debutante balls and charity events. Old money is old news. It's overdone. Why not cover the nouveau riche? The younger and sexier side of New Orleans Society."

Ted smirked and the other two people on the call stared. However, Marlena's eyes brightened, and a wicked smile crossed her lips. For my part, I tried to maintain a poker face, but my heart thumped loud enough to be heard through the computer.

"Keep talking." Marlena steepled her fingers beneath her chin.

The gears in my head spun out of control. "Take the Marchionnis, for example. Five surviving brothers, all of whom own profitable establishments in the French Quarter. Then there are the hotels and other companies outside the Quarter owned by the Marchionni Corporation. They host charity events and are involved in the community, yet no one covers them."

"For good reason." Ted's voice rose. "There've been rumors about the Marchionnis since Joe Sr. started buying failing businesses. Most folks think they're tied to the mob."

People in the south loved to gossip and hated outsiders. A Sicilian family buying up half the French Quarter had sprouted as many tall tales as the old myth of vampires living in the attic at Old Ursuline Convent.

"Is this big enough to do a monthly piece?" Marlena leaned closer to the camera.

"There are many young powerful residents in New Orleans." *Thank God. They liked the idea.* All I had to do was close the deal. "My brother-in-law is the late Joe

Marchionni Jr. and Gabe Marchionni is a *friend* of mine. The first piece will be an exposé on the Marchionni family, each of the following months will feature a different brother. When we run out of Marchionnis, I'll move on to other young up and coming leaders in the city."

Referring to Gabe as my friend made my chest hurt. That line about time healing all wounds was crap. I'd thought of him every single day in the four years since he'd dumped me.

"I don't like the name." Ted tapped his pencil to his lips.

"How about, *The Bourbon Street Bad Boys Club?*" I forced a smile. My best friend, Shanna, had coined the term back when I'd first met Gabe. "The Marchionnis' Mardi Gras Gala is always big news. We can piggy-back the article off the event coverage."

"I love it. A little sexist, but it'll work for the Marchionnis." Marlena clapped. "You'll need to research the corporation, their businesses, their community involvement, and their personal lives. I can see the photos now. Those men are seriously sexy, even Papa Joe."

You have no idea. Images of a skin and sweat and black six-hundred thread count sheets flashed through my mind.

Ted glanced over his shoulder and lowered his voice. "Do you think they're connected to the mob? I mean, is it safe to go snooping into their business?"

"That's a good point. Maggie, given your relationship with the family, are you willing to spill the dirty secrets as well as the pretty ones?" Marlena raised a perfectly sculpted brow.

"I seriously doubt they're involved in organized crime, but they wouldn't be the first to play dirty in New Orleans.

Very few leaders in this city are squeaky clean. I'll write the piece as it should be written—truthfully." My voice might have sounded strong, but my stomach roiled and threatened to return my lunch. I hadn't seen Gabe or his brothers since my sister's funeral over a year before. *What the heck did I just get myself into?*

"Do the research. I want a full proposal by the end of the week. Dennis, get legal involved. We don't want to print anything too risqué and lose sponsors. Ted, get with creative. Let's brand this thing—logos, ads, the works." Marlena barked orders like Meryl Streep in *The Devil Wears Prada*. "The Bourbon Street Bad Boys Club. I love it."

After everyone had their marching orders, I closed the laptop and walked into the bathroom in search of antacids. I didn't love my job as much as I needed it. As a freelancer, they allowed me to work from home. The small amount I took from the children's trust funds each month barely paid the bills, and not paying daycare had helped. Sure, I could use more of their money, but I hated feeling like I'd somehow profited from my sister's death. I took one look at myself in the mirror and groaned. *So much for a professional appearance.*

My hair had drooped and my mascara had bled. One shoulder of my jacket had a white and brown smear. The substance looked suspiciously like the peanut butter and fluff sandwich I'd fed my nephew for lunch. Ryan must have wiped his hands under the table. No wonder Marlena had planned to fire me.

The weight of what I'd done settled on my shoulders. While I knew for sure my sister would never marry into the mob, I hated the idea of investigating Rebecca's in-laws. Gabe was an ass, and I loathed his parents, but the rest of the bunch were good guys—even if they hadn't bothered to check on me and the kids in over a year.

The alarm on my cell phone chirped, reminding me to pick up Ryan from the sitter. In another hour, the house would be full of children, backpacks to check, papers to sign, dinner to cook, baths, and pajamas. I'd never thought of myself as mother material and never imagined I'd be raising three children before my twenty-sixth birthday. Sometimes, no most times, life wasn't fair. However, I'd promised three children we'd make the best of a bad situation, and that's exactly what I intended to do.

First things first, I needed back-up, and my bestie just so happened to work for a private investigator.

"I need a favor," I said the moment Shanna answered the phone.

"Hello, to you too." She laughed.

"I'm sorry. It's been one of those days."

"What can I do?"

I drew a breath. "I need some help finding info on the Marchionni Corporation and the brothers."

"Dare I ask why?"

"Marlena pulled my regular article. I have to put together a proposal for something new this week. I'm thinking about a standing piece on new money families in New Orleans, starting with the Marchionnis."

"Are you crazy?"

"Probably."

"I'll look into it." She hadn't mentioned Gabe, but I had a feeling she would soon enough.

"Thanks, Shanna. I have to run." I smiled despite my mood.

"Uh uh, no way. You're on your cell. Take me with you." She sucked in a breath. "Are you planning to see He-Who-Shall-Not-Be-Named?"

Am I? Can I do the story without coming in contact with Gabe? The part of me who needed closure to see him and demand he tell me the real reason he ended our relationship. That, I could handle. The part of me still completely and utterly in love with the big jerk was an entirely different matter.

"Maggie?" Her voice rose. "Tell me you're not going to see him."

I sighed. "I'm not going to see him."

"Why do I have a feeling I'm going to regret doing this?"

"Because you love me, and you worry."

"I do love you, but I worry because this is Gabe we're talking about."

I grabbed my keys and hurried to the car. "Shoshanna, this is business, not personal."

"It must be if you're using my full name."

Gabe

MY MOTHER SHOWED NO SIGNS OF ENDING HER lecture anytime soon. As it was, she'd damned near paced a rut in the travertine floor.

"I don't understand what I did wrong with the lot of you. Why can't you boys find nice Italian girls to settle down with?" Evelyn patted a rhythm on Ella's diapered bottom. "At least you could find a good Catholic girl."

"Ma, Rebecca was Catholic and you know it."

Evelyn pursed her lips and shook her head. "Irish Catholics are *hardly* the same."

"How is Maggie doing?" I knew better than to ask, but my curiosity had always gotten me into trouble.

My mother's temper went from zero to sixty in a heartbeat. German engineering had nothing on Evelyn Marchionni.

"She's too young to handle three kids. Your father and I are taking her back to court next month. I don't know what Rebecca and Joe were thinking." She paused to do the sign of the cross after mentioning my brother's name. "Our lawyers think we'll win this time. She's two months late on her mortgage. What are we supposed to do? Throw our own grandchildren out on the street?"

"It's not a mortgage. You gave Joe and Rebecca the house as a wedding gift." I ran my hands over my head. Joe had made his wishes clear, but since when did something as trivial as a last will and testament ever stop my parents?

"Yes, but she insisted on paying rent."

"You and Pops have no business taking money from Maggie."

"That's a matter for your father." Her chin rose.

I knew better than to fight this battle, not when I had my own problems. From all reports, Maggie had done a great job with the kids. It'd kill her if she lost custody. "Don't be so hard on her."

"Hmmph." Evelyn pulled the baby from her shoulder and kissed her cheek. "Let's go see Grandfather. He's going to love you. Another baby girl to spoil."

"It'd be better if you watch her while I talk to him—"

"Nonsense. You made this mess. You'll deal with the consequences." My mother marched me toward my father's study as if she were taking me before a firing squad—solemn with a chaser of doom. She rushed inside with Ella, leaving me to watch from the door. "Look what your son has brought home. Poor thing. Her mother left her on the doorstep like a bottle of milk."

Giuseppe Marchionni Sr.—aka Papa Joe—went wide-eyed for half a beat before he smiled.

Evelyn held the baby out to my father and smirked. "I told him he should stay here. He needs help. With the hours he keeps, he can't raise a baby."

I sighed, which drew my father's attention. I didn't dare grin, instead I hung my head and walked into the room. "Hey, Pops. Sorry to spring this on you and Ma. I found out about her today."

If the fact I'd become a father surprised him, he hid it well. "What did you name her?"

"Her mother named her Gabriella Antoinette. She doesn't have our last name, but I intend to change that."

Joe Sr. grinned at Ella. A rumbling laugh started in his gut and spilled into the room. "Is that right, *mio piccolo rosa*? That's a big name for a little rose."

"I call her Ella."

"Where's her mother?" Joe's voice remained playful, even if his words didn't.

"She works on a cruise ship. She left today. Said she's not coming back."

Joe's mouth fell open and snapped shut. "Have you called our lawyer?"

"Not yet. I'll speak to Santiago tomorrow."

"Get this taken care of." Joe glanced at his wife. "Eve, leave us to discuss business."

Evelyn scooped the baby from his arms. "Before I go, since my other grandchildren will be under this roof soon, so should Ella."

No Marchionni had ever moved back home, and I wouldn't be the first. My brothers would never let me live it down. "Ma, I just need a little help getting started. I can and will handle this."

She continued speaking as if she hadn't heard me. "If Gabriel's man enough to get some girl pregnant, he's man enough to fix his mistakes. I think he needs to track her down and make this right."

Not believing my ears, I whipped my head back and forth between them. "No freakin' way."

"This is how you speak to your mother?" My father narrowed his eyes. "Sit down."

I'd come here for help with the baby—the same baby Chantal had abandoned. I'd be damned if I allowed anyone to force me to marry a woman I couldn't stand. All I had to do was drop the name Chantal DuBois, and all talk of marriage would end. My father despised her for a myriad of reason, some I knew and some I didn't. Then again, my parents were old-school Sicilian. My mother could guilt the devil into turning down the heat, and my father held the deed to my bar and the strings to mine and my brothers' finances.

Evelyn shot me a warning look, kissed my father's cheek, and left the room. No doubt, she headed for the kitchen to conspire with Hildie. One thing I knew for certain, I'd be stuck here until after dinner. If I got out at all.

As soon as the door closed, Joe leaned to the side and coughed.

The wet gurgle and high-pitched wheeze made my jaw clench. We never mentioned the C-word in this house, but that hadn't stopped the cancer from setting up residence in his lungs. I stood and placed my hand on my father's shoulder.

"Your mother's right," Joe said, waving me away. "You're not going to be able to raise a kid and keep bar hours."

"I know, Pops." I reclaimed the chair. "But I'm not going to marry Ella's mother. I'll figure something else out."

His eyes brightened, but his jaw tightened. He'd thought of a solution to the problem. "You'll kill two birds with one stone and marry Maggie Guthrie. It'll make your mother happy without the two of us having to raise another litter of kids."

I froze in place. "What? I followed your orders. I haven't spoken to her or gone near Joe's place since the funerals. I doubt she'll speak to me, let alone walk down the aisle."

My father believed the wreck that killed my brother and his wife was no accident. At one point, he'd accused Chantal of playing a part in the deaths in some revenge plot over the bad business deal.

"You had a relationship with Maggie. Rekindle it." Studying me, my dad leaned back in his chair.

How the hell would *that* work? She hated me, and with good reason. I'd told her I wanted to end things so she could follow her dreams or some shit, but in reality, I wanted to protect her from my family and our business associates. Maggie was a stubborn woman. She wouldn't blindly follow orders. My brain spun out of control with the logistics of the situation, but my heart started beating the melody of some ridiculous love song.

My father cleared his throat. "I'll put security back on her and the kids."

Security who would report my every move back to him. No-freaking-thanks. "It's been a year. Nothing's happened. No security. You want me to do this. I'll do it my way. I won't let anything happen to Maggie or the kids."

"Your brother said the same thing, and look how well that turned out."

"I know, Pops. I know." I stared at a picture on my father's desk. Papa Joe stood arm in arm with his eldest son, both smiling. After posing for the picture, the two had a falling out that ripped the family apart. Joe Jr. had died before the rift could be repaired. I didn't know what they'd argued about, only that they'd disagreed over a business decision. After the accident, my father refused to discuss it.

"You do this your way, and you're responsible for my grandchildren's safety."

I pressed my lips together. I would have been looking out for the kids already, if he hadn't ordered me and my brothers to stay away from them.

Joe coughed again and folded his arms across his chest. "It's time for you to step up. Take your place in the company."

I'd also done everything in my power to stay on the law-abiding side of the *family business*. Unfortunately, my father's corporation owned my bar—a situation I'd planned to rectify as soon as possible.

"I'll start working with you part-time this week." I held his gaze. "But my personal life is mine, and I'm keeping the bar."

"Find a manager and be here full-time." My father drummed his fingers on his desk—something he did when he negotiated with business partners.

I didn't dare react and risk him having another coughing fit. "It'll take time. I'll work both jobs until I find someone."

"You'll need help with the baby, for when you travel. Marry the Guthrie girl in the next month or you're moving in here. I won't spend the rest of my days on this earth listening to your mother bitch about how her grandchildren are being raised by some Irish tart."

"Pop, I need more than a month—"

"Too damned bad." He slammed his fist on the desk, his face turning an alarming shade of red. "You'll marry her or bring all four of my grandchildren to your mother. Do I make myself clear?"

I couldn't let on that I needed time to work my way back into Maggie's good graces because I'd screwed things up with her years before. "Yes, sir."

"Good. I'd hate to pull the bar and everything else away from you. If you break your mother's heart, so help me God." He paused to hack into a handkerchief. "You've had it too easy, kid. Joe took care of things for you, but he's gone now. Time for you to man-up."

I rubbed the back of my neck to postpone the oncoming tension headache. "I'd like to stay on the legit side of things. It's not like the old days, Pops."

"We do what we have to do." He opened his desk drawer, pulled out an envelope, and tossed it my way.

"What's this?"

"The Lazios are doing better than we expected. We need to up our operations."

The *operations*, as he put it, were killing my profit margin on liquor. We were the only place in the Quarter that didn't accept credit cards. Great if you launder drug money. Not so much if you intended to steer clear of the Sicilian mafia, aka the Cosa Nostra.

"I'll see what I can do, but the new mayor's making noise—"

"I'll make a call. Remind him of our generous campaign contributions."

I glanced at the picture and promised myself I wouldn't cross the line and end up dead. I'd stick around to see Ella grow up.

"Don't look so glum. It's not such a hardship marrying Maggie Guthrie. Men would kill for those..." My father held his cupped hands in front of his chest, mimicking Maggie's breasts.

"Yeah, she's a looker all right." I stood along with my father. I hated the way he spoke about her, and women in general for that matter, but I'd given up trying to change him years ago. We don't choose our parents. All we can do is love them and fight like hell not to turn into them.

Joe barked out a laugh and clamped a hand on my shoulder. "Do it quick. I want to see you married before I go."

"Pops, this custody hearing."

"Will go away when you walk down the aisle."

"Did you buy the judge?"

He clamped his hand on my shoulder. "Smart men do what they can to keep their wives happy. You'll understand soon enough."

Not trusting my voice, I nodded. It bothered me to see my dad so damned frail. In the couple of weeks since Christmas, he'd dropped a considerable amount of weight, his complexion had paled, and his cough had worsened. The demand that I marry Maggie could turn out to be my father's dying wish.

How can I say no? Better yet, how can I convince her to say yes?

4

Maggie

WITH EACH TICK OF THE CLOCK, MY HEART RACED faster. Still in sweats and a ponytail, I had thirty minutes before the babysitter arrived—a half-hour to make myself presentable for my date. It was early in the relationship, but we seemed to have things in common. Plus, unlike the others I'd gone out with, he didn't smell like sour milk or use a calculator to split the check or kiss like a cow.

Admittedly, my standards were low.

The dog went ballistic in the other room. Judging by the tone of her barks, someone or something had stepped into the yard.

"Aunt Maggie, someone's here," Chloe called from the living room. At nine years old, she was allowed to answer the door, but only if I was home and only after she'd run through her safety procedures. "Who is it?"

I hurried to the front room and wrangled the dog.

"It's Uncle Gabe."

My lungs convulsed, sending all my oxygen out of my

mouth. The absolute last person I expected to see stood on my front porch—the kids' uncle, my brother-in-law's brother, otherwise known as my ex-boyfriend.

This could not happen. Not now, not ever. Sure, I planned to write a column about him, but I'd decided to do it without ever setting foot in the same room with the man. I reminded myself of the reasons I hated him, but none of that seemed to matter to my heart.

Chloe barreled on before I'd decided what to do. Her eyes widened, along with her smile. "What's the password?"

"Snicklefritz," Gabe said through the door.

"Wrong!" The girl chewed her lip, likely to keep from laughing.

"Is Maggie home? It's important." His voice lost its humor.

I eased into the foyer and looked through the peephole. Although I had no idea what he wanted, I knew two things...one, I didn't have time for this, and two, it couldn't be good. "We're a little busy, Gabe."

My niece clamped her hands over her mouth and giggled.

"Come on, Mags. I need to talk to you."

I drew a deep breath and squared my shoulders. Before I'd gathered the courage to turn the knob, Chloe threw the door open. The little girl leaped into his arms and hugged his neck so tight it looked painful, though Gabe didn't seem to mind.

"Hey, munchkin."

"I've missed you." Chloe pulled back, grinning.

"Miss you, too." He kissed her cheek before setting her down.

Even Cocoa seemed happy to see him. She sniffed his calves and the baby in the carrier beside him before sitting at attention.

I did a double take at the infant. My brain struggled to make sense of the situation. Gabe. On my doorstep with a newborn who looked like *him*.

"Hi, Maggie." Gabe ran his hand over the back of his neck, with a grin that still made my traitorous stomach do a somersault.

I had to hand it to him. He hadn't changed a bit in the four years since he'd dumped me. Long, dark hair made for caressing, tanned skin made for licking, and those eyes, God, don't get me started on those piercing green eyes. Unfortunately for Gabe, I was immune to his charms.

He reached down for the carrier. "It's been a long time. How have you—"

"What are you doing here?"

"Can we come in?" His voice might have come out strong, but his slumped shoulders and the dark circles under his eyes betrayed him.

Against my better judgment, I held the door open. "Sorry, surprised to see you. Is that your *daughter*?"

He set the carrier beside the couch. "Yeah, she's mine. Her name's Ella."

Chloe settled beside the baby. "Oh, Ella. Like Cinderella. She's so cute."

"Her real name's Gabriella." Gabe bent and scratched Cocoa behind the ears.

Once again, my body revolted against me. The idea that he'd had a baby with someone who'd loved him enough to name their child after him ripped me in two. Then again, this was *Gabe,* the man who'd taken a sledgehammer to my heart four years ago. Gabriel Anthony Marchionni, the oldest surviving Marchionni brother and biggest ladies' man in New Orleans.

He flashed Chloe a smile that most would find sweet, but I didn't trust it. "You got so big. How old are you now, twenty-six? Are you married?"

"I saw you at Christmas. You know I'm nine." She stood and set her hands on her hips. "Aunt Maggie, can I play Xbox?"

"Sure, but let your little brother play, too."

"Come on, Cocoa." Chloe rolled her eyes and ran toward the playroom. Not even a baby could compete with video games.

The dog sniffed Gabe one last time and followed her pint-sized master.

He opened his mouth as if to speak, but clamped it shut and took a step closer to me. Too close, as if he still had a right to invade my personal space.

I eased back. It's not that I feared Gabe, but I knew better than to get within sniffing distance. I'd never forgotten his scent—sandalwood and cedar and sin.

He frowned and glanced around the room. Children's toys, shoes, stacks of mail cluttered the room. A half-dead Christmas tree sat in the corner surrounded by a halo of dry needles.

The longer he looked, the more my cheeks heated until my embarrassment dissolved into anger. What gave him the right to judge my housekeeping skills? Sure, I wasn't perfect, but I'd damned sure made lemonade out of a barrel of rotten lemons.

He shoved his hands in his jean pockets. "I...uh..."

"Ryan had an ear infection. We haven't gotten much sleep this week." My words had come out far more defensive than I'd intended.

"Is he okay?"

"Yeah, the antibiotics finally kicked in." I cleared piles of folded laundry from the couch and motioned for him to sit.

"What's the story behind the tree?"

"Chloe asked if we could keep it a while longer. This is their first Christmas without their parents. How could I say no?"

"You couldn't...I guess." Gabe stared at *me* the same way he had the living room—assessing the mess.

In bleach-stained sweats and an oversized T-shirt, I looked like I'd rolled out of bed—at dinnertime. I ran a hand over my head to smooth the loose strands back into my ponytail. "I was about to get in the shower."

"Need someone to wash your back?" He flashed me a crooked smile.

An unwelcome memory of our previous bath time activities danced through my mind. *Four years. It's been four years, and he acts like we're still a couple.* "I'm seeing someone. We have a date. I have a date tonight, with my boyfriend."

"A date?" He tilted his head.

"Yes, Gabe. That's what normal people do, go on dates." *All right, it was the third time I'd gone out with this guy, but we'd talked for hours on the phone, often late at night. That had to count for something... Nevertheless, Gabe didn't need to know any of that.* I sat on the edge of the love seat, though every fiber of my being screamed to get him out the door.

"Right." Gabe stared for a moment, sighed, and looked at his hands. "Can Ella and I stay here for a couple weeks?"

"Here? Why? I mean your place is fifteen minutes away." My mouth went dry. Was he serious? No way could Gabe-*freaking*-Marchionni live in the same house as me and the kids. He was my ex, and much to my horror, my body liked the idea of having him under my roof—a lot.

He met my gaze. "I'd like to spend some time—"

"With the kids? Really? It's been a year since their parents died, and none of their so-called uncles have bothered to visit them." I had no idea why I blasted him, but I refused to take it back.

"I was grieving, too. And I've seen them at my folks..."

"We were all grieving."

Gabe sighed. "You're right. I should have been there for them after the accident."

"Why come here? Why not go to your parents?"

"My father's sick."

The sadness in his voice made me second guess myself. "I'm sorry. I heard that he's ill, and he didn't look good the last time I dropped the kids off."

He sat on the couch, rested his elbows on his knees, and bowed his head. "I'll be taking over the business soon."

The business? What about his bar? He loves that place. I clasped my hands to keep from fidgeting, or worse, touching him. "Where's Ella's mother?"

"Not in the picture. It's a long story."

"I have a few minutes." I told myself I asked because I needed information for the article. My curiosity had nothing to do with jealousy. Too bad I didn't believe my own lies.

"I met her at a hospitality event in town. Went out a couple of times, nothing serious. She started acting strange, and I ended things. Then a couple of weeks ago she showed up demanding I take a paternity test." He laughed, a hollow sound that had nothing to do with amusement. "I thought no way it's mine. This afternoon, she handed me the test results, a diaper bag, and the baby."

I held up my hand and took a minute to process what he'd said. "She left the baby with you?"

"Said she didn't want to be a mother and left." His expression reminded me of Cocoa begging to come inside.

Nope. No sad faces. No belly rubs. No feeding strays. I turned my head. Looking into his green eyes felt like looking into the face of a cobra—lulling, mesmerizing, deadly. I didn't know if I wanted to slug him or cry. I went with the safer choice, anger. "And the first thing you do is come here?"

"I figured since you are so good with the kids, you—"

I stood and backed away from him and the infant. "No. No way. I'm not taking responsibility for another kid. Rebecca's three are enough. Jesus, Gabe. What do you think this is? The Baby Humane Society?"

"It's not like that." He grinned. "I'm planning to stay here, too."

Part of me wanted to grab him by the ear and throw him out. I refused to entertain what the other part of me wanted with kids present.

Gabe sighed and pushed to his feet. "Look. You need

help with the bills and to get my folks off your back. I need help with Ella. It's a win-win."

A win-win my ass. It'd taken me almost two years to get over him. I'd be damned if I'd put myself through that again. "I can't do this with you."

5

Gabe

My God, how did I let this woman go? They say contrasts are sexy, and I couldn't agree more. Memories of us flooded my mind. My tan hands on her pale skin, her blonde curls and my dark hair spread out on a pillow, her soft curves against my hard... Sucking in a breath, I forced myself to make a U-turn on Memory Lane and focus on the woman in front of me.

Beauty, brains, and one hell of a temper, she wore her emotions like the sky wore clouds. One look, and I knew Hurricane Maggie was about to make landfall.

I rested my hands on her shoulders. "Mags, please. I'm sorry for the way things ended between us, but I have no clue how to take care of a baby, and my place in the Quarter isn't exactly child proof."

"Get a nanny. You can afford it."

"It'll take time to find someone. Give me two weeks. Enough to get me started." *And long enough to convince you how right we are for one another.*

"Who's running the bar while you're here?"

"My cousin Jessie until I hire a manager."

As if on cue, Ella squirmed and made unhappy noises.

Maggie raised a brow and nodded to the baby.

"Please." I folded my hands and dropped to one knee. Cheesy, I know, but desperate times called for cheddar. "I'm in deep here. I can't even figure out how to get her out of the car seat."

She closed her eyes and shook her head. "You have four younger brothers. How's it possible you're so clueless with children?"

"Not children, just babies." I hated feeling so damned helpless.

"Two weeks, no more."

"Thank you." I moved in for a hug.

Maggie blocked me by squatting and unfastening the buckles and straps holding Ella in the seat. She brought the baby to her shoulder. "I have a *boyfriend*, so don't even think about getting physical. I'm not your nanny, maid, chef, or friend. Do I make myself clear?"

"Did I hurt you that bad?" As usual my mouth got ahead of my brain.

"Don't flatter yourself. Ugh, she's wet." Maggie handed Ella to me.

I'd used port-a-potties that smelled better than the kid. Her diaper weighed more than she did and had leaked through her clothes.

"Change her in the bedroom. I need to cancel the sitter *and* my date. I can't leave you alone with four kids." She spun and walked toward the kitchen.

I adjusted Ella to prevent the mess from seeping into my shirt. "That's crazy. Go out. I'll watch them."

"Isn't learning to take care of a child the reason you're here? I'm canceling the date." She jabbed her finger into my chest. "I want to toss you out on your perfectly sculpted backside, but I can't do that to Ella. She didn't ask her mother to abandon her with a class-A asshole."

I sucked in a breath and took a step back. I'd handled our breakup like a coward. She had every right to her anger, but that didn't make it easier to swallow.

Rather than continuing the argument, I winked. "Nice to know you still think I have a nice ass."

She glared.

Zach, my oldest nephew, came down the hall and did a double take. "Uncle Gabe? What are you doing here?"

I clamped a hand on his shoulder. "I'm going to stay here for a couple of weeks."

"That's great." The teenager motioned to Ella. "Whose baby?"

"She's mine."

"Holy sh—" He gave Maggie a sheepish grin. "I mean, holy cow, you have a kid?"

"I could use some help tonight." I nodded toward the pissed off woman. "Mags has a date."

She sucked in a breath and shook her head. "He's busy with homework and needs to practice his sax."

"Naw, that's cool. I don't mind helping." He poked around in the fridge.

I shifted Ella to my shoulder and wished I hadn't. Urine soaked into my shirt. "See? Zach and I can handle the kids."

"Okay. I'll go." She folded her arms.

I turned my head before she caught me staring at her chest. "Which room do you want me and Ella in?"

Maggie glanced at the baby and sighed. "I'm in the guest room. You can take the master."

"Can she sleep in the bed with me?"

"Uh, no, but Ryan's crib is still in there. He doesn't use it anymore." She snatched her cell phone from the counter and headed for the back of the house.

"You sure?"

"Yeah, it's fine. Let me clear it out."

Unsure what to do, I trailed behind her. Better to keep an eye on her to make sure she didn't start overthinking the situation and throw us out on the street.

Maggie tossed a towel on the floor and took the diaper bag from my arm. "Lay her down."

I knelt and placed Ella in front of her. Maggie had changed since the last time I'd seen her. She smiled less, and the twin wrinkles between her brows had deepened. Raising three kids hadn't been completely unkind. She'd filled out in ways that made me want to slide my hands beneath her T-shirt and explore her new curves.

"Use a wipe, even if she's wet. No powder, no ointment, unless she has diaper rash." She did some sort of ninja move with the diaper.

"Wait, slow down and do that again."

She gave me an impatient look that reminded me of my mother. "It's simple. Put the clean diaper under her bottom before you pull out the dirty one."

"Got it." *I didn't have it.* In fact, I didn't have any clue how she'd pulled it off.

"She should be eating every three to four hours, but don't wake her to feed her. She'll let you know when she's hungry." She pulled a clean pair of pajamas out of the bag and dressed Ella. "Follow the directions on the formula can to make her bottles. They need to be body temperature. Put the bottle in hot water, don't use the microwave. Always test the milk on the inside of your wrist before you give it to her."

"Got it." I lifted my daughter into my arms.

Maggie opened her mouth as if she had something to say but bit her lip.

"Thanks."

She put the wipes back into the bag and pulled out the envelope with Ella's birth certificate. "What's this?"

"Read it. Tell me if it looks legit." As much as I wanted the documents to be bogus, I doubted they were.

Maggie's frown deepened with each page. "They seem that way, but you should call the lab."

"I'll have my attorney look into it, maybe run a second test to be sure."

"Do it soon, before you get more attached." She glanced at the clock and sighed. "I use the master bath. I'll move my stuff out later, but I don't have time to do it right now. I need to get dressed."

Memories of the two of us in my shower hardened my cock—the bastard always did have bad timing. "We can share."

"I'll use the one in the hall." She walked to the door and turned. "You're sure you can handle this?"

Hell no, I'm not sure. "We'll be fine."

She smiled and hurried to her room.

By the time I walked into the kitchen to dump the filthy clothes and diaper into the trash, all three kiddos had converged at the bar.

Chloe cocked her head. "Uncle Gabe, why were you and Aunt Maggie arguing?"

"Adults do that sometimes."

Zach snickered. "Kids do it too. Mind your business, Chloe."

She huffed. "Whatever, bonehead."

The teen glowered at his sister.

I grabbed a bottle of water from the fridge. "All right, munchkins. What's on the agenda for tonight?"

"Jammie party!" Ryan pumped his fist like a three-year-old rock star. "Woot Woot Woot!"

Zach held up his hands. "Nothing personal, but I've got homework."

Chloe motioned for me to come closer and lowered her voice. "Can we stay up past eight and have junk food?"

I glanced over my shoulder as if to make sure no one stood behind me. "It's not a party without pizza and root beer."

A grin split the girl's face. "And ten o'clock bedtime?"

"Sounds reasonable."

"I'm out. Yell if you need me." Zach retreated to his room.

Maggie rushed into the living room in a whirlwind of pink. Her lips, her dress, even her toes were varying shades of girlie. She looked good. Too good.

"Wow, Aunt Maggie, you look pretty," Chloe said.

"Pretty." Ryan nodded.

My chest tightened. Maggie had surpassed pretty and gone straight to gorgeous. So much so, I had a sudden urge to tell her to stay home. Instead, I flashed her my signature grin. "Beautiful."

"Thanks." She blushed, and once again, my cock sat up and took notice.

I walked to the fridge in search of a beer.

She kissed Chloe and Ryan's cheeks. "Are you guys okay with Gabe watching you? I'll only be gone a couple of hours."

Chloe nodded and glanced at me with big doe eyes. "We are going to have a pajama party."

Maggie sighed, obviously rethinking her decision to leave. "I love pajama parties. Maybe I should stay?"

Yes. Stay. We'll have a private party, sans the pajamas. I closed the distance between us and set my hand on the small of her back. Ushering her toward the door before I changed my mind, I whispered, "They already told me you don't allow junk food and bedtime's at eight o'clock. Nothing personal Mags...but your idea of a party sounds like a downer."

Her eyes flashed, and she turned, likely to tell me what I could do with my downer, only to be silenced by the giggling behind me. "Fine, but make sure Ryan doesn't drink too much, or he'll soak through his nighttime Pull-Ups, and you'll be the one stripping wet sheets in the morning."

I winced. My first adventure with Ella's diaper had scarred me. I didn't want to contemplate how much piss a three-year old would produce.

She seemed to have enjoyed my reaction, because she flashed me her first real smile since I'd arrived. "I'll be home by ten. Do you still have my cell phone number?"

"Stay out as long as you want. And yes, I have your

number." I held the door for her and followed her to the porch.

She hesitated. "Don't let them talk you into turning the Christmas tree on."

"Are you kidding? That thing would go up like a Roman Candle. You know it's February, right?"

"Yes, smartass, I do. But I've been busy." She stared for a beat. "Try not to spoil them too much. You're visiting. I'm the one who will have to un-spoil them when you go back to your life."

I'm not going anywhere, sweetheart. "Have fun, Maggie."

6

Maggie

I burst through the doors of the sushi bar and straight into a crowd. I elbowed and excused my way through the sea of people to the hostess stand.

The girl, who looked too young to have a job, let alone wear a top that revealed half her breasts, smiled. "We are on a two hour wait."

"I'm meeting someone." I snagged a tissue and blotted the sweat from my forehead. "His name is Justin, Justin Trudeau."

She covered her mouth to hide her grin.

Surprised someone her age would recognize the name, I leaned closer and lowered my voice. "Not *that* Justin Trudeau. He has an unfortunate name."

Confusion crossed her features, but she shook it off and checked her list. "I'm sorry, but I don't have him on the list."

"Maybe it's under Maggie Guthrie?" I checked the time on my cell. I'd arrived ten minutes late.

"I don't have you either." She stared at my eyebrows.

"The original time was seven-thirty. We rescheduled for eight." My voice went shrill.

She motioned to the crowded dining room. "You're welcome to take a look."

The man behind me grumbled under his breath.

"Thank you." I hurried into the main dining room and spotted Justin near the back.

He turned and smiled, though it didn't reach his eyes. Evidently, he didn't like to be kept waiting.

"Sorry I'm late. New sitter." I bit my lip to keep from apologizing again.

"You're not sick, are you?" He leaned back as if to put distance between himself and my imaginary germs.

"No, I'm fine." I motioned for the server, who ignored me.

"I ordered for both of us. The food should be out soon." Justin gave me a pointed look and wiped his forehead.

"Oh. Um. Did you remember I don't like raw fish?" I hated it when others ordered my food.

"Trying new things is good for you." He reached for my hand. "It's crunch time at work. I'll be working around the clock. We should get away next weekend. Go to the coast and get some sun?"

I jerked back, almost knocking over the soy sauce in the process. This was our third time out together, definitely not long enough to discuss overnight dates. "I can't next weekend. Chloe has a dance recital coming up, which means extra practices. Maybe we can do it after tax season?"

Justin stared at me but somehow never met my gaze. "I think it's great you're such a good mother to those poor kids."

I nodded, dreading the speech. Next, he'd say the inevitable "but" followed by a gentle break up.

"They're lucky to have someone like you caring for them."

"It doesn't bother you that I put the kids first?"

"Why would it bother me?" He eased back to allow the server to put the food on the table.

"You'd be surprised how many guys don't want to date a single mother." I surveyed the various rolls, all of which appeared to contain raw fish.

"You should take time for yourself. Relationships require work. All relationships." His eyes darkened and traveled to my chest. "In fact, why don't we get this to go?"

I forced a laugh. He'd pushed to take our relationship to a physical level since our first date. I thought he'd gotten the message that I intended to take things slow, but it seemed I was wrong about a lot of things. "So... will this be our last date for a while?"

"That depends on your feelings about take out." He wiggled his brows.

I didn't have men beating down my door, but ugh. What a jerk. My thoughts drifted back to Gabe. As much of a horn-dog as he was, he'd never put me in this kind of situation.

"Maggie?"

"I don't know..." *What am I saying? The answer is no. I'm absolutely not ready for sex.* An image of Gabe's body moving over mine popped into my head. *Where the heck had that come from?* "I can't tonight. I have a new roommate."

"You let someone move in?"

"Sort of. My brother-in-law and his daughter are staying at the house for a couple weeks."

Justin arched a brow.

"He's in a rough spot." I stuffed a piece of sushi in my mouth before I said anything else. The flavor of dead fish hit my tongue and curdled my stomach. As discretely as possible, I spat the sushi into my napkin.

"Is this the brother-in-law that dumped you?" Justin curled his lip, but I couldn't tell if my manners or my roomie had caused the reaction.

I nodded and took a swig of water.

Justin pushed back from the table. "I don't think that's a good idea."

"Me either, but it's short-term."

Justin waved his hand, dismissing the topic. "Let's go."

"Justin, I can't—"

"That's bullshit." He shot to his feet and tossed his napkin on the table as if throwing down a gauntlet. "I won't share you with another man. Come with me now or we're over."

People stared and whispered.

I wanted to crawl under the table and hide, but more than that I wanted to punch Justin Trudeau in the balls. He might as well have painted a huge red *A* on my chest.

"Maggie?" He thrust his hand in my face.

I forced a smile. "Stop at the twenty-four-hour pharmacy on the way to your place."

He flashed me a triumphant smile. "I have plenty of condoms."

"How about lube? I hear it helps when jerking off."

He turned and stormed out.

I hung my head and fought to keep my emotions in check. Not that I was sad about the breakup—he could good and truly go screw himself. These were angry tears.

The waitress brought a to-go container and the check. Not only had he demanded sex, he'd left me to pay for food I couldn't stand.

I snatched my napkin from the table to dry my eyes and the half-chewed piece of sushi fell into my cleavage. Let's just say, the tears started and didn't stop until I was safely in my car.

I had nowhere to go and no one to see, but I couldn't go home. I'd rather sit in my car eating cheeseburgers than share my latest disaster with Gabe.

I'd loved him once upon a time. Heck, I thought we'd eventually end up married. For a year, we were the couple everyone envied, if a couple is what you call a whirlwind romance with a scorching hot older man that ended with him giving me a lecture on chasing my dreams, followed by him ghosting me.

I hurried to my car and did what any woman would do in my situation. I called my best friend.

Shanna picked up on the fourth ring. "Hey, Maggie. I thought you had a date with the Mr. Short, Pasty, and Boring?"

"I did..." I'd called for advice, but now that I had her on the line, I didn't know where to start. "Can I come over?"

"Sure, but you hate the French Quarter. Want me to come to you?"

"No. I'll be there in fifteen minutes." I disconnected before she asked me any questions. Some things needed to be discussed face to face.

Thanks to traffic and drunken tourists, it took me a half hour to reach Shanna's condo on Chartres Street. She was right when she said I hated the Quarter, but it wasn't the crowds that bothered me—it was the memories. I'd avoided the area as much as possible since Gabe and I had broken up.

"There you are!" Shanna called from her postage-stamp sized balcony.

I trudged up the flight of stairs and met her at her door. "Sometimes I hate my life."

She took one look at me and covered her mouth, much in the same way the hostess at the sushi bar had. "Oh, honey. You've got a little something..."

"What?"

Shanna pulled bits of tissue from my forehead.

I bit my lower lip to stop it from quivering. That's what the receptionist was laughing about! Justin, the jerk had let me sit through dinner with bits of Kleenex hanging from my eyebrows?

She draped an arm over my shoulder and guided me to her couch. "You look like you could use a drink."

"I have to drive home."

"Okay, but alcohol is why God created ride shares." She plopped down beside me. "What's going on?"

"Justin dumped me because I wouldn't go home with him."

"Correct me if I'm wrong, but this is the guy you said had a tongue like an oversaturated sponge?"

"No, that was the one before Justin." I grinned despite my crappy night.

"I can't keep up with them all." She wiggled her brows.

"What's there been? Ten?"

"Three since He-Who-Shall-Not-Be-Named dumped me, and two of them never got past the first date." I kicked my shoes off and drew my knees to my chest.

"Don't let it get you down. This is New Orleans, there are almost as many men as there are rats." She waved her hand. "You were obviously too good for him."

"I won't miss introducing him."

"Yeah, no kidding. Too bad he didn't look like the other Justin Trudeau." She gave my shoulder a squeeze. "Dating sucks, but at least you got back on the horse."

"I guess." I hadn't ridden anything, equine or otherwise, in four years—a fact that brought me to my next problem. "Gabe Marchionni is babysitting."

Shanna laughed as if waiting for the punchline. When I failed to deliver, she said, "At your house? Gabe, the man who we both hate, is at your house with your kids?"

"They're his niece and nephews too." The defensiveness in my voice surprised me.

She stood, went into the kitchen, and returned with a glass of wine. "Spill it."

I told her everything—well, almost everything. I left out the part about how certain body parts had practically melted at the sound of his voice. "I should go home, right? I mean, it's crazy to leave him alone with the kids."

"Don't you dare. He deserves whatever hell they give him tonight."

Shanna had a point, but worst-case scenarios played through my mind. "They shouldn't get attached to someone who isn't going to be around for long. They've had enough loss."

"I didn't say you should let him stay. I guarantee, four hours alone with the Marchionni brood, and he'll run home to Mommy."

"You're probably right." I wanted to call and check in, but I couldn't bring myself to move.

"I am one hundred percent right." She downed half her glass. "You're already second guessing yourself. That man is trouble on two legs."

Two long, muscular legs... "You're right. I'm asking him to leave tomorrow."

"No. You're telling him to leave."

I nodded, but I knew I wouldn't do it—not when it meant throwing a newborn baby out with him. "Shanna, I need a favor."

"Normally, I'd say anything, but I have the feeling this had something to do with Gabe."

"It does. I need you to do some digging on a woman named Chantal DuBois. Birthdate is August 21st, 1989."

"Mind telling me what this is about?"

"She's his baby's mother."

"How do you know Gabe's baby mama's birthdate?"

I bit my lip and hung my head. "Ella's birth certificate and the paternity test results were in the diaper bag."

"You were snooping?" Shanna choked out a laugh.

"No, I wasn't snooping. He asked me to look at it to see if I thought it looked counterfeit. I can't help it if I remember details." Some people called it a photogenic memory, but I disagreed. My talent only worked with dates and names—a useful skill in history class and trivia nights, not much good for anything else.

Shanna grabbed her phone and hit a couple of buttons.

"Give me her info again."

I gave her Chantal and Ella's information.

She smirked. "Gabriella Antoinette? He named his kid after himself?"

"The mother named the baby. Anyway, can you do some digging and see what you can find out about Chantal DuBois?" I reached for her wine and took a sip.

Shanna refilled the glass. "Such as?"

"Where she is. Who she is. Anything. I need to make sure he's telling me the whole truth. I mean, what kind of woman abandons her baby?"

"I think you should ask yourself, what kind of guy sleeps with someone who would abandon her baby?"

I'd expected Shanna to be hostile toward Gabe but not this hostile.

"I'm sorry. Sure, I'll see what I can find. Anything else I should know?"

"Gabe's going to have his attorney check with the lab that did the paternity tests. I can't think of anything else right now."

"I'll look into this and get the information you need on the Marchionni Corporation, but I'm worried about you."

I thought back to the dark circles under Gabe's eyes and how defeated he'd seemed. "I'm a big girl. I can handle myself around him."

"Uh huh."

"I'm not ready to go home. Let's binge-watch something funny." I tugged Shanna's throw blanket off the back of the couch and settled in. "You're right. A few hours with the kids and Gabe will run for the door."

"If not, I'd be happy to tell him to get lost."

7

Gabe

I SURVEYED THE LIVING ROOM. WITH THE EXCEPTION of the mess, the house looked the same as it had before my brother died. A novel sat on the table beside Joe's leather chair. A scrap of paper marked the place where the reader had stopped. *Too bad my life doesn't have a bookmark telling me where to begin again.*

Chloe and Ryan had sprawled out on a blanket to watch cartoons. Not that I had much time to watch television, but Scooby Doo remained one of my favorites. I settled into the couch to enjoy the goofy dog and his stoner owner.

A split second later, Chloe groaned and covered her face. "Ryan, is that you?"

He shook his head and pointed at Ella.

I winced. "Again?"

It had to happen sooner or later, but I'd preferred later... like after Maggie came home. Scooping the baby in my arms, I went to find reinforcements. "Zach?"

"Yeah?" a voice called from inside the room.

I poked my head inside and grinned. It looked like a

laundry bomb had exploded. Clothing covered every surface including the bed. "Hey man, can you help me with something?"

"Sure. What's up?" Zach blinked a few times as his eyes adjusted to the light in the hallway. At thirteen, he was as tall and lanky as his father had been at that age.

"I need a hand with Ella's diaper."

"So I smell." Zach laughed. "I'll be the wingman, but you're piloting this one."

I laid Ella down on another towel and mentally prepared for battle. Drawing a deep breath, I unsnapped her onesie.

Zach pulled a diaper and wipes from the bag and placed them beside me. "You got this."

"It's coming out the sides." I reached and retreated several times, unsure where to touch her.

"How long has it been since you changed her?" Zach searched through the bag and pulled out tiny pajamas with feet.

"Maggie changed her before she left." I opened the dirty diaper and swayed away from the odor. "My God."

"Dude, that's gross. What are you feeding her?" Zach covered his face.

"I don't know. Formula, I guess."

"She needs a bath, but we need one of those baby tub things."

It seemed like I needed a lot of *things*...changing tables, bathtubs, nose plugs. "I can hold her over the sink while you spray her down."

Zach motioned to me. "Let's use wipes for now. Maggie will know what to do when she gets home."

My hands felt too large for such a small baby. I couldn't figure out how to clean her without going elbow deep in shit. After several attempts, I gave up and dove in. "Is it supposed to smell like that? Why's it green?"

"I don't know. Ryan's stinks pretty bad." Zach took a step back.

"Google it." I pulled more wipes from the container. At this rate, I'd run out before dawn.

The kid whipped out his phone. "This is disturbing."

"Yeah, tell me about it." I couldn't decide if it was better to breathe through my nose and smell it, or my mouth, and risk the odor sticking to the back of my throat.

"No look." He shoved his phone in my line of vision. Pics of baby shit in a rainbow of colors filled the screen.

"Not helping." My gag reflex took over.

He chuckled. "I'm still looking."

Once I had Ella clean, I slid a new diaper under her butt and fumbled with the tabs. It looked looser than the one I'd taken off, but it stayed on. I eased clean PJs under her and stuffed her arm into a sleeve.

Ella cried until she shook, and her face turned an odd shade of magenta. "She's turning purple."

Zach helped me align the snaps along the inside of her legs. "They do that when they are pissed. She's breathing, otherwise she wouldn't be screaming."

"True. Other than the images, did you find anything online?"

He picked her up and settled her against his shoulder. "Two webpages said smelly stools could be a food allergy. Maybe she's allergic to milk?"

Ella quieted to whimpers and hiccupped breaths.

"We should call Maggie." I fished my phone from my pocket.

"No, I'm sure she'll be fine. Maggie doesn't go out much. We shouldn't bug her over poop."

I followed him into the kitchen. If my brothers found out I'd asked the kid for help, they'd never let me live it down, but man-oh-man, was I grateful. "Should I feed her?"

"Yeah, good idea." Zach traded me the baby for a bottle of water and a can of formula.

The instructions seemed simple enough. "This is a four-ounce bottle. The directions say two scoops. I mix drinks for a living. I think I can handle that."

"You have to warm it in hot water." Zach supervised as I made my first meal for my daughter.

I remembered Maggie said to test the temperature on the inside of my wrist. "I think it's good. Now what?"

He took the bottle and brushed the rubber nipple across her lips until Ella got to work. "See, nothing to it."

I couldn't help but smile. I'd made my first bottle, and she seemed to like it. "Thanks. I'm clueless with this stuff."

"You don't have a lot of clothes for her. They go through a lot in a day. Plus, there's poop on the blankets in the carrier."

"I'll put the dirty stuff in the washer." I peeked around the corner at Chloe and Ryan, and glanced back to Zach.

"You need special baby soap." He laughed, shaking his head. "You really are clueless."

"Do me a favor and don't tell your uncles." I wondered if Ella would survive her first day in my care. "How come you know so much about babies?"

"I helped my mom out with Ryan when she had the

baby blues. Do you want to try?" He held the baby up to me.

"Sure." I fumbled to settle Ella into my arms but managed to coax her into finishing most of the bottle before she fell asleep.

"We should try to put her in the crib."

I followed Zach down the hall to Joe and Rebecca's room. The space looked the same as it had before they died, right down to the wedding photo on the nightstand. Why hadn't Maggie changed anything? I'd be sleeping in a mausoleum.

The kid took Ella, laid her on her back, and lifted the side of the crib.

"Does she need a pillow?" I watched her sleep and wished I could crawl in with her. It had been one hell of a day.

"Not unless you want her to suffocate, and you shouldn't use a blanket either. Her feetie-jammies will keep her warm." Zach patted my shoulder. "It's not hard, once you know the rules."

"Thanks again, I owe you one." I pinched the bridge of my nose to stave off a headache. "One down, two to go."

"Those two are easy. Ryan needs a bath, but you have to sit with him. Chloe's attitude will drive you nuts, but she can shower by herself. Make sure they brush their teeth, and Ryan has to pee twice before bed, once after he brushes his teeth and again after you read him a story. Don't give him anything to drink or he floods the bed."

"I can handle that. Listen. I'm sorry I haven't seen you much since your dad died."

Zach shrugged. "You're busy. We see you on holidays at

Grandma Evelyn's. It's all good."

"Are you still playing guitar?"

"Yeah, plus sax in the marching band."

"We should jam sometime. Next time I go home, I'll get my guitar."

"We should do it at your place. Maggie freaks out if I play too loud."

"Duly noted." I returned the living room to check on the other two munchkins.

Maggie had done a remarkable job with the kids, but the house made me claustrophobic. She had piles of stuff on every available surface. I owed her one, a big one. I might not know anything about babies, but I could clean with the best of them.

"All right, troops. Gather around. We are going to do something nice for Maggie." I rubbed my hands together as they approached. "Ryan, pick up your toys, and put them in the playroom."

Ryan looked at me as if I'd grown a second nose. "Why?"

"Because Zach can't vacuum with toys on the floor."

Zach came down the hall. "Wait. How did I get sucked into this?"

"What do I do, Uncle Gabe?" Chloe beamed.

Pretending to consider her question, I tapped my chin. "You can put these clothes away. At least get them to the right bedroom, if you don't know where they go."

To my surprise, the kids got to work without being told twice. I started with the dishes. The tactical position gave me a central location to keep an eye on the munchkins while they worked.

The stacks of mail came next. I sorted what looked like household bills into one pile, personal mail in another, and junk in the garbage.

The kids put away their backpacks, extra shoes and coats. Once Zach vacuumed the fallen needles from the floor, the Christmas tree seemed to stand prouder. The thing really needed to go, but otherwise the place looked good.

I glanced at the clock. We didn't have much time before Maggie came home. "Bath time."

"No bath!" Ryan made a break for it.

I grabbed him around the middle before he could escape. "Oh no you don't, little man."

Giggling and squirming, Ryan squealed, "I want a shower."

I glanced at Zach and quirked a brow. He shook his head.

"Bath it is." I tossed the boy into the air, catching him under his arms. "Chloe, take a shower in Maggie's bathroom."

A devilish expression crossed her face. Judging by the piles of lotions and potions, I doubted Maggie allowed her to shower in the master bathroom. Deciding to pick my battles, I let it go. How much trouble could she possibly get into?

"Zach, take my keys and get the black checkbook out of the glove compartment. Make sure you lock it and don't even think about a joy ride." I carried Ryan down the hall. This parenting thing wasn't so bad.

Fifteen minutes later, I had the little man scrubbed down and in his PJs. The finish line was within my grasp.

All I had to do was supervise teeth brushing and make sure Ryan emptied his bladder.

I walked into the living room and all hope of a moment's peace evaporated.

Chloe hadn't taken a shower. Makeup covered every inch of skin on her face, including her ears. She'd painted her nails, though I couldn't tell if she'd used polish or a paint roller. She wore one of Maggie's silk robes, also splattered with makeup, and a pair of her high heels. The girl looked like a miniature vampire, drag queen.

"Am I gorgeous, darling?" She preened.

For the first time in my life, I understood why animals ate their young.

"Is that nail polish?" Stupid question, the scent of chemicals hung in the air.

Chloe nodded.

"Are you allowed to play in Maggie's makeup?" Also a stupid question. The woman didn't allow junk food. She'd never consent to *this*.

Chloe bit her lower lip and shook her head.

"Go take a shower and wash that off your face before Maggie gets home. I'll help you with the nail polish when you're done."

Chloe started toward the master bedroom, but I put my hand on her head and pointed her in the direction of the kids' bathroom. "Uh uh. No way. Be careful, the floor is wet."

The clock chimed ten times.

How the hell does Maggie do this alone day in and day out? I'd double down on convincing her to marry me. Whether she knew it or not, we needed each other.

8

Maggie

I walked through the front door, still thinking about the evening. It took me a moment to realize someone had cleaned the house. Even the two-month old Christmas tree looked better.

"Did you have a good time?" Gabe asked from the kitchen.

"Yes, I did. How are the kids?" I rounded the corner and found him at the island nursing a glass of whiskey.

"Chloe got into your makeup and nail polish, but I think I got it all off the countertop and floor. I couldn't have done it without Zach. I gave him twenty bucks for his help. Otherwise, they're bathed, tucked in, teeth brushed, and bladders emptied."

"Sounds like you had fun." I eyed his glass. "Where did you find that?"

He stood slowly, as if his muscles had stiffened from sitting too long. "Joe's stash is still in the garage closet. Want a drink?"

"Really?" I'd gone through every inch of the house, except the garage. "Just one. I don't drink much anymore."

"I think Ella might be allergic to milk. Can you help me get her an appointment with a pediatrician?"

"I can, but are you staying?"

"Why would I change my mind?"

Why, indeed. So much for the kids freaking him out. "I'll call the pediatrician first thing Monday, unless you think it's an emergency."

"Her poop is blackish-green and smells like the river, but she's eating."

"It's probably nothing, but I'll keep an eye on her."

"I started a grocery list and one for things I need for the baby. I hope you don't mind I used your computer."

"That's fine." I glanced at the stack of papers on the bar. My hand trembled as I picked up the second notice from the power company. "You paid my bills?"

"No. Your *personal* mail is unopened on the desk. I paid the household expenses."

I started to speak, but he interrupted. "Consider it rent."

I couldn't believe it. Part of me wanted to yell at him for invading my privacy, but the other part wanted to hug him. It'd been a long time since someone had done something so nice for me. "Thank you."

"When did you start dating?" Gabe pulled down a glass, poured a respectable amount of whiskey and topped it off with a splash of Coke to add color.

"Thanks." I sipped the drink and gasped.

"You're welcome." He chuckled and reclaimed his barstool. "Are you avoiding my question?"

"A few months ago, on a dare." I eased onto the stool next to him.

"A dare?" He ran his hand over his stubbly chin. "What kind of dare?"

Not wanting to go there, I shrugged. "How's work?"

"Don't change the subject. Tell me about this dare."

"Shanna dared me to sign up for an online dating service. I went out with two guys from the site but took down my profile when I met Justin."

He smirked as he refilled our glasses. "And it's working out?"

Nope. "I guess."

Gabe grew quiet.

I waited until I couldn't stand the silence. "Three weeks is a long time to be away from your place."

"If it's an inconvenience, I'll figure out something else."

"Like what?"

"I don't know. I could use a vacation. Florida's nice this time of year."

I loved the idea of a few days with nothing to do except work and sleep. "The kids have next Monday off of school..."

"You're pretty excited over a hypothetical trip." He nudged me with his shoulder. "Or is it a couple of nights in a hotel with me?"

"You could take the kids to Disney with your parents. Your mother has them every other weekend anyway. Plus, you said you needed to talk to your dad. That way, I could get some work done and have a sleepover with Justin." I had no idea why I'd suggested that—not when I'd rather sleep with Attila the Hun.

"Ella's too young to travel." Gabe grinned, seeming to hold back laughter. "Besides, Chloe told me your sleepovers end at eight-thirty, remember?"

I lifted my glass and downed half its contents. "My sleepovers are a lot of fun."

"They used to be." He flashed me a crooked grin and wiggled his brows.

"Not that I remember what a grown-up sleepover is like." I ignored his damned grin and his eyes and his biceps. Instead, I focused on the countertop.

"How long has it been?" He emptied the remainder of the whiskey into my glass.

"Um..." I stared at the ceiling, making a show of counting on my fingers. "When did you dump me again?"

He choked on his whiskey. "What? Wait. You haven't slept with anyone since me?"

Damn it, I should've lied. "I didn't want to do the rebound thing. Then I was busy with school. Then Rebecca died...and the rest is history."

He seemed to consider my words. "I thought you had a boyfriend now?"

"We're taking it slow." *Why am I lying to him?*

"Glaciers move faster, Mags."

My face heated, though I doubted it had anything to do with blushing. The alcohol had gone straight to my head faster than this conversation had gone into the gutter. "I can't..."

"Can't what?" He turned to face me.

"Actually, he dumped me, but that's not all. He did it loudly in a crowded restaurant and left me with the check." I shot him what I hoped was a withering glare. "I spent the rest of the night at Shanna's watching bad cable and eating ice cream."

"The guy sounds like an asshole."

"He's not the first asshole I've run across." I folded my arms.

"I should have returned your calls." Gabe reached for my shoulder.

"Water under the bridge." I dodged his hand and went for my drink.

Gabe scooted the glass out of my grasp. "Is it?"

"Yes." *At least I thought it was until he'd showed up looking all sexy and cleaned my house and paid my electric bill.* "Besides, I can't jump in the sack with anyone. Your mother watches me like a hawk. She's taking me back to court next month. If I start sleeping around, I'll lose the kids quicker than the Baptists make it to Sunday brunch."

Gabe slid the drink in my direction. "She doesn't need to know."

I raised the glass for a toast. "Here's to your mother getting a new hobby besides harassing me."

"Is she that bad?"

"She's on me like a tick on a two-legged hound dog." Imagining Evelyn clinging to a dog like a starving vampire made me giggle.

Gabe snorted and motioned to my glass. "More whiskey? You're more fun drunk."

"Why, thank you."

"How's work going? Are you writing another crime novel?"

I downed the remainder of my drink. "No. I haven't had

time to work on another book. I write society pieces. They're garbage."

"I've read your articles. They're not garbage."

"No one reads reviews for cultural events in New Orleans. Locals know what they like, and most tourists come for booze, boobs, and beads." I winked. "Oh sorry, that's right up your alley."

"Just because I run a bar doesn't mean I don't appreciate culture."

"I remember the ballet turned you on."

"Thinking about what I would do to you *after* the ballet turned me on."

I narrowed my eyes and tried to think of a snarky remark but snapped my mouth shut. *Damn him, and his after-the-ballet sex talk.*

Gabe grew quiet, which made me nervous. "I'm sorry I hurt you."

"Don't be. I chalked it up to a learning experience. I'm over it."

"Are you?"

"We've already covered this. Water under the table. Bridge. I mean water under the table, and I can still drink you under the bridge." I turned too fast and teetered, only to be caught around the middle by his strong arms. Pressed against his muscular chest, I glanced up a split second before his lips came down on mine.

Unlike the quick exchanges I'd shared with Justin, Gabe kissed me like a man with a PhD in seduction. He cupped my face and invaded my mouth. My defenses crumpled, along with my knees. A sound of surrender escaped me. But rather than claiming victory—Gabe retreated.

"Something wrong?" I whispered, holding the counter for support.

"I'm beat." Gabe's hand brushed over my hip.

I wanted to kiss him again or hold him or invite him to my room. On the other hand, I wanted to throat punch him and toss him out of my house. I couldn't go down this road with him again. I wouldn't survive it.

As if he'd read my mind, Gabe frowned and ran his over the back of his neck. "Good night, Maggie."

"Good night."

Drunk and exhausted, I should have fallen asleep the moment I closed my eyes. Instead, I stared at the ceiling and tried to think about anything but the man in the room across the hall.

9

Gabe

FIRE SHOT CLOSE ENOUGH TO MY HAND TO SINGE THE hair on my knuckles. Cursing, I grabbed the tongs and moved the steaks away from the flare up. No matter what I did, I couldn't put out the flames.

"Son of a bitch." I eased back from the fire. "Hey Leo, I could use a spray bottle out here."

"Don't use water. It'll extinguish the coals or get ash on the meat." My brother pushed me out of the way and placed the cover on the grill.

"I've never had a problem with it before."

He smirked. "Carbon seals in the juices. Don't be afraid of a little fire."

"I can handle the heat." I downed half my beer.

My mother would probably call it a sin, but Leo was my favorite brother. Joe, the eldest and the golden child, had treated me more like an underling than an equal. Leo, born ten months after me, was more like a best friend than a sibling. I trusted him to give it to me straight.

"You look like shit." He opened the grill to check on the steaks.

I glanced over his rooftop patio. He lived in quintessential French Quarter apartment, an old mansion that was later turned into a multifamily home. I envied his rooftop oasis, but I had almost twice the square footage. "Have you spoken to Ma?"

"She called the other day. Something about a family dinner."

"Figures." I made a mental note to speak with the rest of my brothers soon, or I'd have to face them as a group. The three of them, plus my parents, would be a verbal blood bath.

"You gonna tell me or do I have to call Ma?"

"Could you keep an eye on the steaks? I need another beer for this." I shook my empty bottle.

"Uh uh, bro. Spill it."

I looked him square in the eye. "I have a kid."

He froze for a couple of seconds and laughed. "Holy shit, man. Congrats, but you know they make condoms to prevent this sort of thing."

"As it turns out, condoms are only ninety-nine percent effective."

Leo plopped down on a lounge chair. "What are you going to do with a kid?"

"Raise her." I turned back to the grill, but my thoughts drifted to Maggie. *I should call to let her know I'll be late.*

"Not for nothing, but do you even know how to change a diaper?" Leo shuddered.

"Yeah, smart ass, I do." Never mind that a thirteen year old had taught me how.

"How often do you see her?" He'd spoken as if from experience but turned his attention to the rooftops of the French Quarter.

I nudged his shoulder. "Something *you* want to tell *me?*"

Leo startled, but tried to cover it with a dumbass smile. "Don't put your shit on me. This is all you."

Right. "Ella lives with me."

"Where's her mother?" He cocked his head. "*Who's* her mother?"

"She works on a cruise ship..." I told him the rest of the story while I pulled the steaks off the grill, but I left out one tiny detail—Chantal's name. I needed to get through the *I-have-a-kid* part before I dropped another bomb on him.

"Jesus, Gabe. Is she coming back?"

"Don't know. Don't care. I'm going for full custody. Besides abandoning her child, she's nuts. Lucky for me, I'd ended it before things got too serious."

"Not soon enough." He stood and walked to the table.

"The timing could be better, and the circumstances suck, but I don't regret having a kid."

"Yeah, I get that." His voice cracked.

What's up with him? I took a seat and unwrapped my baked potato. "Sure, you don't have anything you want to tell me?"

"I'm good." He picked at his salad. "Where's the little bundle of joy?"

"Maggie's watching her tonight." My stomach twisted. I'd finally come to the subject I needed to discuss.

"Maggie. As in Rebecca's sister, Maggie?"

"The one and only."

"Shit, Gabe. I thought Pops told us to stay away from Joe's kids."

"It's been a year. Nothing's happened." I shoved a piece of steak into my mouth, chewed, and took a swig of beer. "Besides, you and I both know Pop's prime suspect had an iron-clad alibi..."

Leo furrowed his brow and glanced away. The moment he put it all together, his mouth fell open. "For fuck's sake, tell me the mother of your kid isn't Chantal DuBois."

"Guilty."

He dragged his hand down his face. "Jesus, does Pops know?"

"No, and I'd like to keep it that way for now." *Forever if I can help it.*

My father wouldn't need to worry about lung cancer. He'd drop dead of a coronary if he knew I'd slept with the person he suspected of causing my brother's accident.

"Do you think she got knocked up on purpose?" He pegged me with a glare.

"Hell if I know. I mean, I suited up every time."

"Accidents happen, I guess. Where does Maggie fit into this?" Leo consumed his meal like he hadn't seen food in weeks.

"I'm going to marry her."

He choked on his potato.

I pushed my plate to the side and set my elbows on the table. "It was that, move home, or lose my bar."

"I need something stronger before we get into this." Leo finished his beer, went inside, and returned with a bottle of Jack and two glasses. "A little birdie told me you're planning to take over for Pops."

A little birdie named Enzo. Three years younger, Enzo made it his life's goal to know everyone's business.

"It's not as if I have a choice. Pops isn't doing well."

Leo poured two shots. "I'd like to believe we all have a choice, but I know better."

I downed the whiskey. "I'll learn the ropes, do what I have to, and get all of us out as soon as I can."

"And if you can't?"

"I can." I poured myself another and stared into the amber liquid. The Marchionni family had been tied to the Cosa Nostra since the 1800s, but the internet, more savvy investigation techniques, and RICO laws made organized crime even riskier. Thankfully, the majority of our wealth came from legitimate business ventures nowadays. We could stand on our own. The question was—would the other families allow it?

"Gabe, not for nothin' but you don't have anything to prove. Joe's dead. The rivalry's over. No good will come from trying to fill his shoes."

His words stung like rubbing alcohol on road rash. "That's not what this is about. Joe was good with the status quo. I'm not. Fuck the sins of our father, we're going legit."

"I'm behind you one hundred percent on that." He furrowed his brow and took another bite of steak.

"You got something else you want to say?" I half-expected him to bring up more psychobabble bullshit about needing mommy and daddy's approval.

"Are you sure about this thing with Maggie?"

"I love her. Always have." The words rolled off my tongue without hesitation.

"No shit. But last time I checked, she wanted your head

on a pike. How'd you get her to agree to marry you?"

I knocked back my second shot. "I haven't asked her yet."

Leo rubbed his forehead, a habit he shared with my father, and a sure sign I'd lost him.

"I will, but I have to tell her why I broke things off the first time around. She needs to know what she's walking into." *And I have to convince her she's still in love with me.*

"You mean tell her about the *business*." He set his fork down.

"Yep."

"Bad idea." He pressed his hand to his gut. "Rebecca changed once she found out. To hear Ma tell it, her post-partem depression had more to do with Joe coming clean than hormones."

I folded my arms. I'd heard my mother's side of the story, but I'd also spent time with Joe's wife. She'd known the truth long before her youngest son was born. "That's bullshit."

"It's been years since you and Maggie broke up. How well do you know her now? What makes you think she won't run to the cops? Or worse, write a story about it in the *Picayune*?"

"Good point." I doubted she'd go to the police, but I hadn't considered the paper. "But she deserves to know the truth. Even if she throws me out on my ass, she's raising the next generation of Marchionni men. Sooner or later, the *business* will touch them."

"Unless you get us out free and clear."

"Free and clear's a long shot. I'll settle for legit without bloodshed."

10

Maggie

CHILDREN'S LAUGHTER AND THE SCENT OF FRESH baked cookies filled the house, but nothing cheered me up. Though I couldn't put my finger on what had me in such a foul mood, all signs pointed to Gabe Marchionni.

I struggled to focus on the Bourbon Street Bad Boys Club proposal I'd drafted for Marlena. It wasn't my best work. It reeked of passive aggression as if I'd taken all of my frustrations with Gabe, his family, and life in general and wrapped them up in one tidy document. I held my breath and hit *send* on the email.

In the week since Gabe had arrived, he'd worked nights at the bar and days with his father. At least that's what he told me. He could have been anywhere with anyone, and I'd never be the wiser. *Not that it's any of my business.*

Our kiss haunted me day and night. I'd tried to blame my response on the whiskey, but it was a lie. I'd wanted it. I'd wanted him.

My phone rang. The name and number on the screen caused my pulse to race. I'd only sent the proposal a few minutes ago. Marlena either loved or hated it. I pressed answer.

My boss's voice boomed through the connection before I had a chance to say hello. "Maggie, I swear on the life of my Christian Louboutins, you have outdone yourself!"

"I'm glad you liked it." I hurried out the back door. On the off-chance Gabe had woken, I didn't want him to overhear the conversation. "Is there anything you want changed?"

"Not a thing, darling. Get me what you've outlined, and I'll find a place for you on staff. Telecommuting of course, with a raise and benefits. Whatever you want, just get the story."

I'd waited a year to hear her say those words. A regular paycheck and health insurance would solve a lot of my problems, but the articles could cause a whole lot more. *No. Screw my guilty conscience. I can do this.* "I've already started working on it."

"Good to hear. I'd like to run the first article the day of the Mardi Gras Gala. Can you pull it together by then?"

Three weeks? Is she kidding? "That shouldn't be a problem."

"Perfect. Keep me posted. I'm counting on you." Marlena disconnected the call.

I hung my head and went inside. On days like this I self-medicated with carbs—homemade carbs filled with chocolate. I'd already eaten half a dozen cookies, but after the call, I ate three more.

My stomach churned. The sugar hadn't eased my stress. In short, I still felt like crap. To atone for my food sins and save my waistline, I resorted to angry cleaning. Nothing like taking your frustrations out on the carpet.

I ran the vacuum down the hall, banging it into the master bedroom door a couple of times before moving on. *Oh, so sorry, sir. Did I wake you?*

"Maggie?" Gabe called over the noise.

Ignoring him, I turned the corner and redid the living room floor.

"Maggie?"

The vacuum went dead.

Oh no he did not! I rounded on him with my hands on my hips. "What?"

Still holding the cord, he frowned. "Would you mind doing that later?"

I smirked and let my gaze travel from his face to his bare feet and up again. "You look like ten pounds of shit in a five-pound bag."

"I feel like it."

"Your hangover isn't my concern. I have to clean the house this morning."

Gabe shook his head and walked into the kitchen.

Realizing he wasn't going to plug the vacuum back into the wall, I huffed and followed him. "Look. If you're going to stay here, we need to lay down some ground rules."

"Like not running the vacuum before ten?" He stuffed a cookie into his mouth.

"Like from this point forward we're friends, which means hands off." I had no idea why I'd said that, but my heart broke a little.

"Friends, got it." He ate two more cookies.

I pulled the plate away from him. "There are kids in the

house. They hear and see everything. You're an adult, if you want to eat cookies for breakfast that's your business, but it isn't setting a good example."

"I'll be the model of a responsible adult." He stuck his head in the fridge, pulled out the milk, and took a swig from the carton.

I made a sound in the back of my throat and balled my fists.

He took one look at me and laughed, spitting a mouthful of milk into the sink. "Relax, Mags. I'm the only person in the house that drinks regular milk."

"You're trying to piss me off." I closed my eyes and counted to ten.

"Not really, but it's so damned easy." He chuckled and put the milk away.

"You shouldn't cuss either."

His brows rose. "Pot calling the kettle black on that one?"

I pinched the bridge of my nose. "I'm serious."

"I got it—no touching, no drinking from the milk carton, no cookies for breakfast, no potty mouth. Anything else?"

"Yes. You don't need to ask my permission to go out, but I'd appreciate knowing when you're leaving and about when you'll be back. I planned dinner last night, and you didn't come home before going to the bar. I had Ella all day."

"I told you it would be a long one. Asked if you wanted me to take her to my folks."

"I know, and I appreciate it. Still, a phone call would have been nice."

"Any more rules?"

"Don't bring women here." I regretted it as soon as I'd said it.

The humor faded from his eyes. "Got it."

I'd crossed a line. He was a player, but he knew better than to bring the game near the kids. "Now that's settled, can I get you some breakfast?"

I used food like an olive branch. Hopefully, an omelet would make him forget all about my crankiness.

"No, I'm good." Gabe held the coffee cup with two hands with his shoulder slumped forward as if trying to garner every ounce of warmth from the mug.

I moved closer. "The sitter's coming tonight. I made plans last week."

"I'm off tonight. I can watch the kids, unless you're worried I'll corrupt them. You know, cookies for dinner with chasers from the carton."

"Are you sure you'll be up for it? You look rough." I set my hand on his forehead.

He pulled away. "I'll be fine once I get some sleep."

"Sorry. I'll try to keep it down in the mornings until you get into a normal routine."

"Going on another internet date?"

"Girls' night with Shanna, if you must know." I refilled his coffee.

"Thanks." He hunched over his cup again. "Like I said, I can handle the kids."

"I'll cancel the sitter." I left to put the vacuum away. Try as I might, I couldn't figure out why I let him get under my skin. Then again, I'd become rather adept at lying to myself.

I wandered into my room for a moment's peace and to

get as far away from him as possible. As soon as I sat, the doorbell rang, the dog started barking, and the kids came down the stairs like a herd of elephants. By the time I'd returned to the front room, Chloe had opened the door and had ushered my mother into the house.

"Mimi!" Ryan launched himself at his grandmother.

"Mom?" Wondering where Gabe had gone, I glanced toward the kitchen.

No matter how temporary the situation, or the circumstances, my mother would not approve of me shacking up with a man.

She hugged the kids and gave the dog a quick pat, all while surveying the house. By the time she got to me, her smile had faded. She smoothed her designer jacket and patted her perfectly coifed hair. "Mary Margaret."

My heart sank along with my mother's smile. The house was as clean as it was ever going to be, but it would never be enough—*I* would never be enough.

"So good to see you." I gave her a half hug and locked eyes with Gabe, who'd chosen that moment to step into the room.

"Who're you?" My mother tilted her head as if trying to place the face.

I'd managed to keep my previous relationship with Gabe from my mom, mostly because she never asked. However, she *had* met Gabe at least twice, once at Rebecca's wedding and again at her funeral. Both occasions had been emotional days for all involved, but I'd bet my right arm my mother had recognized him.

"This is my uncle, Gabe. He lives with us now." Chloe

took Gabe's hand. The little girl beamed. "Uncle Gabe, this is my Mimi. Her real name is Nadine."

I prayed to God for a lightning bolt to strike me dead. *This cannot be happening.*

He cleared his throat. "Nadine, nice to see you again."

She paled beneath her expertly applied makeup.

I set my hand on my mother's shoulder to draw her attention away from him. "You remember Gabe? He's Joe's brother."

"Oh, yes." She forced a smile. "What brings you to Algiers Point?"

"I'm staying here while some work is done on my house in the Quarter," he said without hesitation.

I forced my shoulders to relax. Gabe had lied so smoothly. I wondered if he actually planned to renovate his place. "Mom, I wasn't expecting you."

"Isn't today Chloe's recital?"

"No, it's next weekend." I motioned for her to sit.

"Mary Margaret, I'm quite sure you told me it was today. You need to get yourself together. Buy a planner."

"Mimi, can I spend the night with you?" Chloe pressed her hands together in front of her chest. "Please."

"Of course, darling. Go pack a bag for you and Ryan." Nadine smiled as if the matter had been settled regardless of my thoughts.

"I'll go help them pack." Gabe lifted Ryan and followed Chloe out of the room.

"Nice to see you again." Nadine called after him, then turned her gaze on me. Her lips pursed and she shook her head ever-so-slightly. "Please tell me that man isn't staying here."

"It's Joe and Rebecca's house," I whispered.

"That doesn't give him the right to stay here. You know how I feel about the Marchionni family. They're responsible for your sister's death."

"Joe and Rebecca had an accident." I hated that she'd never accepted the truth. "Besides, it's only for a short while, and he'll be on his way."

"Good. The last thing you need to do is get a crush on someone like him." Nadine sniffed and turned her head.

"He's not my type, mother." I sighed, remembering the year Gabe had been exactly my type.

Nadine patted my hand. "No, he isn't. A man like that dates women like Rebecca. He'd never be happy with you."

"I know." I smiled to reassure my mother, but something fragile inside me curled into a tight ball and died.

11

Gabe

I HADN'T SEEN MAGGIE SINCE THE DEBACLE WITH HER mother that morning. And I thought I had it bad? Nadine made my mom look like Mary-Fucking-Poppins.

I listened at her door for signs of life and knocked. "Mags? What time are you heading out?"

"I'm not going anywhere," she called from inside the room.

"Why?" I frowned and set my hand on the knob. "Can I come in?"

"No. I don't feel well." Her voice sounded nasally like she'd spent the afternoon crying.

"I'm coming in." Ignoring her puffy eyes, I sat on the edge of the bed. "What happened to girls' night?"

"I cancelled." She blew her nose into a tissue, then set it with a pile of others on the nightstand.

I pressed my hand to her forehead. "You don't have a fever."

"That's good, I guess.

"Come on, get up." I stood and tugged her hand. I

refused to let her wallow. She needed cheering up, and I needed dinner. A win-win in my book.

"Why?" She sank deeper into the covers.

"We're going out." I released her, flipped the light on, and opened her closet. "You'll feel better once you're out of the house."

"What? No. What are you doing? Get out of there."

"I didn't hear a rule about not going into each other's stuff. Get in the shower. I'm starving."

"I'm not hungry." She hopped out of bed and positioned herself between me and her clothes.

Score one for me. She's out of bed. I stared into her blue eyes and grinned. "Please? I hate eating alone."

"Where's Ella?"

"My mother came for her and Zach a couple of hours ago. I may need the National Guard to get her back, but Zach will call if she tries to take Ella out of the country."

Maggie hung her head. "Fine. Where are we going?"

"Don't know yet." I knew exactly where I'd take her.

She glanced between me and the bed. "Give me fifteen minutes to get dressed."

No way would I give her to the chance to crawl back under the blankets. "I'm not leaving you until you're in the shower."

"Fine." She gave me an eye roll that put Chloe to shame and shambled to the bathroom.

"You're adorable when you pout."

"Go to hell." She slammed the door.

My father was right. There were definitely worse things than marrying Maggie Guthrie.

My phone rang, and I answered without looking at the screen. "Marchionni."

"Gabe, its Chantal. I need to talk to you."

I glanced at the bathroom door and walked into the living room. "Talk."

"I got a call from your lawyer."

"I know."

"I'll sign the papers, but I need something from you."

I stared at the ceiling. My attorney had told me to expect a cash grab. "Go on."

"Your family ruined my life. I lost everything. I want what's owed to me."

"I told you I would set you up in a place close by so you could be a part of Ella's life."

"No. I can't see... I can't... No."

"Right. You can't be a mother, but you expect me to buy my daughter? How much?"

"Five-Hundred Thousand"

"Sign the papers, Chantal." I disconnected the call and slid the phone into my pocket. I could get the money, but it would mean dipping into the savings I'd set aside to buy my bar from the Marchionni Corporation. My only other choice was to go to my father, but Satan would build an igloo before that happened.

Maggie walked into the hall. "Everything okay?"

One look at her and my frustration melted. Even in jeans and a T-shirt, with almost no makeup, she stole my breath. "It is now."

"Yeah, okay." She gave me side-eye.

Until that morning, I'd never understood why she couldn't

take a compliment. When I'd overheard the tail end of the conversation between her and her mother, it'd taken all of my restraint not to tell the woman to go to hell—no mother should speak to their daughter like that. But I'd recently learned it took more than giving birth to make a woman a mother.

No wonder my ending our relationship the way I did had hurt her so deeply. She had to know I was lying about my reasons and had filled in the blanks with God knows what.

I decided then and there to make it my mission to make her see her beauty. "You look nice."

Maggie shrugged. "It's as good as it's going to get."

I opened the front door for her. "Looks good to me."

She ignored my remark. "Where are we going?"

"You'll see."

Maggie's shoulders tensed, but she got into my car.

I kept my mouth shut during the drive. She glanced in my direction when we went over the Crescent City Bridge and exited on Camp Street, but didn't say a word.

The woman needed to let loose and have fun, and there was no better place to do it than the French Quarter.

"It's late, most kitchens close at ten..." She sounded like she wanted to bolt.

"I know a place that stays open late. The food's great, but the owner's a dick."

Maggie shot me a dubious look.

"I'm kidding. Trust me." I pulled into a parking spot behind the building.

"This is reserved for owner. There's a sign."

"I won't get towed."

Maggie motioned to the line of people stretching out the

main door and down Ursuline Street. "We'll never get a table."

"You're going to have to learn to trust me." I ducked into the service entrance.

"Uh huh." She glanced around the busy kitchen and smiled.

"Gabe!" Enzo embraced me, something he hadn't done since our brother's funeral. I didn't trust it. "How are you, man? I heard you're a dad. Congrats."

I slapped him on the back harder than necessary and pulled out of the hug. "Thanks. Ma called the entire family?"

"Yeah, you could say that." Enzo smirked. "As for the other half of the news, good luck. I'll believe it when I see it."

My mouth went dry. Had my mother told people I was engaged, too?

Recognition dawned on my brother's face. "Maggie Guthrie? My God, it is you. It's been a while. How are you doing with all this?"

Maggie's smile faded. "I'm all right. You should stop in and visit the kids."

"I've been meaning too. I'm sorry, without Joe..." He drew her into a tight hug and kissed her cheek. "You're a good woman. What are you doing with this loser? I never would have guessed he'd be shacking up with you."

"Why don't you quit hitting on my date and get us a table, will you?" I laced my fingers with hers.

Much to my surprise, Maggie didn't pull her hand free.

Enzo considered the two of us for a moment and shook

his head. "We're standing room only. Let me see what I can do."

"You do that. Technically, I'm the owner of this fine establishment, and I have the parking place to prove it." I couldn't resist giving him a hard time.

My brother nodded toward Maggie as if daring me to push my luck.

I winked, and he stormed away. He might play the role of perfect host, but I knew better. Beneath that chef coat beat the heart of a man who put his ambitions above all else.

She furrowed her brow. "What was that about?"

"Parking here's a bitch."

"Uh huh." She opened her mouth to speak, but a waitress came to show us to our table.

Maggie ordered a drink as soon as we sat. Between her knee bobbing under the table and her fidgeting with her phone, her anxiety began to rub off on me.

I clasped my hands to keep from reaching for her bouncing leg. "Everything's good here, but the steak Florentine is off the charts."

She glanced at me and sighed. "I'll have a salad and the gumbo."

Not only had she decided on the fastest items on the menu, I recognized the look in her eyes—she wanted to leave. I had to do something, so I blurted out the first thing that came to mind. "I like your hair down."

"Thanks."

The server delivered our cocktails. "The usual, Gabe?"

"Not tonight. We'll both have the house salad and a bowl of gumbo." I latched onto the glass like a drowning man gripped a life preserver.

Maggie took a large drink and seemed to look every-where except at me.

This is ridiculous. I leaned closer. "Are you still pissed at me?"

"No, why?"

"You haven't said much since we got in the car."

"I'm sorry. I have a lot on my mind. Enzo looks good though. This is his place?"

Her question surprised me. Enzo's was one of the hottest restaurants in the Quarter. "Yeah. You've never been here?"

"No. I don't come to this part of town often." She turned her attention to her drink.

"You used to love the Quarter. What changed?"

"I don't know, Gabe. Maybe it had something to do with not wanting to run into you after we broke up?"

The verbal bitch-slap left me reeling. I'd never get anywhere with her if I didn't tell her the truth. "I'm sorry. If it's any consolation, I couldn't walk a block without passing a place that reminded me of you...of us."

She stared at me for a long moment before glancing away. "I can't talk about this. Not tonight. Not here."

"I understand but listen. I've been thinking a lot about our situation."

"We have a situation?" She sat back and folded her arms.

I'd never been so grateful for a meal to arrive. It gave me something else to put in my mouth besides my foot. "Another time then. Let's eat."

The woman was killing me one sharp word at a time. I wasn't stupid back then. I knew breaking things off would hurt her, but I'd done it for her own good. She deserved so much better than me. Hell, she still did, but things were different now. I was finally in a position to break free of the Cosa Nostra and be a better man.

We remained quiet during dinner—uncomfortable, but not unbearable thanks to the noise from the bar crowd in the adjacent room.

By the time the server cleared our plates, Maggie had finished her second drink. Her mood had improved. "Okay, you can say it."

"What?" I thought I knew she'd say *I told you so*, but I didn't want to risk missing the mark and pissing her off.

"I told you so. I needed to get out of the house."

My freaking stomach fluttered. Whether she cared to admit it or not, I knew her inside and out. I leaned across the table and cupped my ear. "What? Are you saying I was right?"

"Don't get used to it. I'm sure it won't happen again."

"Come on." I threw some cash on the table and pulled her to her feet.

"Where are we going now?"

"Already skeptical?" I made a tsking sound, set my hand on the small of her back, and led her to the bar in the next room.

"What's that noise? It sounds like someone strangling a raccoon with a cat."

"That would be karaoke."

Maggie slid onto a stool.

I snaked my arm around her and ordered another round of drinks—whiskey on the rocks for her, water for me. After working in a bar for years, I knew the drill. If I didn't make it obvious I had a date, the women would circle. I refused to risk sending her fragile self-confidence into the toilet.

She leaned close, still half shouting, "Why are we here?"

Rubbing my cheek against hers, I spoke into her ear. "To dance our cares away."

"Dance to karaoke? No way." She turned her attention to the half-dressed woman on the stage singing "Don't Stop Believin.'"

"Come on, Mags. It'll be fun."

"You do remember that I can't dance, don't you?"

I laughed knowing good and well the woman had moves. "Then you leave me no choice. Stay here. I'll be right back."

"Where are you going?"

I winked and walked to the edge of the stage.

The older woman queuing the next song glanced up at me and smiled.

A little flirting, name dropping, and a well-placed compliment later, she agreed to let me cut in line.

Maggie shifted her weight on the stool and chewed her lip. She seemed uneasy, but I doubted she'd run away before I finished the song.

Mic in hand, I made my way on stage. Three notes into the song, Maggie's spine stiffened, and her gorgeous blue eyes widened. Not surprising, considering I'd chosen to sing "When I Was Your Man" by Bruno Mars. Not only was he one of her favorite artists, the lyrics expressed my feelings better than I ever could—except for the part about wishing her new guy would buy her flowers and hold her hand. *Fuck that.*

I loved singing in front of a crowd. I'd sung and played guitar or piano at my father's clubs, including my bar, since high school. Getting the right pitch and rasp to pull off Bruno Mars presented a challenge. The smoky air, along with the growing tension in my chest, helped roughen my voice. Not to mention, Maggie's flaming-red cheeks and the glisten in her eyes urged me on.

How is it possible she's more beautiful now than when we were together?

Women swarmed the stage, but I kept my eyes on my girl. Halfway through the song, I wished I'd chosen a shorter tune. I wanted nothing more than to kiss away every tear she'd ever, or would ever, shed.

As if he had a bad timing detector, Enzo came out of the kitchen and sidled next to Maggie. The bastard took her attention off me by draping Mardi Gras beads over her head. My heart skipped a beat. If Enzo told her about my father's mandate, I'd never get her to trust me.

Thank Christ, the song ended. I fought my way back to Maggie and took her chin between my thumb and forefinger. She met my eyes and licked her lips, sending a bolt of electricity through me. I leaned in and brushed my lips across hers before she had time to argue. She tasted like peaches and whiskey—intoxicating.

Enzo smirked and turned to speak to the woman at his right.

Maggie, on the other hand, gave me a look that promised pain.

I needed to get her out of there before she laid into me in front of my brother. "Let's go home."

She tugged her purse on her shoulder and marched for the door like a woman on a mission.

I took advantage of the situation and winked at Enzo, who looked as stunned as if I'd groped the Virgin Mary herself. So what if he'd misread the situation? If it kept his damned mouth shut, I'd take it.

Outside, Maggie rounded on me. "I can't go home with you, and don't kiss me again without permission."

"I'm staying at your house. It's a no-brainer you're going home with me. And I'll be sure to ask next time my lips come in contact with your body." I used my bedroom voice on the last bit. I liked her drunk, but she was fun as hell when she was angry.

"Don't you dare speak to me in that tone. You don't know me anymore. We're practically strangers. Things are complicated enough without adding physical stuff in the mix."

Strangers who know every square inch of each other's bodies.

"You're right." As much as I wanted to rekindle things with Maggie, I knew better than to push her. Not yet anyway. "How about a walk? I should check in with my staff."

"Sure, why not." She folded and unfolded her arms before stuffing her hands in her pockets. The woman had something to say and from the looks of it, something I wouldn't like.

"What's on your mind?"

"You had to pick that song. Didn't you?"

I stopped and turned to her. "I couldn't have expressed my feelings better if I'd tried."

If she'd rolled her eyes any harder, they would have done a three-sixty.

"Mags, I'm serious. I'm ashamed of the way I handled things with you. I never should have—"

She walked away.

Maggie didn't want to talk about it. Point taken. "So was it good for you?"

"What?"

"The kiss."

She punched my arm. Hard. "I should have turned my head when you came at me all puckered up. My morals go out the window when I'm around you."

"Don't blame me for your lack of morals. Blame the whiskey." I chuckled to cover my frustration and guided her up Ursuline toward Bourbon.

12

Maggie

PEOPLE CROWDED THE SIDEWALKS, AND MORE WOULD arrive in the coming weeks. Fat Tuesday, the biggest party in the city, would swell the city's population by millions. Walking with Gabe here reminded me of better days. Days when we'd been happy together. Although much of our time together had involved a bed, we'd spent many hours enjoying the French Quarter.

We entered his bar on Bourbon Street and ran into a wall of noise. The body heat alone made the space twenty degrees warmer than the sidewalk. Gabe guided me to a stool behind the bar and said something to the female bartender.

She glanced at me and nodded.

Recognizing the tall brunette, I grinned and waved at Gabe's cousin, Jessie.

He pulled his phone from his pocket and frowned at the screen.

"Trouble?" I motioned to his cell.

"No." Leaning in close, he fondled the beads between

my breasts. "I need to go in back and check tomorrow's delivery schedule. Are you okay here for a few minutes?"

"I'm good here with Jessie. I love people watching."

"Ten minutes tops." Gabe winked and disappeared around the corner.

I startled when a man waved a ten-dollar bill in front of my face. "Oh. I don't work here."

"I need a vodka cranberry," he said louder.

I waved at Jessie but couldn't get her attention. While I didn't know how to run the register, or how much the drinks cost, I could pour a proper vodka cranberry. I hopped off the stool and pulled the brand name vodka from the top shelf.

The customer nodded.

The liquor bottle in one hand, the dispenser in the other, I poured a long ounce into the glass of ice and topped it off with juice. The technique gave the illusion of equal parts juice and alcohol. I finished with a lime wedge and set the drink on the bar.

"Damn, girl. Good pour." Jessie smiled and took the cash from the bar.

"Thanks. Gabe taught me eons ago. Bar tips helped pay for my last two years of college."

"Well, brands are eight bucks, top shelves are ten. Beers are five in the bottle and four from the tap. Everything's cash. Call me if you can't find something." Jessie winked and took another order.

I shrugged and turned to the next customer. Gabe had paid my bills. Helping out tonight seemed fair.

A few moments later, the rush ended, and Jessie nudged my shoulder. "We're looking for another bartender. It's that time of year. If you want a job, talk to Gabe."

I grinned as she pulled a bottle of whiskey from beneath the counter. *This would be a great way to get info for my article.* "I'll talk to him about it."

As if afraid I'd change my mind, Jessie nodded toward the back. "If you're serious, ask him now. I could use some help later this week."

"Sure. Why not?" I turned on my heel and hurried down the hall to find Gabe but slowed at the sound of voices.

"It's all there. There's no need to count it." Gabe's tone made the hairs on my arms stand on end. He didn't sound pleased.

"You're too smart to short me, Marchionni. I'll see you next month."

I had no idea what I'd overhead, but I knew it couldn't be good. I ducked into what looked like an employee break-room and fiddled with the coffee maker.

"Maggie?"

I turned to find Gabe and a uniformed New Orleans police officer staring. My heart thudded against my sternum. *Had he paid off a cop?* "There you are. Could you show me how to use this? It's not like the one at home."

"I'll leave you to it." The cop grinned and continued down the hall.

Gabe moved beside me and lowered his voice. "How much of that did you overhear?"

I swallowed hard. "More than I should have."

"I slip him a little something to avoid problems."

I reached for the counter and realized my hands were shaking. "Are you finished with tomorrow's orders?"

"Almost." He embraced me. "You're trembling. Mags, it

looked far dirtier than it is."

I plastered on a smile and ducked out of his arms. "I'll help Jessie until you're finished."

Gabe sighed and motioned to the door.

I slid behind the bar and tried to convince myself I'd overreacted. Heck, how many times had I commented on the crooked politicians in the city?

"Two Coronas, no lime," a familiar voice called from behind me.

I turned, and Justin's eyes went wide.

"Maggie?" He looked as if he'd swallowed a bee. "You work here?"

A dark-haired woman slid her arm around Justin's waist and kissed his ear.

He went from pale, to red, to a shade of green.

"Who's your friend?" My throat tightened, making my voice sound clipped.

"I'm Denise, his *wife*. Who the hell are you?"

My brain stuttered. I took a step back, bumping into Gabe in the process. "This is Justin and his wife, Denise."

Gabe's eyes darkened and the small muscle in his jaw flexed. Justin looked unimpressed, but Denise stared at Gabe like he was the crab legs on an all-you-can-eat buffet.

Justin laughed and kissed the woman's cheek. "This is Maggie from accounts receivable. She's upset because we have a strict no moonlighting rule. Isn't that right, Maggie?"

"Yes." I turned to take another drink order.

"A table just opened up. Grab it. I'll get the drinks." He patted her backside.

Denise cast me one more dirty look and stormed away.

Turning my head, I swallowed hard and willed the tears

to stay in my eyes. No way would I let the cheating jerk see me cry—angry tears or not.

Gabe pulled me aside. "Are you okay?"

Glaring, Justin whispered, "Really, Maggie? This guy?"

My mouth fell open. For the life of me I couldn't understand where *he* got off judging *me*. Besides the fact he was married, we'd only dated a few times.

Something snapped. It could have been the pen in Gabe's hand, or his last shred of patience. He leaped over the bar and grabbed Justin by the collar. He clawed at Gabe's arms, struggling to break free. Nearby patrons scurried away from danger. In the process, they spilled drinks and alerted others to the situation.

I ran around the bar and set my hand on Gabe's bicep. "Let him go. He's not worth it."

Gabe glanced at me and shoved Justin a foot or so; it didn't matter as long as the argument ended without violence.

Straightening his shirt, Justin muttered under his breath. "Fucking bitch."

The right hook caught Justin in the jaw, sending him careening into the bar. I gasped and took a step away from Gabe. I'd never seen him so angry. For that matter, I'd never seen someone punch someone else in the face.

Struggling to gain his footing on the wet floor, Justin put his hand to his jaw and glared.

At some point during the scuffle, his wife returned. "What the hell happened?

"Call the police," Justin whined and spat blood on the floor.

"She doesn't work in accounting, does she?" Denise

pointed at me. "Are you cheating on me with that?"

"No! Damn it. Look at her!"

Gabe's expression grew dangerous. "Get the hell out of my bar."

Tears running down his cheeks, Justin screamed, "I'm going to press charges."

Gabe chuckled and looked over the crowd. "Anyone see who hit this jackass?"

The patrons responded with laughter, several *no's,* and shakes of the head. Most of the onlookers went back to partying while others stared with amused grins.

Watching Justin turn and walk out, Gabe drew me to his side. "You okay?"

"I think so."

Denise gave Gabe one last, longing look, glared at me, and followed her husband.

"I can't believe you hit him." My voice cracked.

Gabe looked down at me and winked. "I can't believe you didn't."

If anyone walked into the room, they'd never have guessed a fight had broken out moments before. The music played, laughter filled the air, and life went on. I blew out a relieved breath and pressed closer to Gabe. As much as I wanted to be irritated with him for resorting to violence, I couldn't. No one had stood up for me before, in a strange way—I felt safe.

The short drive home gave me enough time to wrap my brain around Justin cheating on his wife with me.

How could I have been so wrong about him? He seemed so nice. Why am I always someone's second best? Why am I never good enough?

"He's an idiot." Gabe shifted the car into fifth gear and sped down the highway.

"I'm the idiot." I rubbed my eyes.

"Bullshit. Even if you'd known he was married, and obviously you didn't, he's the one that made a vow, not you." His eyes on the road, Gabe squeezed my hand.

"Thanks." I turned to him. "You shouldn't have hit him. We should have left. What if someone would have called the police?"

"I couldn't stand there and let him disrespect you. And I'm not worried about the cops."

Because he'd bought their cooperation. I pushed the thought from my mind. "Jessie offered me a job."

"You were great when you used to help me out. Interested?"

Thankful to have something to think about besides cheaters or fights or bribes, I smiled. "Maybe. I could use the money. I'd have to work days and find a sitter for Ryan."

"I can take him with me to my folks. My mother's already watching Ella. I'm sure she'd love having both of them."

"You need help during the nightshift, don't you?"

"Not necessarily. Most of my staff hate working before the sun sets. The tips aren't as good." Gabe pulled into the driveway, cut the engine, and brushed his fingers across my cheek. "Look at me."

I turned and before I talk myself out of it, I kissed him. Be it the stress of the night, Justin's dishonesty, my mother's comment, or the fact I'd wanted to jump him from the moment he'd rang my doorbell, I wanted this. I wanted him —if only for the night.

13

Gabe

WHAT THE HELL ARE YOU DOING, MARCHIONNI. SLOW IT the fuck down.

As much as I wanted to carry Maggie into the bedroom and make her forget the name of every man on the planet except mine, it was wrong. So damned wrong.

Sure, she'd kissed me, and judging by the way her hands shook when she tried to unlock the door, she had sex on the brain. However, I wasn't the kind of guy who enjoyed screwing a woman who had someone else on her mind.

I took the key from her. "Let me."

Once inside, she wrapped her arms around my neck and tugged me down for another kiss. I had to put a stop to this before I gave in and did something she'd regret.

"Slow down, sweetheart." I ran my fingers through the length of her hair.

My words seemed to sober her. She took a step back and nodded. "You're right. I'm just..."

I drew her into my arms. "You've had a rough night. Let's go watch a movie."

"Have you spent time with Ella's mother since you showed up here?"

Where the hell did that come from? "No."

"I'm sorry. I don't mean to be such a drama queen."

"You're far from a drama queen." I thanked God I'd stopped things from getting any hotter. No matter how much I wanted to lick every inch of her luscious body, I had to earn her trust before any nakedness happened. "Put on sweats and one of those giant T-shirts. I'll meet you in your room in ten minutes."

"Sweats?"

"It'll help me keep my hands to myself." I sat and unlaced my boots.

Maggie stood there staring at me as if I'd taken off my pants instead of my socks.

This woman's killing me. A grin tugged the corners of my mouth. "Sweats now."

"Ten minutes." She turned and headed down the hall.

I walked to my room and listened to the dozen or so voicemails Chantal had left over the previous twenty-four hours. For the most part, they all contained the same demands—money, money, and more money—but her latest text made my blood run cold.

A friend sent me this. Thought you preferred tall brunettes to chubby blondes. Does she know what you do for a living? She seems nice. It'd be a shame if something happened to her.

I clicked on the attachment. "Son of a bitch."

Someone had taken a pic of me and Maggie at Enzo's.

Chantal had gone from using Ella to blackmail me to threatening Maggie. *This has to stop.*

I knew people who could put an end to the situation, and to Chantal, permanently. One call to my father's guys and I'd never have to worry about her again, but I couldn't do that to Ella. As much as I'd grown to despise the woman, I couldn't ignore the fact she was the mother of my child.

I walked into the garage and called the one person I could count on for advice that wouldn't end in bloodshed —Leo.

"Bro, do you own a clock?" The grit in his voice told me I'd woken him.

"Chantal upped her game." I checked to make sure Maggie hadn't come into the kitchen and relayed the latest drama to my brother.

"You think she's following you?" Leo sounded wide awake and as freaked out as I felt.

"No clue. She told me she was leaving town, but she could have someone else following me. Either way, I need to know where she is."

"I'll find out." He paused and lowered his voice. "What are you going to tell Maggie?"

I imagined telling her the truth about Chantal, the threats, the family business, all of it. I had a good idea how she would react, and it made my blood run cold. What if she threw me out? I couldn't handle it if she never spoke to me again. "Nothing. I can't protect her if she tosses me out on my ass."

Leo remained quiet.

"You there?"

"I'm thinking." He sighed. "You two aren't together twenty-four-seven. What happens when she goes out?"

My first thought was to cancel her side gig at the bar and order her to stay in the damned house, but that would go over as well as a pregnant nun at mass. "I'll call in some favors. Get her some security."

"If you meant what you said about going legit, let me make the calls. You need to keep your nose clean. Start the way you intend to fly, bro."

And stop paying off dirty cops. I ran my hand down my face. "Thanks, Leo. Just make sure they're invisible."

"Will do." He disconnected.

I had one more call to make, my attorney. I would have felt bad for bugging the guy so late, but my father compensated him well for the inconvenience. I'd miss this part of the business—the ability to get shit done.

Sal Santiago, the family lawyer since before my folks had left Sicily, answered the phone like it was a Monday afternoon. "Gabe, I was going to call you in the morning. The paternity tests we ran are in. She's your daughter."

A silver lining in a cloud of shit. "Thanks, but we have another problem."

Other than an occasional *mmm hmm* or sigh to let me know he was on the line, Sal remained quiet while I gave him the rundown of Chantal's latest bullshit.

"I'm putting security on Maggie."

"And Joe's kids?" He perked up a bit, but I suspected it had more to do with him representing my mother in her custody case than helping me out. "Your father took the guards off them a couple of months ago. If they're in danger because of the threat to Miss Guthrie—"

"You're tap dancing into conflict of interest territory, Sal."

"My concern is for the children."

I counted to five to clear my head. It didn't work. "The only kid you need to worry about right now is Ella. I want Chantal's parental rights terminated by the end of the month."

"These things take time, Gabe. I filed the motion to establish legal paternity. Now we wait."

"Will the courts speed things up now that she's made threats against innocent people?"

"We have to be careful. The judge may not look favorably on you living with Miss Guthrie. I could make the case if you two were married, or even engaged." He went quiet for a few seconds. "Have you considered handling this the old-world way?"

I pinched the bridge of my nose. Was he seriously suggesting I order a hit on Ella's mother? "That's not an option. Get this done, Sal. Legally."

"I'll be in touch. In the meantime, don't take her calls or delete any of her messages."

"Understood." Praying I'd made the right decision, I shoved the phone into my pocket and went to find Maggie.

Maggie

TEN MINUTES SEEMED LIKE TWO HOURS. I'D CHANGED clothes, washed my face, and crawled into bed, but I'd seen no sign of Gabe. After another five minutes, I peeked out the window to make sure his car was still in the driveway.

It was.

Get a grip, Maggie.

I opened the Netflix app and scrolled through the never-ending list of movies. The extra time gave me a chance to replay the previous few hours in my mind. Other than the weirdness with the police officer, Gabe had seemed happy to spend time with me.

Heaven help me, I'd enjoyed him tonight. And that Bruno Mars song, my God, what woman wouldn't melt after that? Not even the crap with Justin and his wife could stop the constant fluttering in my stomach. I could easily fall in love with him again, but what if my mother was right? What if Gabe dumped me like before? This time I had three kids and a possible job to consider.

This is a bad idea.

Gabe knocked and poked his head into the room. "Sorry about that. I had some business to handle."

"Maybe we should call it a night. It's been a long day." I forced a smile.

"Not for nothing, Mags, but you're giving me whiplash." He stepped into the room, and my willpower short circuited—he'd lost his shirt somewhere between his room and mine. Years ago, he'd made my mouth water, but now... My God, he'd filled out. Six-pack didn't quite describe the ripples of muscle down his abdomen. I could spend hours exploring the peaks and valleys. A dusting of dark hair started at his belly button and disappeared beneath his low-slung jeans.

"Sorry." I wanted to keep my distance, but I couldn't stop staring at his damned chest. "Stay. We can watch a movie."

He plopped down beside me. "Uh huh. What's on your mind?"

"I don't know. I mean, maybe you staying here isn't a good idea. It's bringing up all sorts of things for me."

"Come here." He held his arm out.

As much as I wanted to curl up against him, I couldn't will myself to move.

"Stop worrying so damned much. I don't bite."

I knew exactly how and where he liked to bite. "Easier said than done. I haven't talked to you in years and ten minutes ago you had your tongue down my throat."

"If memory serves, you started it." He pulled me toward him and massaged my shoulders. "What do you want to talk about?"

I dropped my chin to my chest to give him better access

to my pressure points. *This is my chance. I have to take it.* "I don't know. Tell me about your new job. What exactly is the family business?"

His hands stilled as if he needed a minute to figure out how to answer. "My father's company does acquisitions, mostly in the hospitality industry—bars, restaurants, hotels. We find properties in trouble or on the verge of bankruptcy. The owners are generally eager to sell. We buy them, fix them up, and turn them for a profit." He nudged me. "Lay down."

"What if they don't want to sell?" I stretched out on my belly.

He shifted his weight as if reaching for something, then moved to straddle me.

A squishy sound told me he'd found my lotion.

Gabe slid his slick hands under my T-shirt and worked the knots in my lower back. "They always want to sell."

"Sounds a little strong arm to me. Do you ever keep the properties?"

"Only in New Orleans. My father owns several boutique hotels. Leo and Enzo have restaurants, and I have the bar."

I made a mental note to jot the information down. "What about your other brothers?"

"Before he died, Joe worked on acquisitions with my father. Marco is a corporate attorney for the business, and Dante is still in grad school."

"Where does he go to college?" My body relaxed, but my brain kicked into high gear. I'd assumed the younger two Marchionni boys were business owners when I'd written the proposal for Marlena. I'd have to do some tweaking to make it work.

"LSU." Gabe worked the long muscles on either side of my spine. "I'm buying my bar from my father. It's almost paid off." His voice deepened as if he were proud of himself.

The change of subject surprised me. I glanced over my shoulder. "Did he cut you a deal?"

"I'm paying fair market, but he holds the loan. Like the arrangement Joe had on this house. Pretty much everything goes through the folks, whether we want it to or not." He pushed my shirt to my shoulders. "Take this off."

Careful not to flash him my boobs or Pooh belly, I pulled the T-shirt over my head. "Why would you want to give that up to take your father's job?"

"I don't want to give it up, but how can I say no? His company is his life's work. I can't turn him down. It would have gone to Joe, now it falls to me." He straddled my thighs.

Gabe had always had a competitive streak with his brothers, especially Joe. That, coupled with his constant need to please his parents, had caused most of the problems in our relationship.

NOLA Society readers would love a peek into his psyche, but I wouldn't go there. No, I'd find a different angle for his article. "How sad."

"It's not sad—it's life. You of all people should get that. You gave up your dreams to come here and raise the kids."

I shook my head. "I always wanted to be an author. I haven't given it up, but it's taking longer to write the new novel than I'd hoped."

"How about the mother part?"

"I never imagined it would happen like this, but I wouldn't trade it for the world."

"Didn't you want kids of your own?" He pressed his fingers into my neck in slow circles.

"I never thought much about it, but I'm okay with what I have. I mean, how many women can have three kids and no stretch marks?"

Gabe moved his hands back to my shoulders. "How do you know you won't want more one day?"

"I guess I don't."

He leaned forward and whispered into my ear, "Relax."

"I'm trying." I laughed, but it would have been easier without his thighs on either side of me, not to mention his breath in my ear.

Gabe's phone rang.

"Are you going to answer?"

"No." His voice deepened.

I would never be a neat freak, but certain things bugged me. Cabinets left open, clothes hanging out of drawers, and unanswered calls.

Gabe fought a losing battle to work the tension from my muscles. "I know you're writing the cultural reviews, but I didn't know you were working on another novel. What's it about?"

I sighed and tried to relax again. "The same as the last four. Female James Bond. International espionage. The publisher's breathing down my neck, but it's hard to find time to write. I don't want to put Ryan in daycare and it's hard to be creative with a preschooler running around. I'll finish it soon."

"Do you enjoy writing?"

The question took me off guard. "Fiction, yes. The free-lance stuff, no, not really."

"Still thinking about Justin?" His hands moved to my lower back.

"I wasn't until you said his name." I grinned against the mattress. "I feel like an ass. I mean we only went out a couple times, but we talked on the phone until late at night. I never suspected he was married."

He made a sound behind me that made me want to turn around, but he rubbed a tender spot, and it felt too good to move.

"Were you falling for him?"

"I thought he was a nice guy. Older, steady..."

"You didn't answer my question."

"I've only ever been in love with one person."

Gabe's hands stilled.

I'd said too much. Or maybe I hadn't said enough. "Are you dating anyone?"

He sighed and got back to work. "I haven't had time."

I turned and gave him a *yeah-right* look.

"I'm serious." He put his hand on my head and pushed me back down.

"What's it been, a month?" I bit my lip to hold back laughter.

"Ten months give or take."

Holy crap. I should have let the subject go, but I wanted answers now that I had him talking. "Did you love her? Ella's mother?"

"We barely knew each other." He pressed harder, as if taking out his frustration on my muscles.

I made a pained sound, and he eased the pressure.

"Sorry, bad subject." Gabe moved off me and reached for my shirt.

I couldn't stand the lost look in his eyes or the fact that I'd put it there. I did my best to slip into my shirt without flashing him, but I must have given him a glimpse of side boob or something. The man stared at me as if I were the star of his fantasies.

My mom didn't know shit. Not about Gabe. Fifteen extra pounds or not, he liked what he'd seen.

I tilted my head. "You okay over there?"

He licked his lips. "I'm rethinking the sweats."

I winced before I could stop myself. "This is what I mean about bring up old feelings. Sometimes this feels like it used to, but sometimes it's like we're strangers. I don't want to get hurt again."

"I'm not Justin, and I'm not the same jerk from four years ago. I'm not going to hurt you..." He must have seen something in my expression because he sighed and glanced away. "Sleep beside me tonight."

"Just sleep?"

He crossed his heart. "Like you said, it's been a tough day. The kids aren't here to catch us. I don't know about you, but I'd rather not be alone."

Knowing better than to give in, I curled against him. It wouldn't end well. We wouldn't end well. But damn it, I wanted one night to believe we'd beat the odds.

15

Gabe

FOR THE SECOND SATURDAY IN A ROW, I WOKE TO A CAR door slamming and the dog going nuts in the living room. Cocoa ran from the window to the door, and back in a figure eight pattern that, along with her deep barks, set my teeth on edge.

Saturday. Shit. It's little-girl-dance-recital day.

I extracted myself from Chloe and Ryan, who'd crawled into my bed during the night. A habit Maggie said I'd have to break sooner or later, but I didn't have the heart to do it now. I got it. They missed their dad, and I missed my big brother.

The two weeks since Chantal had dropped Ella into my life had flown by. Maggie and I had established a comfortable routine. We pulled opposite shifts, which sucked, but it gave me an excuse to crawl into her bed when I came home. We'd talk about the kids, the bar, life in general until she fell back asleep. Then I'd return to my room alone—though I seldom woke that way.

Maggie worried about the kids finding us in bed

together, but I was smart enough to know she had other reasons. Reasons like, the more we shared a bed, the more likely we'd have sex. I'd told her I'd wait, and I would, but my father's ultimatum hung over my head—not to mention my balls had gone from sky blue to cobalt.

"Enough, Cocoa!" The damned dog made enough noise to wake the entire house. It had to be my mother coming early to check on Chloe. Who else would visit before eight on a Saturday morning?

Still in my pajama bottoms, I opened the door.

Nadine took me in from my bare feet to my unshaved face and bed rumpled hair. "Where's Mary Margaret?"

"Maggie's sleeping in. She was up late." I took a step back and motioned for her to come in.

"Where are the children? Today's Chloe's recital. Shouldn't they be up by now?" She nudged the dog out of her way, pulled her purse higher on her shoulder, and headed toward the hall.

I stepped into her path. "The recital's not until ten-thirty. I'd rather you not wake Maggie. She doesn't get a chance to sleep in often."

"Who are you to tell me about my daughter?"

"Someone who cares a lot about her." I folded my arms.

Nadine took another step forward, but I held my ground. We glared at each other until the doorbell rang. Again.

I grinned and went to the door. My grin didn't last long.

"Jesus, Mary, and Joseph, Gabriel. Is this how you open the door? Half-dressed?" My mother pushed into the house, looking over Mrs. Guthrie like last week's leftovers. "Nadine. Nice to see you again."

"Evelyn." Nadine narrowed her eyes.

"Where's Maggie? We're supposed to go to breakfast before the recital." My mother dropped her purse on the sofa.

"She's sleeping. Ella kept us up most of the night." *Maggie's going to flip. I gotta get them out of here.*

"The poor dear. Did the pediatrician change her formula?"

"Yeah, she's on soy now."

She kissed my cheek—likely for Nadine's benefit. "Where are my grandchildren?"

"Everyone's still sleeping." I ran my hand over the back of my neck. Nadine made me nuts, but Nadine and Evelyn together were more than anyone should have to endure. "Have a seat, I'll start some coffee."

Maggie staggered down the hallway in one of her over-sized T-shirts and little else. She offered me a sleepy smile on her way to the coffee pot.

I nodded toward the living room, but she didn't take the hint.

Nadine cleared her throat. Maggie turned her head and her face paled.

I leaned close and whispered, "Our mothers are here. We're supposed to have breakfast before the recital."

"Oh no, what time is it?" Maggie went from sleep-deprived zombie to alert and freaking out in no time flat.

"Eight fifteen." Nadine said from the bar.

Maggie turned and looked between Nadine and Evelyn, and then shot *me* a dirty look. "I'll get the kids up."

What the hell did I do this time? I kept my eyes on the pot while the coffee brewed.

"Where are the kids?" Maggie called from upstairs.

"In my room." I answered before I thought the better of it.

Nadine huffed. "Where did you sleep?"

Evelyn's smile changed from forced to downright cheerful. While she wanted me to bring all of her grandchildren under her roof and for the Guthrie women to disappear, she wouldn't pass up the chance to rub Nadine's nose in mine and Maggie's relationship. "With Maggie. Where else? They're getting—"

"To know each other. We're getting to know each other. And no. We aren't sharing a bed." I shot my mom a warning look. The last thing I needed was her blabbing about the engagement before I'd gotten around to talking to Maggie about it.

Nadine narrowed her eyes and glanced between us. "Don't tell me you approve of this situation."

Evelyn shrugged. "What's to approve of? They're adults. As long as they're happy and the kids are taken care of, I think it's wonderful."

It's too early for this. "Coffee?"

Either they hadn't heard or they ignored me.

The mood in the house had gone from cold to downright hostile in a matter of moments. If something didn't change, I'd be refereeing a senior citizen cage match. Thankfully, Zach shuffled into the kitchen, hugged each of his grandmothers, and wandered to the coffee pot.

"Good morning." I grinned. With his rumpled hair and drowsy smile, he reminded me of my older brother.

"Is it?" Zach yawned and filled his mug.

Ryan emerged next, raring to go. "Grandmas!"

Nadine and my mother held their arms out to the boy, but he bypassed them and went straight to me.

"Hey, little man. Hungry?" I picked him up. It might have been wrong to use a small child as a human shield, but I'd take what I could get. I poured two cups of coffee and set one in front of each mother. "I should get Ella dressed."

"You aren't bringing a newborn to a dance recital, are you?" Nadine raised her chin and looked down her nose.

"Why shouldn't he? Ella's a good baby. Hardly makes a sound." Evelyn turned and glared.

Nadine huffed. "It's rude. People are there to watch their children dance, not to listen to a baby cry."

God love her, my mother laughed and raised the tension in the room to DEFCON five. "I've been to enough of these things to know she won't be the only crying baby in the building."

"Oh, so she *will* be crying?" Nadine smirked. "My daughter has enough to deal with, getting Chloe ready. She doesn't have time to take care of an infant."

Evelyn pushed into the other woman's personal space. "My son will take care of his child."

"Enough. Ladies." I used the same tone as I had with the dog. "It's too early in the morning for this. Why don't you two go have breakfast? We'll meet you at the auditorium."

"I'm not leaving until I speak with my daughter." Nadine put her hands on her hips.

"You're right, Mrs. Guthrie. Maggie has enough to deal with this morning." I set Ryan down and moved around the bar. One hand on each woman's shoulder, I guided them to the living room. "You two need to go. Enjoy breakfast together. We'll meet you there."

"Of course." Evelyn smiled and plucked her purse from the couch. "Put Ella in the adorable pink dress I bought her."

"I will." I kissed my mother's cheek and opened the door.

Nadine's frown deepened, but she left.

Even with the door closed, their voices carried inside the house.

Zach shook his head and took his coffee to his room. Meanwhile, Ryan crawled onto a bar stool and picked up Nadine's abandoned mug.

"Oh no you don't." I took the cup from his hands. "How about some cereal?"

"Pancakes?" Ryan giggled.

"Cereal." I pulled the box out of the pantry.

"Pancakes." The boy folded his arms and gave me a look that promised a tantrum if I didn't comply.

"Pancakes it is." I added *stop giving in to the three-year-old terrorist* to my list of shit to do.

Fifteen minutes later, I set a plate of pancakes in front of Ryan.

"These are weird." The kid eyed his breakfast. "Cereal, please."

I closed my eyes and counted to ten. "You're killing me, little dude."

"Do I smell pancakes?" Zach came back out of his cave.

I took the plate from mini-Bin Laden and slid them to the teen.

Dragging her dance bag behind her, Chloe walked

down the hall.

"Good morning, Princess. Want some pancakes?" One look at her and my smile faded. She looked like hell in a pink leotard and black tutu.

Before I could ask, Chloe grabbed her stomach and barfed on the carpet. The room erupted in movement. The boys groaned and abandoned their breakfasts. Ryan's milk spilled during the melee. I knelt beside Chloe, and she showered my chest in vomit.

Maggie ran into the room. She took one look at the situation, turned, and ran toward the bathroom.

Chloe glanced down at her ruined dance costume and burst into tears. "No!"

I'd seen war veterans go into a post-traumatic fugue state but had never experienced one myself—until then. My mind blanked.

"My tutu!"

"Come with me." I tossed my shirt in the laundry, took her hand, and led her to the bathroom.

"I don't feel good." Chloe sobbed while I mopped the puke from her tutu with a frilly white hand towel. One of Maggie's special, decorative-only hand towels. *Shit.*

"I know, sweetie." I wiped the carnage from my chest and started a shower. "Do you feel like you're going to throw up again?"

"I don't think so."

"Okay, let's get you cleaned up."

Chloe nodded, her shoulders shaking with each sob.

I placed my hand on her forehead and frowned. She had a fever. "Do you want me to stay here or do you need privacy?"

"Privacy."

I worried she'd fall or vomit again and freak out, but I understood. "I'll get you some PJs and wait in the hall in case you need me."

"I love you, Uncle Gabe."

My heart melted. Getting puked on was worth it—almost. "Love you, too, munchkin."

After the quick bath, I tucked the girl into bed. Her forehead didn't feel as warm as it had and her color looked better, but I hated to leave her alone.

Tears leaked from Chloe's eyes.

"What's the matter?" I smoothed her hair back from her face.

"I'm going to miss my recital."

"What if we hold another one? We'll invite the family. It'll be a one woman show."

"Will there be a stage?" Her expression brightened, and I knew she'd be okay.

"Of course."

"And a pink costume with wings?"

I booped her nose. "Is there any other kind?"

Chloe snuggled into her pillow. "Okay."

"I need to check on Ella and Maggie. Will you be okay for a few minutes?"

She nodded and patted the side of the bed.

The chocolate lab hopped up and curled against the little girl. The dog and I shared a look. Cocoa was a pain in the ass, but she'd keep an eye on her master.

I stepped into the master bedroom and peeked into the crib. Sound asleep, Ella sucked an imaginary bottle. I could have watched her sleep for hours, but a noise from the bathroom drew my attention.

I leaned close to the door and lowered my voice. "Maggie?" When she didn't respond, I poked my head inside. "Mags?"

She'd fallen asleep while spooning the toilet.

I touched her shoulder. "Wake up, sweetheart."

She raised her head with the most pitiful expression I'd ever seen. "Help me to my bedroom. I don't want Ella to get sick."

I slid an arm around her waist, hoisted her to her feet, and half-carried her to my bed. "Stay in here. It's closer to the bathroom. Chloe's in bed."

"Is she okay?" She started to get up, more than likely planning to check on the girl.

"She's fine. Cocoa's keeping an eye on her."

Maggie curled into the pillows. "Aren't our mothers still here?"

"No. I threw them out for bad behavior." I pulled the blankets to her chin.

"They hate each other."

Gee, I hadn't noticed. "I know."

"Check to see if the boys have a fever. If not, send them to my mom."

"Would it be all right if they went to my parents' instead?"

"Why?"

"The look Nadine gave me on her way out..."

She nodded against the pillow and whispered, "Call your mom, but promise me you'll testify if she uses this against me in the custody hearing."

16

Maggie

WITH CHLOE SLEEPING, AND THE REST OF THE KIDDOS at their grandmother's for the night, the house was quiet—too quiet. I had nothing to do, so I'd spent the day feeling like garbage and thinking about my life. Under the circumstances, *that* wasn't a good idea. To distract myself, I retrieved my laptop from my room. Maybe I could squeeze out a couple of chapters on my new book before I went back to sleep.

An email from Shanna caught my eye. From the looks of it, she'd spent a considerable amount of time researching the Marchionni family. I scrolled through genealogy records that made my head spin. Names and dates and places. Births and deaths and marriages—too much to comprehend in one sitting.

My phone rang, and I nearly toppled out of bed trying to reach it. "Hello?"

"You're going to die, bitch." The caller hung up.

I glanced at the screen. Blocked number. "I thought prank calls died sometime in the nineties."

"Mags?" Gabe knocked and opened the door.

I dropped my cell and snapped the laptop closed. "Is Chloe okay?"

He gave me the same look he had when he'd stared at my boobs. Crazy man. Sure, I was in bed, but there was nothing sexy about my reading glasses and ponytail.

I pulled the blanket higher on my chest.

"She's sleeping. Can I come in?" His gaze drifted to my shoulders.

"Sure, it's your room."

He plopped down in the chair near the window. "Want to watch a movie?"

"I'm really tired. I'm going to sleep once I finished checking my email."

"We could watch a chick-flick." He wiggled his brows.

"Just so you know, porn isn't the same thing as a chick-flick."

"I beg to differ, but that's not what I had in mind. Come on Mags. You can pick the movie." Biting his lower lip, Gabe dipped his chin and peered through his lashes. The expression would have looked feminine on most men, but he wasn't most men.

"Don't give me puppy-eyes. We'll do it another time. I promise." I wanted nothing more than to curl up beside him, but I had work to do. "Oh. I've been meaning to ask you. What happens to your bar once you take over for your dad?"

"You know...I asked Joe a similar question in this exact spot." He stood as if to leave.

My reporter's instincts kicked in. I'd hit a nerve. "When was that?"

Gabe hesitated and picked up a photo of my sister and her husband. "Shortly after Zach was born. Joe planned to start working with our father. I pointed out he'd be traveling a lot."

I nodded, though I couldn't shake the feeling he'd lied, or at very least, held something back.

"How can you stand to be in this room?" Speaking through gritted teeth, he slammed the picture face down on the dresser.

Once again, his reaction surprised me. "I feel strange getting rid of their stuff. I don't usually stay in here."

"I get that, but I don't think anyone would mind if you changed things to your taste." He motioned from the collection of family photos to the stack of books on the nightstand.

Joe and Rebecca wouldn't mind because they were dead, but the kids might have a problem with me messing with their parents' things. "I'd rather not—"

"Do you like it here?" Chin raised, he stared down at me.

I wrapped my arms around my middle. *Why is he so upset?* "It's okay."

Gabe seemed to pick up on my distress and softened his tone. "If you ever decide you want to move, I'd be happy to help you and the kids get a new house."

"I couldn't ask you to do that." I forced myself to meet his gaze. "Besides, this is their home. How could I move them when they have been through so much?"

"Maybe they need a new beginning as much as you do." He walked to the door. "Sweet dreams, Maggie."

That's it? He's leaving? "Wait, you didn't answer my

question. I think I have a right to know what happens to your bar since I'm an employee now."

"We can talk tomorrow. I'm going to turn in. Should I sleep in your bed?"

The change in his demeanor concerned me, but it also told me where to dig for information on the story.

"I'll move." I grabbed my laptop and marched to my room.

Gabe followed. "Maggie, wait. I didn't mean to chase you off."

I set the computer on my nightstand. "It's fine. I'm sick, and you're tired. We both need some rest."

"I'd rather not think about giving up my bar."

His expression reminded me of Zach's any time he talked about his parents. Gabe mourned the loss of his bar. It made sense, but it broke my heart. I understood family obligations better than most people, but I couldn't understand him turning his back on his dream.

I slid beneath the blankets and plucked the remote from the nightstand. "Still up for a movie? You can choose."

"Sure, but what I could really use is a Jack and Coke and sex."

I wanted to call him out for avoiding questions any time they hit too close to a nerve. However, he chose that moment to strip out of his jeans and climbed in beside me in his boxer briefs.

My stomach did a backflip that had nothing to do with the virus rampaging through my body. "I can't drink, or I might throw up again, and sex is off the table."

"Okay. How about a blowjob?" He poked my side.

"That's sex."

"No, it's not. Everyone knows that. Bill Clinton made it legally not sex back in the nineties."

I smacked his arm and curled up beside him.

"I'm kidding." He flipped through the channels.

My phone rang from the other room.

"Crap."

"I'll get it." Gabe hopped out of bed.

Fighting off exhaustion, I ran through my to-do list. I didn't have time to get sick. I needed to finish the damned article and get paid before the custody hearing.

"Missed the call. It was a blocked number." He tossed the cell to me, and it dinged with a voicemail alert.

I hit replay and listened to the same raspy voice call me every name for a female of questionable morals I'd ever heard, and some I hadn't.

"Mags?"

"Second prank call tonight." I deleted the message.

He frowned and stretched out beside me. "I can have the calls traced."

"I'm sure it's nothing." I had a feeling it was something, but after the day I'd had, I didn't want to get into it. Nuzzling into the pillow, I flashed him a smile to butter him up. "Are you up for watching the kids Wednesday morning?"

"Sure, but where are you going?"

"I have to do some research for a new piece I'm working on. Then I have a shift at the bar."

"What happened with the cultural reviews?" Gabe rolled to face me.

"They pulled my article. I'm on a new assignment. I have to finish it soon."

"I can watch them." He brushed my hair back from my face.

"Thank you. I'll write down everyone's schedule. I should be home by three."

"Have you spoken to your lawyer about the hearing?"

I closed my eyes and debated on how to answer. Lying or avoiding seemed like the best options, but he'd find out the truth sooner or later. "Attorneys cost money."

"Now that I'm living here, my folks should back off."

My stomach did another somersault. I'd owe him big time if he managed to get Evelyn off my case. "That'd be great, but I'll believe it when I see it."

He drew his brows together and tensed his jaw, an expression I knew meant he had something unpleasant to discuss.

"What's wrong?" Nerves thinned my voice.

"Nothing." He glanced back to the television. "How's it going at the bar?"

"It's fun." I sincerely doubted he'd intended to talk about my second job.

"How do you feel about hiring a nanny? I could change our schedules so we would see more of each other."

Ah-ha. I knew it. I eased back from him. "I don't want a nanny."

"If I didn't know better, I'd think you were trying to avoid me by working different shifts." He grinned, likely to hide the insecurity in his words.

Once again, his expression made me pause. Gabe was a lot of things, but unsure of himself? Never. "I like having you here, now that you're not drinking from the milk carton."

He tugged my body against his. "Think about it, Mags. When it slows down at the bar, you could use the time to finish the novel. Hell, you could even go back to school."

"I can't afford a nanny, and you're going back to your life in another week or so." Although, I could use the time to finish my novel. Lord knew, I needed the check from the publisher. Still, I didn't feel right about pawning the kids off on someone else. Rebecca had left them in my hands, not a nanny's.

"About that..." Gabe pulled back enough to meet my gaze. "I don't want to move out. Let's make *us* official."

A million questions popped into my head. What did he mean official? Dating? Would I wear his class ring and letterman jacket? Was that an off-handed proposal? What would the kids think? Could I do this again with him?

Gabe's cell rang. He leaned over the bed, pulled it from his jeans, and hit the ignore button.

Memories of the weeks and months after our break-up crashed over me. I couldn't help but wonder who called him at all hours of the day and night, and why he never answered. I sat up and scooted away. "You have a bad habit of not answering your cell."

"Blocked number." He clasped his hands behind his head, the picture of relaxed. "Maybe your prankster moved on to me."

I knew him. I recognized the tension in his jaw, and that his grin hadn't crinkled the corners of his eyes. Gabe had lied to me.

"You should go. Chloe might come looking for me, or

my mother could show up in the morning." The thought of my mother finding him in my bed made my head hurt almost as much as his dishonesty.

"Your mother already thinks we're sleeping together."

My throat tightened. "Why does she think that?"

"She got the wrong idea this morning." He shrugged and nudged my side. "May as well do the deed. I'm sure both our mothers already lit candles for our sinful souls."

"Perfect." I drew my knees to my chest. "One more thing your mom can use against me in court."

"I'll get her to drop the custody case, but it would be easier to do if you had my ring on your finger."

Blood rushed behind my eardrums. *That was definitely an off-handed proposal.*

His phone rang again. This time he cursed and turned it off.

My nerves sparked like downed powerlines. "Who keeps calling you?

"It's another blocked number. Probably a solicitor." He reached for my hand. "I want this. I want you. Let's go ring shopping."

"I can't marry you. We're just now getting to know each other again." Part of me wanted to laugh, the other wanted to cry. I'd never stopped loving him, but he'd broken my heart. I couldn't go through that again. I wouldn't survive it.

Gabe's expression grew more serious. "She's wrong, you know."

"Who?"

"Your mother. Guys like me do fall for women like you."

My mouth moved though no sound came out. I stared for a beat and dipped my chin. I couldn't look at him, not when I felt so damned humiliated. "You heard that?"

"Yeah." He took my hand and pulled until I rested against his chest. "Nothing personal, but your mother's a bitch. Took everything I had to not toss her out on her skinny ass last week. And man-oh-man, did I enjoy kicking her out this morning."

"She's had a tough time since her divorce and worries about me getting hurt." I hated myself for defending her, but she was my mom.

"There's no excuse." He ran hand up my back. "Let me hold you tonight. We'll talk about the rest in the morning."

I weighed my options. Chloe might come downstairs, but I could always lock the bedroom door. I sighed, preparing to turn him down when it hit me—I didn't want him to leave. Not tonight. Not ever. I'd always loved him, but at some point since he showed up on my doorstep, I'd tripped and fallen back *in love* with him. "Stay."

"That was too easy. Are you sure?" He nuzzled his face into my hair.

"Are you trying to talk me out of it?"

"No." Gabe chuckled. "Close your eyes and get some rest."

"I feel better."

"Good."

"You convinced me to sleep with you and all you want to do is *sleep*?" I slid my hand down his back to his ass.

"Crazy what we do for love, isn't it?" He kissed the top of my head. "Good night, Maggie."

He used the L-word! It seemed silly that those four letters could make my pulse race faster than it had when he'd all but asked me to marry him. For once in my life, I settled into the warm-fuzzy feeling of belonging without the fear of it all coming down around me. "Good night, Gabe."

17

Gabe

THE DIGITAL CLOCK ON THE NIGHTSTAND PROVED FAR less entertaining than the fully clothed woman in my arms, but I stared at it anyway. I needed the distraction to keep my mind and my hands still. She'd taken me by surprise when she'd asked me to stay.

Hell, I'd surprised myself with the half-assed proposal. I should have known better than to spring it on her like that. She deserved better, but Maggie had a way of making me act before I thought.

When we'd dated before, her intensity had scared me. Not that I minded smart women, quite the contrary, but in my line of work, a strong-willed woman didn't last long. She'd ask questions and demand answers—answers I couldn't give.

At twenty-one, her optimism shined like the sun. She believed she could change the world, and I had no doubt she would succeed. The woman had every conceivable detail of her future planned out. When I realized those plans included me, I made the decision to let her go for her own good. *Who was I to tie her to a world she would never understand, let alone accept? Only the man who regretted pushing her away every fucking day of my life.*

I'd avoided her until Joe and Rebecca's funeral. Maggie had seemed so different then. She'd matured in the years we'd spent apart. Oddly enough, she'd taken on more of Rebecca's softer, more nurturing personality. Lately, she even looked more like her sister. Maggie had traded in her sexy skinny jeans and high heels for yoga pants and sneakers.

Since the funeral, it seemed like she'd focused all of her energy and determination on a single goal—being a surrogate mother and father to three grieving children.

As much as I hated to admit it, I missed the old Maggie. The girl with fire in her veins. The gorgeous, self-confident woman who wouldn't let anyone or anything stop her from reaching her dreams. She was in there somewhere—all I had to do was draw her out.

Maggie's phone rang.

She bolted upright and nearly broke my nose in the process. "Sorry. Are you okay?"

Pain bloomed in my face and my vision blurred. "I'll live."

She searched for her phone. "Where's my cell? It could be about the kids."

I plucked it from the nightstand and handed it to her.

"This better be good, Shanna. It's five in the morning." She listened a moment.

A garbled female voice came across the line, but I couldn't make out what she'd said.

Maggie nodded several times and turned to me.

One word rang out loud and clear, "Marchionni."

"Shanna, this isn't funny." Maggie's brow furrowed and the color drained from her face. "He's right here. I need to go."

Her complexion changed from pale to angry red. "That was Shanna. She's close with Dahlia, your brother's friend. Would you mind telling me why half of New Orleans thinks we're engaged?"

"Already?" Once again, my mouth got ahead of my brain.

"What do you mean *already*?" Maggie crawled out of the bed and paced. "What in the hell is going on? Why are you really here?"

My temples throbbed, along with my nose. "Slow down, Mags. Let me explain."

"I don't want to hear it. Put some freaking clothes on and get out." She turned her back to me, but she couldn't hide the fact she was crying.

"Maggie, I—"

"We have court in two days. Did your mother put you up to this?" She rounded on me.

"Not exactly."

"What do you mean, not exactly?" Her voice had quieted several notches, but her anger bubbled beneath the surface. "How does anyone know anything about this? You just mentioned a ring last night. By the way, that was a piss-poor proposal, *if* that's what you meant it to be."

"It was. It is." I eased closer to her. "I went to my folks when Ella's mother—"

"This is bad. If the magazine finds out..." She hugged herself and bent at the waist.

"Sweetheart, you need to calm down." I rested my hand between her shoulders.

Maggie stood upright, but her gaze flitted around the room. "What do your parents have to do with this?"

"You know how they are. I showed up with a baby. They insisted I get married."

"To Ella's mother, right? How did I get dragged into this?"

I dug my fingers into my temples. "That's what I'm trying to explain."

She pressed her lips together and nodded.

I sat on the edge of the bed. "You have to understand. You were the first person I thought about when I found out about Ella."

She gave me a look.

"I swear on my grandmother's grave." I took her hand. "I always wanted kids, but I wanted them with you."

She opened her mouth, likely to argue.

I put my finger to her full lips. "Let me finish. When my folks started in on the *if you're man enough to be a father, you're man enough to marry the mother speech*, I panicked. I told them I wouldn't marry Chantal. My father...he knew how I felt about you before—"

"But we weren't even speaking to each other, let alone a couple."

But, sweetheart, I wanted to be. I wanted you every day of my life. "I know, but this is my father we're talking about. He saw a means to an end and took it. He'll take my bar if I don't marry you."

"Can he do that?" Her eyes widened.

"Yes. He can call the loan any time." I sighed and took

her hands in mine. "Maggie, think about it. We can make it work."

She flinched as if I'd hit her. "What you said last night... This has nothing to do with how you feel about me. You're trying to hold onto your bar."

"I am, but didn't you hear me when I said you were the first person I thought about?"

"I need you to leave."

"We have to do this. They'll take the kids from you if we don't." I regretted my words as soon as I'd said them.

Maggie's mouth fell open. She turned and stormed out of the room.

I followed, taking her arm before she reached the kitchen. "Maggie, wait."

She pulled away. "Don't. I thought maybe you'd changed. It's bad enough you're using me, but to hold the kids over my head?"

"I'm not using you." I took a step back to give her space. "This could be good for both of us."

Maggie folded her arms. "Do you actually expect me to play along with this?"

"Hear me out. This isn't about the bar. I'm going to lose it anyway."

She turned her head.

"You're struggling to make ends meet. You hate your job, and I bet you'd love to finish your novel. Maybe go back to grad school? I'm struggling with Ella. I have to give up a job I love and take one I may hate. My father told me to marry you or bring all four grandkids to my mother. They're never going to stop fighting you for custody...but if we get married, they'll back off."

"What about Ella's mother? What if she comes back?"

"Listen to me. Chantal made it clear she wants nothing to do with raising a child. She isn't coming back and even if she did, it wouldn't change anything." My bluntness seemed to surprise her.

"You should've told me the truth from the beginning."

"I know, and I'm sorry." I struggled to find the right words, not wanting to piss her off even more. "But it could work. You could make rules. Think about it, Mags—no more worrying about bills, no more looking over your shoulder worrying about my mother."

"Bullshit. She'd be even more in my business as my mother-in-law. Plus, I'm Catholic."

"What?" It took my brain a minute to catch up to her. "So what? So am I."

"We don't do divorce." Her voice softened.

I wanted to pull her into my arms and kiss her stupid. Maybe then she'd understand how much I loved her. "Catholics aren't supposed to have premarital sex or use birth control either. Besides, I don't plan to get divorced."

Maggie's brows climbed into her hairline. "Do you expect me to believe you actually want to marry me?"

I wanted to tell her I loved her, but doubted she'd believe me. I'd never felt so off my game. Running my hand over the back of my neck, I searched for the right words. The words that would make this beautiful creature understand.

Maggie turned, walked to her bedroom, and shut the door.

My nose ached to the point I could feel my heartbeat in my nostrils. I needed to ice it, but I followed her. "Dammit,

Maggie. I know I'm screwing this up. Would you just listen?"

"Please, go. I need time to think before the boys come home."

"No." I searched the top of the door frame for the key and turned the lock.

She shot to her feet. "If you don't get out, I'm going to call the police."

"Do what you have to do, but they'll take one look at my face and arrest you for domestic abuse."

18

Maggie

HE WOULDN'T!

Gabe was a lot of things, but he wasn't the kind of man who would allow a woman to be arrested for something she didn't do. Then again, I never thought he'd play with my feelings to save his precious bar or reputation or whatever he was doing here.

I shut my eyes because looking at him hurt, and I needed time to sort out my feelings before I said something I couldn't take back. "Please leave."

He closed the distance and pulled me against him. "Since you won't listen, let me try a different tactic."

"That's the problem. You shouldn't have to use tactics in a—" One moment I struggled to break free, the next his lips were on mine.

Pulling back enough to meet my gaze, he whispered, "Damn it, Maggie. I love you."

I wanted to believe him. I needed to believe him. And I suppose, I *did* believe him. I loved him, too, and always had, but was that enough?

Gabe didn't give me the chance to respond. He curled his fingers in my hair and yanked my head back.

I gasped. The moment my lips parted, he delved into my mouth. My body melted, but my brain revolted. I'd dreamed of this for four years—the same four years I'd spent sobbing into my pillow. Gabe's kiss felt like home, but part of me wanted to run away and join the circus.

He pulled back and held my gaze. "Don't overthink this."

"What?"

He slid his hand beneath my sweats and grabbed my butt. Half-lifting and half-pressing, he ground his hips into mine.

"Oh, that." I murmured against his lips.

Gabe released me, turned me around, and pressed his chest to my back. With one hand across my belly, he slipped the other under my shirt and cupped my breast.

This is happening. Oh God, this is happening now? "Gabe?"

"Hmm?" He nipped at my earlobe.

Between his fingers toying with my nipple and his cock pressed against my lower back, I thought I might climax before he touched me below the waist. "What are you doing?"

He licked the hollow behind my ear. "Trying to turn you on..."

I shivered and reached back to caress his hip. "It's working."

"Good."

He felt as good as I'd remembered. In fact, he seemed to recall exactly how I liked to be touched and where.

Gabe tugged my sweats. "Take these off."

I hesitated, and he pinched my nipple hard enough to elicit a yelp.

"Get out of your head."

I slid my pants and boy shorts over my hips and kicked them off. I tried to turn to face him, but he held me in place.

"Not yet."

Before I could protest, he distracted me by tracing slow circles down, down, down my body until he'd zeroed in on his target. One touch and I forgot how to breathe, two more and I thought I'd spontaneously combust.

"Like that, baby?"

"God, yes." I arched my back and wiggled hoping he'd take the hint. "But I need more."

He released my breast and turned my face toward his. "You're so beautiful."

I parted my lips, and he wasted no time in claiming my mouth. The awkward position made the kiss seem more erotic—our tongues struggling in the space between us. I tried to turn in his arms, but he broke the kiss and tightened his grip.

The pressure built inside me, and I knew it wouldn't be long before I came. At lease I hoped it wouldn't. It had been forever since I'd done this with another person. Four years since he'd turned me into a puddle. My belly trembled against his forearm. *So close, so damned close.*

He switched from circles to firm strokes, and my knees threatened to give out. "Let go, baby."

"I can't." I hated the desperation in my voice, but I knew my body. The pleasure hung on the line between bliss and pain—too sensitive, too intense, too everything for me to let go.

Gabe turned me to face him and walked me backward to the bed. His gaze fixed on mine; he yanked his boxers down.

I wanted to tell him I'd missed him, that I'd thought about this, about him, about us, but he pressed a finger to my lips.

"If you talk, you'll think, and you'll second guess yourself."

Grinning, I ran my tongue around the tip of his finger.

"Mags..." He slid his hands under my thighs. Bending me in two, he pressed his cock against my entrance. "Is this what you want?"

I nodded.

Cursing under his breath, Gabe released my legs. "Do you have a condom?"

Rather than speaking, I pointed toward the nightstand drawer.

"Good girl." He rewarded me with a grin. The man enjoyed taking charge in the bedroom as much as I enjoyed surrendering.

A moment later, he poised himself over me again. This time he wasted no time asking questions. He drew both my thighs up and buried himself inside me in one quick stroke.

I saw stars; pleasure and pain mixed together into a strong cocktail that left me intoxicated.

Still sheathed inside me, he whispered, "More?"

I closed my eyes. "Yes."

"Look at me, beautiful." Gabe set a leisurely rhythm.

I watched the lines of his face sharpen with concentration. We'd had a lot of sex in our time together, and he'd rarely taken the slow and steady route. He had to be holding back for my benefit.

Lying half on top of me, he released one thigh and buried his face in my hair. "You feel so damned good."

"Please..." I skimmed my nails down his back.

"Please what, baby?"

"Stop being so careful." I thrust my hips against his.

He sucked in a breath and increased his speed. Once again, the pressure built inside me. I wrapped my legs around him tight enough to restrict his movement, but he seemed to take it as a challenge and thrust harder.

"Come for me." Gabe growled into my ear.

I obeyed. My entire body shook with the force of the orgasm. Keenly aware we had a child upstairs, I bit the inside of my mouth to keep from crying out.

Before I could recover, Gabe pulled back and flipped me to my stomach. Tugging me to all fours, his fingers dug into my hips.

I grasped the sheets until my knuckles paled from the effort. Once again, I lost myself somewhere between pleasure and pain. I hadn't felt so alive since we'd broken up.

Gabe slapped my ass hard enough to leave a handprint.

The shock of it sent me over the edge again, and he followed.

He collapsed beside me, but I couldn't bring myself to move. I laid still with my arms folded beneath my chest and my hands balled under my chin. He caressed my back.

Smiling through the hair covering my face, I whispered, "Hi."

"Hi." He pulled me close and kissed my brow. "Did I hurt you?"

"A good kind of hurt." I buried my face in his chest. "Gabe?"

"Hmm?" He eased back until he could see my face.

"Can we do that again when we don't have any kids in the house?"

"Which part?"

"All of it."

He chuckled and kissed me. "Yes, and often...on one condition...marry me."

"I'll think about it, but I need to sleep first." I nuzzled against him.

"I love you, Maggie."

"I love you, too." If something went wrong, I'd blame this entire conversation on the post-orgasm hormones, but I did love him—and yes, I would marry him...one day.

19

Gabe

WEDNESDAY MORNING, THE ALARM SCREAMED AT FIVE forty-five. Exhausted, I reached to turn off the alarm and couldn't find it. The realization that I'd slept in a strange bed woke me quicker than an ice bath. I smelled a familiar perfume and reached behind me to find a curvy hip —Maggie.

The way her sweet little body fit against mine made me smile, and the need to protect her overwhelmed me. She had a quiet strength about her, and a fragile heart I intended to nurture.

Maggie hadn't accepted my proposal, but she hadn't said no. She would be mine, she had to be—not because of my parents or money or to win a custody battle—because we belonged together.

As much as I hated to leave her, I had shit to do. I eased out of bed doing my damnedest not to wake her, and grabbed my jeans.

Still buttoning my fly, I stepped into the hall and ran

into Zach. The kid was thirteen. He had to know what happened behind closed doors.

"Morning." I ran my hand over the back of my neck.

Zach coughed. "Yeah. Um. I need some cash for lunch."

I went into my room, pulled two twenties from my wallet, and handed them to the kid.

"That's enough for a month." Zach gaped at the cash.

"Keep it. Take your girl out for ice cream after school." I'd bribed the kid into silence, so what?

"She's pretty great, huh?" Zach grinned.

"You tell me, I haven't met her."

He shook his head, seeming to enjoy having the upper hand. "No, I mean Maggie. She's great."

"Oh, yeah. She's something special."

Zach's expression hardened. "Look, you hurt her and I'll hurt you. I might be a kid and it might take years, but I *will* make you suffer."

"I don't intend to hurt her." I clamped a hand on Zach's boney shoulder. "Men take care of their women. Do you look after your sister like you look after Maggie?"

Zach shrugged. "I punched the kid down the street for making Chloe wreck her bike, but Maggie grounded me for a week."

"Women don't understand these things. Besides, a week in your room with your Xbox and computer? Big deal."

"No man, she took all of it out, even the television."

I chuckled. "Harsh, but your sister's worth it."

He nodded and followed me into the kitchen. "I'm glad you're here."

"Me too." Inspiration struck me at the oddest times. I

had an idea, a good one, but I'd need his help. "What do you think about playing a guitar accompaniment while your sister dances?"

"Depends. I can't exactly pull off Swan Lake on a six string."

"I'm thinking Clapton at the Mardi Gras Gala. I'll sing and play rhythm."

The kid's eyes widened for a split second before he slipped back into teenaged indifference. "Yeah, that could work."

"Cool. We'll need to start working on the piece." I rummaged through the pantry. "I'm never up this early. What does she feed you guys for breakfast?"

"Ryan and Chloe eat oatmeal, or eggs and toast. Maggie makes them eat fruit too."

The doorbell rang. The damned dog barked and hauled ass to the foyer and the window and back again.

With one hand on Cocoa's collar, I opened the door and let Evelyn inside.

Zach kissed his grandmother on the way out. "I gotta run. Early band practice."

"Bye, Zachary." Evelyn smiled and handed me a bag of baby clothes. "I went shopping for Ella yesterday."

I set the fancy paper sack on the couch. "I see that."

She shoved a glass container of still warm food into my free hand. "I remembered you said you were getting the kids off to school this morning. I made you a frittata."

"Thanks, Ma." I smiled, though I had my doubts the munchkins would eat it.

"It was no trouble. I wish I could stay and visit, but I

have to get your father to Baton Rouge for a doctor appointment. Is everyone feeling better?"

"Yeah, it must have been a twenty-four-hour virus. Maggie and Chloe are fine."

"Good. Poor Chloe missing her recital."

"I promised her we would hold a private performance. Could we do it at the gala?"

"She could dance at the wedding."

"Very funny."

"I'll inform the event planners my granddaughter will be dancing."

"Could you find her a pink costume with wings?"

"Consider it done." She patted my cheek and headed for the door.

"Drive safe, Ma." Following her, I grinned to keep the mood light and launched a verbal hand grenade. "When will you call off the custody hearing?"

"When will you set a date?"

It was too fucking early in the morning for this. "Weddings take time to plan..."

She gave me the same look she'd given me when I was a kid trying to lie my way out of a beating. "I love you, but I'm not dropping the case until the two of you are married."

"Don't be ridiculous. The hearing is tomorrow. It takes longer than that to get a marriage license."

"Your lack of planning isn't my fault." She smirked. "And there will be no running off to Vegas."

"You should know, I plan to testify on Maggie's behalf."

"We'll see what your father has to say about that." Evelyn headed for her car.

Cursing under my breath, I waved to my father.

He motioned for me to come to the car.

My mother, the good mafia wife, backtracked into the house. "I'll watch the kids."

Joe rolled down his window. "There's a little matter of a loose-lipped, and sticky-fingered employee I'd like you to take care of."

I hung my head. "Pops, I—"

"It's not like you have to get your hands dirty. It's a call and a car ride." He set his jaw. "You need to be there. Power only holds when our enemies know we are strong."

A call to arrange someone's execution, and a car ride to witness the murder. "I have a family to consider. What happens to them if I go away?"

He barked out a laugh. "We take care of our own. End of story. Get it done."

My nod cost me a piece of my soul. I could only imagine what the actual deed would rob from me. I passed my mother on the way back inside but couldn't meet her gaze.

Sweet sounds of a waking baby came through the monitor. I snuck into my room to grab her before Ella realized she had a wet diaper and woke the rest of the house. "Hey, sweet pea."

Ella answered with an ear-piercing scream that turned her face from red to a strange shade of blue.

Not now, honey. Please not now. I held her to my shoulder. "Shit. Shhh. Shhh. Shhh. It's okay, little one."

After changing her, I returned to the kitchen to prepare a bottle. Holding her upright, I did a sort of bob and weave dance as I worked.

Ryan came into the kitchen with a huge wet spot down the front, and back, of his pajamas. "I peed."

"I see that." *This is not my fucking day*. I tilted my head and considered how to fix this with one hand. "Can you take your clothes off by yourself?"

Ryan nodded and stripped quicker than I would have thought possible.

I wrapped my free arm around the kid's waist and hoisted him into the kitchen sink. The little guy looked at me as if I'd lost my mind but squatted like a quarterback waiting to receive the ball.

I used the sprayer to hose down Ryan's butt and legs. Still holding the baby, I grabbed a dish cloth, patted him dry, and set him on the floor.

Chloe stood near the kitchen door with her hands on her hips and a look of pure disgust on her face. "Gross."

"I agree, but my options were limited." I popped the lid on my mother's frittata. "Look what grandma Evelyn dropped off."

Both kids screwed up their faces.

Ryan said, "It has green stuff."

"Yeah, it does, doesn't it? I'll figure something else out." I motioned toward the stairs. "Go get dressed, little man. Chloe, sweetie. Can you put Ryan's pajamas and the dish towel in the laundry room?"

"Eww. No way." She shook her head. "I'd rather eat broccoli frittata than touch pee pants."

It's too freaking early for this. Struggling to function with one hand, I pulled a box of frozen waffles from the freezer and dropped two into the toaster.

At least Ella had quieted down. She seemed amused by the chaos.

Chloe pointed at the toaster. "Those are for Saturdays only."

"Give me a break. I can't find the instant oatmeal."

My niece's expression reminded me of Maggie's when I'd chugged milk from the carton. It seemed they both thought me a moron.

"Because it's not instant." She shook her head and went back to her bedroom.

I considered the baby in my arms and frowned. I'd never thought about the difference between raising boys and girls. "You better be a tomboy when you grow up."

Ryan came back to the kitchen wearing a lot of clothes, none of which matched. Since the kid didn't have to leave the house, I didn't mention his choice of wardrobe.

I poured syrup on the waffles and set the plate on the bar in front of Ryan. Remembering what Zach said about fruit, I added a banana.

Ryan shrugged, picked up the waffle whole, and ate it like a piece of toast.

Chloe returned with a brush and hair ties. She took one look at Ryan and rolled her eyes at *me*.

What the hell did I do now?

Obviously doubting my intelligence, she eyed me. "I need a bun today. I have dance class after school."

"Okay, let's see." I buckled Ella into her carrier, tossed Ryan's wet pajamas into the laundry room, and washed my hands.

The girl wrinkled her nose. "I'll go ask Aunt Maggie to do it."

"I got it." Taking the brush from Chloe, I hesitated. I wore a ponytail on most days, but I'd never pulled someone else's hair back, let alone a bun. I brushed her long brown hair, secured it near the base of her skull.

Chloe pulled a brown band from her wrist and handed it to me. "You have to twist it and put this around it."

I vaguely remembered Maggie doing something similar. I wound Chloe's hair until it coiled into a knot and stretched the second tie around the base. "How's that?"

Chloe pressed her fingers against the messy bun and nodded. "It's good. Thank you."

"Remember I told you we would do a private recital?"

She gave me a pirate's smile. "Uh huh."

"Would you like to dance at Grandma Evelyn and Papa Joe's Mardi Gras party?"

Her mouth fell open. "The masked ball? Like Cinderella? Really? Can I stay and dance with the grown-ups after?"

"Anything you want, except a pumpkin carriage. I don't think I can pull that off."

The little girl smirked. "Duh. Only princesses have fairy godmothers."

Peals of laughter filled the kitchen. The damned dog had pinned Ryan down and was licking the syrup from his face.

"No, Cocoa. Bad dog." Chloe grabbed the mutt by her collar and pulled her off the boy.

I picked Ryan off the floor and washed his face and hands with a clean dish cloth. "Chloe, eat your waffles before they get cold."

Ella started to fuss in her carrier, and the house phone rang in the midst of the chaos. I snatched it from the wall.

Holding the handset to my ear with my shoulder, I grabbed the baby formula out of the pantry. "Hello."

"You're engaged?" Chantal's voice drilled into my eardrum.

"Hang on." I motioned for Chloe to eat, put a pacifier in the baby's mouth, waited to make sure she didn't spit it out, and walked toward the garage.

"Maggie Guthrie? Keeping it in the family, Gabe?"

How the hell did she find out? I whispered through gritted teeth, "How did you get this number?"

"Is this why you refuse to give me the money your family owes me?"

"Sign the papers, Chantal."

"Screw that. I'm coming to get *my* daughter."

I sucked in a breath and counted to five. My lawyer had warned me not to argue with her until the judge approved the custody request. Then again, he'd also suggested I have her eliminated. *I'm going to kill one, why not kill two? Hell. Why not put a bullet in anyone who pissed me off? My father would be proud.* "Think about what's best for the baby."

"You love her?" Chantal's voice dripped with sarcasm.

"Of course, I love her. How can I not love my daughter?"

"Not the baby. Do you love *her*?"

"Yes, I do, and she's good with Ella. Please, sign the papers."

Chantal laughed and disconnected.

I walked back into the kitchen.

Chloe frowned and set her dishes in the sink. "Who were you yelling at?"

"I didn't yell."

She shrugged. "Sounded like it to me."

I checked the time. "When does the bus come?"

"Seven-thirty." Standing at the end of the hall, Maggie looked from Ryan, to the syrupy plate, and finally at me. "Who called?"

20

Maggie

I COULD EXCUSE FEEDING THE KIDS A SUGARY breakfast. Waffles were quick and easy. I could ignore the bag of frilly pink clothes that told me Evelyn had already come and gone. Heck, I could ignore Ryan wearing six outfits at once, but I couldn't handle the guilty expression on Gabe's face. "Who called?"

"No one." He turned and finished preparing Ella's bottle.

Always the peacekeeper, Chloe interrupted. "Look, Aunt Maggie. My Uncle Gabe put my hair in a bun."

"Very pretty." I smiled; it probably looked like a snarl. "Hurry up. The bus will be here soon, and you still need to brush your teeth and get shoes on."

"I know, I know, but it's hard to think about school when I have to plan my recital." She ran down the hall giggling.

I arched a brow at Gabe.

"I promised her a one woman show. Still working out the details."

Normally, I'd volunteer to help, but I couldn't add anything else to my list. "Sounds great."

"Feed the baby while I make coffee?" He asked with a hopeful lift in his voice.

I thought about refusing until he answered my question, but that would only hurt Ella. I pulled the baby out of the carrier. "Before you make coffee, get the port-a-crib set up in the living room. It'll make things easier to have a safe place to put her down."

"You bought a port-a-crib?"

"It was Ryan's. I got tired of Cocoa eating Ella's pacifiers and brought it down from the attic." I took the bottle from him and offered it to the baby.

"I would have done that." He scratched the side of his head. "Where is it?"

"In the garage. Looks like a bag of golf clubs." I turned my attention to Ella.

"I'm ready." Chloe came back into the kitchen and wrinkled her nose. "You might want to clean the sink. Uncle Gabe washed Ryan's pee off in it."

I winced. "Gross."

Chloe threw her hands up. "That's what I said."

Despite my mood, I laughed and gave her a half hug. "Do you want me to wait outside with you?"

"Nah, I got it." Chloe kissed my cheek and Ella's head. She grabbed her bag and hurried to the garage.

I listened as she told Gabe goodbye before she walked out front to catch the bus *alone*. I didn't like it one bit. Chloe never went to the bus without me. Too many things had changed too quickly.

"Your phone's ringing." I called to Gabe.

"Ignore it." He disappeared around the corner with the port-a-crib.

I glanced at the screen and the room tilted.

Chantal had called him.

On a hunch, I checked the call log on the house phone. The same number appeared. *How in the hell did Chantal get my number?*

"What time's your meeting?" Gabe took Ella from me and brushed his lying lips across mine.

Okay, maybe he hadn't lied, but he hadn't shared all the pertinent information either. He had to have seen her, or at least spoken to her. How else would she have my number? "In a half hour. I need to run or I'll miss the ferry."

"You okay?" He stacked dirty plates in the sink as if hiding the evidence would solve the problem. "I can drive you to the Quarter. I have to pick up last night's receipts from the bar."

"You have your hands full. Want me to get them while I'm out?"

"Thanks. I'll let Jessie know you're stopping by." He turned his attention to the breakfast plates. "Have a good one."

"Yep. See you tonight." Even elbow-deep in dishwater, the man made my pulse race. *He lied to me and all I want to do it jump his bones? I need a therapist.*

I'd speed-walked three blocks to the ferry terminal when my phone rang. Figuring it was Gabe, I answered without checking the screen. Big Mistake. "Hello?"

"Good morning, Maggie."

My mouth went dry. I hadn't spoken to Justin since meeting his wife. "Why are you calling me?"

"To congratulate you on your engagement. I didn't realize the guy at the bar was Gabe Marchionni."

"What?" I pressed a hand to my chest and stepped off the curb.

Justin replied, but screeching tires and a blaring horn drowned out his words.

Unable to make sense of what had just happened, I stared at the cursing driver several heartbeats before crossing the street.

"...they're loaded. I had to go to the hospital for my jaw... medical bills... pain... payment... he owes me—"

I disconnected the call and hurried to board the ferry. I had enough on my plate without worrying about Justin Trudeau.

***

SHANNA WAVED AS I APPROACHED THE CAFÉ. NOT THAT I needed any help spotting my best friend. Her hair was bright purple and cut in short layers that stuck out in all directions. I envied her. Shanna had something I desperately wished I had—self-confidence.

"Hey, love the new look." I embraced her a little too tight.

"Thanks. I wanted something different. It'll be great for Fat Tuesday." She pulled away and gave me a quick once over. "Everything good?"

"Everything's great." I groaned to myself. My least favorite thing about living in New Orleans had to be Mardi Gras. "But I'll be working in a bar during that craziness."

"Are you still doing that? What happened to the magazine?"

"It's field research." I raised the menu to hide my expression.

Shanna pulled it down. "I hate to ruin your morning, but did you see the announcement in the paper?"

Little did she know my morning already sucked. "What announcement?"

She lowered her voice. "Your engagement announcement."

My heart fell into my shoes. "It's in the paper?"

Shanna handed me her phone.

For the second time that day, my world tilted on its axis. I stared at a photo of me and Gabe with our names, along with the word *engaged*, printed in bold beneath it. The picture had been taken years before when we were dating—the perfect image of a happy, betrothed couple. "Oh God."

Shanna set the cell on the table between us. "What's going on? You said the engagement was a misunderstanding."

"Yes and no, but I didn't leak it to the paper." Is this how Chantal found out about us? Had she gotten my number from someone other than Gabe? Had Justin seen it? Was that why he'd called?

"Yes and no? Either you are or you aren't." She sat back and folded her arms.

"It's complicated."

"Everything's complicated with that family." Shanna rolled her eyes.

"I need info for the article. Plus, he's going to get Evelyn and Joe to drop the custody case."

"You're going through with the article?" Her eyes widened.

I could count on one hand the number of times I'd seen Shanna look frightened, and for some reason, this was one of them.

"Marlena approved my proposal to do the exposé about the Marchionni family and their businesses."

"Like I said before, are you nuts? Evelyn already wants you dead so she can have the kids, and let's not forget you're engaged to Gabe."

"She doesn't want me dead." I laughed, but it sounded hollow.

"Not yet. If you start airing their dirty laundry to the world, things could get worse. When's the custody hearing?"

"Tomorrow." I'd done my best to trust Gabe when he'd said he'd get his parents to back off, but so far nothing had changed.

"Prince Charming better get his ass in gear. Evelyn and Papa Joe are the last people who need to be raising kids."

"Tell that to the judge."

My phone lit with another call from a blocked number. I answered and listened for half a heartbeat before I hung up. I really didn't need to know all the body parts the person wanted to cut off me.

Shanna touched my hand. "You okay?"

Not even a little okay. "I'm fine. Wrong number."

"I hate to add to your shitty morning." She pulled an envelope from her bag. "You need to take a look at this before you go any further with the article or into court."

"Is it that bad?"

Shanna shrugged. "That's your call."

I opened the thick file and began skimming through personal and business records of the Marchionni family. My eyes bugged out at the size of the dollar figures. I knew they had money, but holy smokes. "You got the police report, too?"

"Sure did. There are several clipped together."

Barely paying attention, I flipped through the pages until a familiar name caught my eye.

I glanced at Shanna, then back at the police report. "Rebecca..."

"Don't read anything into it, the authorities ruled the crash an accident," Shanna said.

"I know." I swallowed past the lump in my throat and closed the folder. Bad news piled upon more bad news. "I'll read it later. What's your gut saying? Is the family as bad as the rumors say?"

Shanna took a sip of coffee. "Ask me again after you've had time to go through it all."

"You think they're part of some organized crime syndicate?"

Her usual carefree expression melted into a frown. "Maybe. It's hard to tell. Whatever they are, people they do business with don't seem happy afterwards."

"How so?" I eyed the file with a sinking feeling.

"Several reports have been filed against the corporation, and more against Papa Joe, accusing them of sabotaging businesses in order to force owners to sell."

"Shit."

"With that many enemies, it's not surprising he insisted someone caused Joe and Rebecca's crash."

I refused to consider what something like that could mean for Gabe, or me and the kids if we were married. *This has to be a mistake. She's exaggerating.* "I'll be judicious with the information I include in the article. Besides, maybe I can dig up enough dirt to stop the custody battle? I mean, if the engagement thing doesn't work out."

"Maybe." Shanna didn't seem convinced. She sat back in her chair. "What's really up with you and Gabe?"

I raised my menu again.

Shanna snatched it from me and tossed it on an empty table. "You slept with him?"

My face heated. "I wouldn't say we slept."

"I can't believe you let him talk you into sex...again. It's bad enough he has you rooked into an *engagement of convenience*." Shanna looked as if she'd chugged a half-gallon of soured milk.

"He's changed." At least, I thought he'd changed until Chantal had called my house.

"Oh, I bet he has. Have you forgotten the part where he dug your heart out with a spoon and pissed on it?" Shanna waved the waiter away, leaning closer to me again. "You cried for months."

"Weeks." I lied. In reality, I'd cried off and on over Gabe until he'd walked back into my life. "I haven't forgotten. We're in a strange situation. We sort of need each other. The rest will sort itself out in time."

"I'll tell you what he needs. A good swift kick in the balls." Shanna smirked. "Tell me about the sex."

I set my elbows on the table and smiled. "He hasn't lost his touch."

The waiter reappeared before the conversation got too raunchy.

"I'll have the beignets." Smiling, I handed him the menu.

"Creole omelet, home fries, and a side of bacon." Shanna turned back to me and narrowed her eyes.

I lowered my gaze and fidgeted with my napkin.

"I knew it. You're marrying him for the orgasms." She laughed loud enough for several people to turn in our direction. "What happened to the vibrator I gave you for your birthday?"

I wanted to hide under the table, but it was no use and she'd probably follow me. "People are watching us."

She turned and glared at the onlookers.

Thankfully, I knew how to get Shanna off the subject of Gabe. "How's your dating life?"

"Non-freaking-existent. After the last debacle, I pulled my profile off the dating sites. I've decided to live a celibate life, focus on work. I want my PI license." She drummed her fingers on the table. "I could take the course now. It's only forty hours."

"You should."

We had this conversation many times before, but she'd always chickened out at the last minute.

"I'd have more credibility with clients if I finished my degree." Shanna lowered her voice. "All I have left is the English and math courses. With my dyslexia, I can get help with the reading and writing. Would you tutor me in math?"

"Of course." I hated math more than I hated the extra weight I carried in my hips and the fact I had pimples and wrinkles at the same time, but I'd do anything for her. God knows, she's done worse for me.

"Thanks, Maggie. I'm hoping to get into classes this fall."

The waiter delivered our food, but I ignored the powdered sugar-coated balls of deliciousness.

"Why aren't you eating?" Shanna eyed me.

"I'm too stressed out."

"Bullshit. You're the definition of a stress eater. Tell me you aren't starving yourself for that asshole."

Most of the time I treasured having a friend who knew me inside and out, but not when it came to my weight. "I'm not. Chloe and I had a stomach virus over the weekend. I took one look at the beignet and felt queasy."

"Stay on your side of the table." Shanna stole a beignet from my plate. "Now that I have the Marchionni stuff wrapped up, I'll start working on Gabe's baby momma."

I'd all but decided to tell her not to investigate Chantal, but the more I thought about it, the more I convinced myself I needed to know. He'd lied about the call, and I suspected it wasn't the first time.

"I know that look." She grabbed my hand. "Tell me you're not falling in love with him again."

"I would, but you'd see right through me."

Shanna muttered a slew of curses that would make a pirate blush.

"It gets worse. Chantal called my house, and he lied about it." I blurted it out before I thought the better of it.

"That son of a bitch. He's already cheating on you?"

I'd always heard of eyes flashing red when someone was angry, but until that moment, I thought it was BS. Shanna was about to lose her mind. "No. I mean, when does he have time? Maybe she saw the announcement in the paper?"

My best friend in the world gave me a look that told me I'd skyrocketed to the top of her shit list—right beside Gabe.

I checked the time and sucked down the rest of my coffee. "I'm late. I have to swing by the bar before I head to the office."

"Go. I'll get the check." Shanna folded her arms. "Just don't do anything *else* stupid."

"I'll try."

I made a show of walking fast until I was out of view of the café. Other than the occasional deadline, I had no clock to punch. I didn't really need to go into the office, except I wanted to check up on a few things, and I needed a public place to read the file Shanna had given me. Sure, I could do it at home, but I'd cry less if surrounded by professional journalists—or so I hoped.

Maggie

THE CONVERSATION WITH SHANNA HAD SHAKEN ME, but being back in the French Quarter rattled me to my core. I used to love Jackson Square with its tarot readers and fun shops. I'd been baptized and taken my first communion at Saint Louis Cathedral, but I hadn't set foot inside the building since my sister and brother-in-law's funerals.

I would have loved to light a candle for them, but I had too much to do—plus I kept getting this creepy crawly sensation between my shoulder blades and the hair on the back of my neck stood on end.

The prank caller's words pinged around in my skull to the point of paranoia. Was someone following me?

I'd seen enough movies to know better than to keep looking over my shoulder, but I couldn't help myself. No one stood out as particularly menacing in the crowd, nor did I notice the same people twice. *That's it. I'm losing my mind.*

Thankfully, the bar was only a couple of blocks from

the café. I punched the security code on the backdoor and poked my head into the break room. A woman stood with her back to the door reading the notices on the bulletin board.

I cleared my throat. "Can I help you?"

"Oh, sorry. I know I'm not supposed to be back here, but the side door was open. I was looking for the owner." She smiled a smile that reminded me of a news anchor. Pretty, but pretend.

"The owner's working from home today." I'd seen her here before though I didn't know her name. "Were you looking at the job postings?"

After a brief silence, she nodded. "Are you still hiring?"

"I think so, but you'll need to speak to Jessie."

"Thanks, I will." She turned for the door.

"I'll show you out."

"No need."

I followed her anyway. Something about the conversation felt off, besides the fact she'd let herself into a closed bar. Why would a leggy blonde be waiting here for Gabe like they had a standing Wednesday morning date?

Once I locked the door behind her, I headed for the office.

Jessie glanced up from her paperwork and removed her earbuds. "Hey. Didn't hear you come in."

I motioned behind me like an idiot. How had she been here the entire time and not realized someone had wandered in? "There was a woman in the break room."

Her eyes widened. "When? Just now?"

"She said the side door was unlocked." I didn't know Jessie well, but she'd never struck me as the careless type.

"I came in through the employee entrance about an hour ago. I haven't been up front, and I *know* I locked the doors last night." She ran her hands over her arms. "I'll make sure nothing's missing. Do me a favor and don't mention this to Gabe. The family's already giving him grief about me working here."

By the family, I assumed she meant Papa Joe. The man was a notorious misogynist. "Want me to stick around to make sure everything's okay?"

"I'm expecting a friend any minute." She blushed and handed me a folder labeled *receipts*. "He brings me coffee on weekdays."

"Your secrets are safe with me." I tucked the file into my bag.

THERE ARE SOME THINGS THAT ONE SIMPLY SHOULD not see by the light of day—Bourbon Street is one of them. I ignored the gaudy strip clubs, and piles of garbage, but I couldn't help doing some quick window shopping at a couple of the sex shops.

What can I say? Living with Gabe had woken my dormant hormones.

My skin prickled, and the sensation that someone was watching me returned. I ducked my head and picked up my pace. Every block or so, I glanced over my shoulder, but no one stood out.

I turned the corner on Poydras Street and ducked beneath the awning of a souvenir shop. A man in a leather jacket followed, made eye contact, and continued on his way. He looked back at me twice but smiled each time.

Is he following me or flirting?

I blew it off as paranoia after the conversation with Shanna and walked the rest of the way to the *NOLA Society News* offices.

I didn't have an office or know many of the employees milling about, but no one questioned my presence. The badge hanging from my lapel gave me the right to use the research computers with access to many of the city record databases.

My first search turned up general information about the Marchionni Corporation. I took notes on their holdings and the members of the board of directors. Next, I conducted individual searches on each of the properties owned by Gabe's brothers, and jotted down names associated with the businesses.

I'd become so engrossed in my work that I didn't hear my boss approaching until Marlena set a hand on my shoulder. I jumped out of my chair. "You scared the stuffing out me."

"I've been practicing my stealth moves." Marlena cackled and met my gaze. "You should have told us you captured one of New Orleans sexiest bachelors. It killed me to read it in the competition."

"I didn't place the announcement in the *Picayune*." My cheeks heated. I had a good idea who'd leaked the story and fully intended to have a word with my would-be mother-in-law. "As for the engagement, it's complicated."

"If I was in your shoes, I'd march that man down the

aisle so quick he'd need a seat belt and helmet." Marlena leaned in and gave me a half-hug. "Though many women are mourning his loss, myself included... Congratulations."

I couldn't help but smile. "Thanks. You should know, my relationship with Gabe won't affect the piece."

"Of course it will, but given your personal relationship, I trust you'll come up with something that's a different flavor of delicious." She leaned forward to read the screen.

"I'm not changing my tactics. The piece will be honest, and from the looks of it, gritty."

Marlene's frown started in her eyes and worked its way down her face. "Did you find something?"

"Not yet, but I have a private source who's doing some digging into financial records. I'm focusing on identifying the key players outside the family." I closed Shanna's file to keep Marlena's eagle-eyes off the police report.

"Smart. If there are dirty secrets, you're more likely to find them on the periphery, but are you certain you want to go this route?"

"Absolutely. I also took a part-time job in a Marchionni establishment."

Marlena's perfectly shaped brow rose. "Oh?"

"I thought it would be interesting to get an insider's perspective. See what their employees have to say about the men behind the myths."

She pursed her lips and glanced over the bank of computers. "Maggie, given the circumstances, you should use a pseudonym on this piece. If it turns out to be more than the typical story, I'm going to sell it to the highest bidder. You'll want anonymity."

"I appreciate that, if not for Gabe's sake, then for my sister's children."

"You're a talented young woman. Too talented to be writing fluff for a local magazine. If you ever decide to spread your wings, I hope you know I would write you one hell of a reference letter."

Ah yes, the old follow your dreams speech. What was it with people using it while trying to get rid of me? It stung, and that pissed me off. "If I'm so talented why were you about to fire me not too long ago?"

Marlena tilted her head. "To force you to come up with something new, or to push you into looking for a position that will challenge you."

"Thanks, but I have all the challenges I need right now." *If she only knew.*

"Being engaged to Gabe Marchionni will do that." She winked and walked away.

I waited until she disappeared around the corner and opened Shanna's file.

An hour later, I'd created a list of over twenty known associates of the Marchionni family who'd been convicted of crimes ranging from racketeering to RICO violations to murder. Another dozen or so associates had died violent deaths or were missing.

I flipped to the police reports concerning my sister's death. Page after page of descriptions of the scene, my sister and brother-in-law, the car—crushed bodies, severed brake lines, broken lives.

One name caught my attention, Chantal DuBois. Papa Joe named her as a disgruntled business partner, but the woman had an alibi the night of the accident. Papa Joe believed someone had murdered them. The reports all but agreed, and yet the police had ruled it an accident.

By the time I'd finished reading, I knew two things for certain—I needed to find out who was making the threatening phone calls, and I needed to talk to Gabe.

22

Gabe

AFTER MY DISASTROUS MORNING, I'D CALLED IN reinforcements. Hildie, mine and my brothers' former nanny, arrived within the hour, which freed me up to do my father's bidding.

I glanced at the man sitting next to me—a man about to take his last breath.

"Please. If I could explain." Artie Guzman, accountant at the Marchionni Corporation for the previous six years, smelled like tuna fish and cheap cologne.

I'd never done this sort of thing, but I'd hung around people who had since I'd started sprouting pubic hair. Tough guys, the kind you wouldn't want to sit next to on a bus, who seldom spoke and rarely smiled. The type of man I never wanted myself or my brothers to become.

I clenched my jaw and stared straight ahead.

Artie Guzman had no wife or kids or family other than two prize-winning poodles. I knew this because he'd reached for his wallet to show me a picture of his dogs a split second before my father's go-to-guy broke Artie's fingers.

"I didn't mean anything by it. It was a joke in the break room. Accountant humor." His voice warbled between terror and laughter. "I didn't steal anything."

Every criminal sang the I-didn't-do-it tune, but this felt different. I believed him. It took serious balls to steal from a man like my father. Artie Guzman didn't seem the type.

The thug beside him slammed his fist into Artie's jaw hard enough to break bone. Blood and spit splattered across my six-hundred-dollar Ralph Lauren dress shirt.

I focused on a drop of crimson on the back of the seat in front of me and thought about Maggie. Her smile. Her laugh. Her hair. Then I thought about my father and his possible motives for ordering this murder. Was Guzman a pawn in Papa Joe's plan to rope me into the business?

The driver came to a stop. No longer able to speak, Artie's moans turned to howls.

I glanced at my phone. An image of Maggie and Ella smiled at me from the screen. *Dear God, I can't allow this.*

"You ready, boss?" My father's guy stepped out and tugged the accountant toward him.

I stepped from the car; humid Louisiana air and the musty odor of swamp hit me like a freight train. I squared my shoulders and walked to the back bumper. I had the beginnings of a plan, but I had no way of knowing how the other men would react. "Stay here. I'll handle this alone."

The large man arched a skeptical brow. "He's bleeding. I'll drag him down to the river for you. No sense in ruining your fancy clothes."

I motioned for him to get on with it.

Artie went, but he didn't go quietly. I wondered if I'd behave the same way in his shoes. I would like to think I'd have more dignity, but no one knew how they'd react to being kidnapped and dragged to their death.

The thug shoved Mr. Guzman to his knees in the soggy earth, turned, and handed me his gun. "I'll be in the car."

I'd held firearms before, but the weight of this one sent a chill down my spine.

"Please." Artie's stare bore into me.

I glanced over my shoulder to make sure my father's guy had gone and squatted beside the accountant. "I'm not going to hurt you, but I need some assurances."

The man's swollen eyes widened. "Thank you. Yes. Anything."

"You have to disappear. Today. Don't go home. You have to run and never return."

He nodded, but I could almost see the wheels turning in his head. "My dogs..."

"I'll make sure they're taken care of until you've found a place." Making a mental note to call Leo about the poodles, I pulled out my wallet and handed him a few hundred bucks along with my personal card. "Call me from a *new* number when you're safely outside the city. I'll get you enough money to start over, but you have to stay gone. Got it?"

Artie stared at the black embossed card with my name and cell phone number. "Yeah...yes...thank you."

"Wait here until you're sure we've gone."

He nodded again.

"Screw this up and we're both dead." I fired two shots into the water before walking back to the car.

"THANKS AGAIN. IF THIS DOESN'T CONVINCE HER TO hire a nanny, I don't know what will." I hugged Hildie for the third time. Not because I loved and appreciated her, which I did, but because I desperately needed to return to some sense of normalcy.

I'd taken a huge risk letting Guzman go, and I prayed I wouldn't live to regret it.

"Mmm hmmm." Hildie patted my cheek. Her gaze fell to the blood on my shirt, but she glanced away without comment.

Smart woman. I didn't know what to say. She'd scrubbed every inch of the house, somehow removed the long-dead Christmas tree, and made supper in the time it'd taken me to oversee my first would-be murder.

"I left contact information on the counter for a woman I know who's looking for a nanny position. She's a good, God-fearing soul and will care for the children like they're her own."

"I'll give her a call." I folded my arms and rocked on the balls of my feet, a habit I thought I'd lost once I'd hit puberty. Spending time with Hildie made me feel like I was eight years old again. Only this time, I felt like an eight year old who'd almost done the unspeakable.

I waited until she pulled away, waved, and walked back into the house—and into what smelled like a sewer.

Ella tensed and turned red from the top of her head to her tiny toes.

I groaned. "You couldn't have done that five minutes ago?"

The baby's mouth hung open a solid five seconds before she worked up the wail, but when she did, I shot into action.

I grabbed a diaper and the wipes and settled the infant on the changing table I'd pulled out of the attic.

A car door shut outside, but the dog didn't bark. It had to be Maggie.

I stripped out of the ruined shirt and shoved it under the bed.

The front door closed. "Gabe?"

"I'm changing Ella."

Maggie came down the hall but stopped before she came in the room. "Can we talk?"

"Sure, give me a sec. You don't want to come in here. She's toxic." I glanced over my shoulder and stilled.

Maggie didn't look happy. "I'll be in my room."

Oh boy. Not now. Not today. I finished diaper duty, settled Ella into her crib, and went to find Maggie. "Rough day?"

She shrugged. "Can we talk a minute?"

"What's up, gorgeous?" I sat on the edge of the bed.

"How are the kids?"

I had the feeling she hadn't asked me in here to talk about the kids. "I had a situation that had to be dealt with in the office. I had Hildie come sit with them."

Maggie sighed and dipped her chin to her chest. "This isn't working."

"Where the hell is this coming from? I thought we were good?"

"We're far from good." She shook her head and stood. "Since you got here, everything is different. Someone put an engagement announcement in the paper. My boss and most of New Orleans saw it. You seduce me, sleep in my bed, make me nuts with your stupid grins and compliments, and the kids are getting too attached. I think you need to go."

I listened to everything she had to say. By the time she quieted, I had to unclench my jaw to speak. "My turn?"

She shrugged.

"I don't want to leave." My voice cracked.

She stared as if waiting for me to say more, but I'd cut through all of the bullshit and said what I needed to.

Unfortunately, Maggie disagreed. The woman exploded. "That's it? That's all you have to say? Of course, you don't want to leave. Too bad, Gabe. We don't always get what we want."

"Ah, there it is." I stood.

"There *what* is?"

I knew better than to argue with her when she was like this, but that didn't stop me. "You're pissed because I screwed up your perfectly planned out life."

"What plan? I haven't had a plan since Rebecca and Joe died." She tilted her head and studied me like I was one of her books.

I had no intention of going anywhere for long, but we both needed time to cool off. "I'll leave if that's what you want, but don't lie to me or yourself."

"It's true." Maggie's voice cracked. "I have no idea what I'm doing with the house, or the kids, or you."

I lowered my voice. "Do you want to know why I ended things with you?"

She stared at her hands. "I remember every word you said to me, but go ahead and tell me again."

"You had a plan for everything. I couldn't figure out

where I fit into it. You didn't want kids. I want a house full. You wanted to live in New York. I live here."

"That's crap. I loved you. It killed me when you threw me away with the whole—*you deserve a chance to follow your dreams*—routine. I always thought you'd found someone else, that you'd woken up and realized I wasn't good enough for you."

My mouth fell open. How could she be so wrong? She acted as if we'd lived through two different relationships. Sure, I'd ended things, but I'd always regretted it. "There has never been anyone else for me."

"Then why did you never return my calls?"

"I thought it'd be easier for you. A clean break."

"No, Gabe, it was easier for *you*." She turned her back to me. "I was twenty-one and stupid. I had big dreams, but I would have changed them for you."

"And I was twenty-six and loved you too much to ask you to do that." I swallowed past the lump in my throat. "I've never stopped loving you."

"You honestly expect me to believe that? I've been back in New Orleans for a year. You never called or stopped by. Not until you needed something from me."

"It killed me knowing you were so close and hurting, but I couldn't see you."

"Why? What was stopping you?"

I couldn't tell her, not without telling her everything. Today wasn't the day for it, not after what had happened in the swamp. "I had no choice."

"Let me guess. Your father forbade you? Why? Because he thought someone murdered my sister?" She stalked to her computer bag, pulled out a stack of folded up papers, and threw them on the bed. "There's the police report, but it's wrong, isn't it?"

Fuck me. This is what this is about? I can't get into this with her. Not now, not like this. It didn't take a degree in female psychology to figure out that none of the shit she'd said up until that point had anything to do with her telling me to leave. That was all ancient history, but this business with her sister...was an entirely different animal. "Maggie... the police ruled—"

"I want the truth." She balled her hands. "Was it a mob hit?"

My brain stuttered. I'd always known she'd figure it out, but I found myself ill-prepared to explain the situation. Instead, I dodged. "Why would you ask me that?"

"What did Chantal have to do with it?"

"Nothing." Before I could explain, Maggie continued the barrage.

"Was my sister murdered?"

"I don't know for sure what caused Joe *and* Rebecca's accident. None of us do. But you're right. My father assigned a security detail on the kids and ordered us to stay away."

She folded in on herself. "I want you out of this house."

A stone wall rose between us. Even the temperature in the room grew a few degrees cooler. As much as I wanted to reach out to her, I couldn't. If she reacted to the truth about my family like she had the accident, Maggie would have yet another target on her back.

Call it self-preservation or cowardice, but I needed a break. I took a breath and forced myself to speak in a professional tone. "I'm going to check on the kids. We'll finish the conversation when we've both calmed down."

"It won't make a difference." Maggie sighed.

I ignored her and walked into the living room.

"Uncle Gabe." Chloe ran toward me and wrapped her arms around my waist.

"Hey, munchkin, when did you get home?" I knelt to put myself at eye level with her.

"A little bit ago. Why were you and Aunt Maggie arguing?" She set one hand on each of my cheeks and pressed her brow to mine until our noses touched.

I'd never felt like such as asshole. I'd blown it. I never should have let things get so heated. "Grown-ups do that sometimes."

"Are you leaving us and going back to heaven?"

My heart shattered like tempered glass, only sharper. "Is that where you think I've been?"

She nodded. "I thought you went with Mommy and Daddy to heaven. You didn't come back after the funeral, except at Christmas...like an angel or something."

My throat began to close before I could swallow back my emotions. Maggie had been right about one thing. These kids had suffered enough loss for two lifetimes. I refused to add to their pain. "Here's the thing. Once you go to heaven, you can't come back. If I went there, I wouldn't be able to visit you or your brothers. Your mom and dad are doing fine up there with the angels. I think I'll hang around here and look after you guys for a while. Okay?"

"Okay." Chloe smiled, showing teeth that looked too big for her mouth. "I like having you here. It's almost like having my daddy back."

I stood and she slid her hand into mine. Chloe was the spitting image of Rebecca, except her eyes. She had the same green eyes as me and my brothers. I'd always loved her, but in that moment, I wanted her to be mine.

Maggie sniffled from the hall.

I nodded in her direction and spoke to Chloe. "I need to *talk* to Aunt Maggie real quick. Can you go keep an eye on Ryan?"

Chloe gave me a knowing look and nodded. If I didn't know better, I would have sworn she had played me. The girl skipped through the kitchen and headed upstairs.

Judging from the look on her face, Maggie's mood hadn't improved. She folded her arms.

I closed the distance and lowered my voice. "I'm staying."

"The hell you are."

"Did you know Chloe thought I died and went to heaven with Joe and Becca?"

Maggie's eyes widened.

"I stayed away too long." Leaning closer, I whispered, "I'm not going to walk away from them again. It's a big house. We can both behave like adults until we figure things out."

"And if I say no?"

"You won't, because you would walk through fire for those kids. It'll hurt them if I leave." I'd played dirty, but I didn't give a shit.

Maggie chewed her bottom lip. "You're only prolonging the inevitable."

"Honey, I don't walk out on my commitments. I may not have planned to be Ella's father, or a stand-in-dad to

Joe's three, but I am. Like it or not, we love each other, and we're going to work this out."

She frowned, but for once in her life she didn't have anything to say.

I shoved my hands in my pockets to keep from reaching for her. "Go wash your face. We're going to sit down and eat dinner at the table like a normal family. The kids deserve that much."

Maggie nodded and walked down the hall.

One thing had gone my way the entire fucking day.

23

Gabe

COURTROOMS AND CHURCHES HAD THE SAME SMELL—
wood soap, old papers, and desperation. I placed my hand
on Maggie's knee to stop it from shaking the table. "We've
got this."

We didn't have this. Not with her representing herself.
Not if my father had bought the judge. But I had to believe
it would work out in the end.

She nodded, but her gaze slid past me to my parents and
their attorney.

I put my face in her sight line. "Don't look at them.
Focus on me."

Her eyes danced back and forth like her knee had
moments before.

Even in her current state, her beauty quickened my
pulse, but her inner strength humbled me. There were
plenty of pretty faces in the world, but precious few could
match my girl when it came to courage. She was the total
package, the real deal, the whole enchilada.

"Maggie," Zach whisper-shouted from the first row of the gallery.

She turned toward the kids.

He gave her a thumbs up. "Don't worry. You've got this. We love you."

I may not have had a part in making him, but I'd never been prouder of the kid. He sat tall between his sister and baby brother and held each of their hands.

"You got this!" Ryan pumped his fist.

Nadine shushed the kids and moved to Maggie's side. "Mary Margret. You must sit up. No judge will give custody to someone who slouches."

I'd never wanted to smack a woman more in my life, but this wasn't the time, and it certainly wasn't the place. "Thank you, Nadine. Maybe you could keep your comments to yourself until after this is over?"

Maggie gasped, but her mother took the freaking hint and sat her ass down.

Thankfully, the judge came into the courtroom before Maggie had a chance to chastise me for calling Nadine out.

I risked a glance toward my parents. Evelyn stared straight ahead, but my father met my gaze. His blazer hung loose on his shoulders and dark circles shadowed his eyes. He needed to be home with his feet up, not in a courtroom listening to family drama.

"This is LA-07-337, in the matter of Evelyn Marchionni and Mary Margaret Guthrie. I understand the petitioner filed a motion for the children to be interviewed during the formal proceedings. Motion denied."

Maggie exhaled a breath.

Santiago whispered something to my mother, who

nodded. Neither appeared happy by the judge's decision. But what did they expect? Putting the kids on the stand and making them choose between their grandparents and Maggie would have been traumatic for everyone.

The judge flipped through several pages before glancing up. "I will send the children out of the courtroom during the formal proceedings."

Santiago shot to his feet. The judge's order seemed to have surprised him. "Will you interview the children after the hearing or simply review their affidavits?"

"Affidavits?" The color drained from Maggie's cheeks. She leaned close and whispered. "When did Evelyn get affidavits?"

"No clue." I turned and glared at my mother.

"Yes. Section 770.04 states the court, in its discretion, may consider the wishes of a child to his guardian. This is to ensure neither party had unduly influenced the child's testimony." He eyed my parents, and then Maggie. "Not that I'm suggesting this happened here."

Thank Christ. I eased back in my chair and stared at my father. Whether he'd tried and failed, or had been bullshitting me, he hadn't gotten the judge in his pocket.

Maggie stood. "Your Honor, I was not given copies of the children's affidavits by opposing counsel. Nor was I aware of their existence."

The judge nodded. "Another reason for the court to interview the children in chambers. The transcripts of the recordings will be sealed. Neither party will be given a chance to review the statements."

Nadine and the children followed an official-looking woman from the room.

Maggie slumped into the chair but seemed to remember her mother's words and sat ramrod straight.

I took her hand under the table, but had to release it when we were sworn in. I'd only been to court once in my life. I had been twelve and Leo had been eleven. We'd been up on shoplifting charges for stealing a couple of boxes of candy out of the back of a delivery truck. The experience had scared me shitless—much like today's proceedings.

The judge motioned to Santiago. "Counselor, are you ready to proceed?"

"Yes, your Honor. I'd like to call Gabriel Marchionni to the stand."

My mouth went dry. I turned to Maggie, who looked as stunned as I felt.

The judge said, "Mr. Marchionni, please take the stand."

I walked forward, though I had no idea how my feet had moved, considering my brain had gone into convulsions. I stated and spelled my name and verified that I'd sworn in.

"Mr. Marchionni, you are currently cohabitating with Ms. Guthrie, are you not?"

I glanced to the judge as if he'd save me.

He nodded.

"Yes."

"Would you describe your sleeping arrangements?"

That fucker. I narrowed my eyes at Santiago, but I knew how this worked. My mother had put him up to this. "I sleep in the master bedroom. My infant daughter sleeps in a crib two feet from the bed."

"And do you sleep alone in the bed?"

"Yes."

"Does Chloe, the nine-year-old, ever sleep with you?" Sal had the good sense to avoid my eyes.

I took a breath and counted to five. *This is how they wanted to play it?* "My niece and youngest nephew have nightmares about their deceased—"

"If you could answer the question, Mr. Marchionni. The court is aware the children's parents are deceased, otherwise we would not be here."

I glanced at Maggie. Big mistake. She'd gone as white as a marshmallow and looked like she'd melt into the floor at any moment. "The kids come into my room once, maybe twice a week. They miss their parents."

"Has Chloe ever come into your room alone?"

"No."

"Have you ever slept in her bed?"

"Fu... I mean, no." I stared at my mother until she glanced away.

Santiago cleared his throat. "Could you tell the court the state of the household bills when you first moved into Ms. Guthrie's home?"

How the hell did he know... My bank account. My fucking mother was on my account. She'd insisted in case something happened to me. "The bills were current, with the exception of the electric. It was one month past due."

"What about the mortgage? Was it current?"

I smiled for the first time since I'd walked into the room. He'd screwed up, and I planned to take full-fucking advantage of it. "There is *no* mortgage on the house. My brother owned it free and clear."

"You mean the Marchionni Corporation owns the

house and privately financed a mortgage to Miss Guthrie after your brother passed away?"

I turned to the judge. "My folks insist we keep all of the family assets under the business name for tax purposes. My brother paid off the note on the house. Maggie, Miss Guthrie, wanted to pay something for rent so no one would accuse her of profiting from her sister's death."

Santiago stood with his back to my parents and winked at me. He'd given me a gift, and we both knew it. "I have nothing further."

The judge said, "Miss Guthrie, do you have any questions for the witness?"

"I do, Your Honor." She stood and moved from behind the table. "Mr. Marchionni, would you tell the court where Chloe thought you'd been over the previous fourteen months?"

I stared at my father. "She thought I'd gone to heaven with her mom and dad."

Evelyn gasped and pressed her hand to her chest.

"And why is that?" Maggie glanced back at her soon to be mother-in-law.

"My father urged my brothers and me to stay away from the children."

She went back to her table, grabbed a stack of papers and handed them to the clerk. "Your Honor, I'd like to submit the police reports from Giuseppe Marchionni Jr. and Rebecca Guthrie Marchionni's automobile accident."

Santiago stood. "The reports are already in evidence."

"Not these, Your Honor. I've secured the preliminary notes and handwritten reports from the responding officers, as well as phone logs detailing Giuseppe Marchionni Sr.'s concerns about the *accident*."

My parents and Santiago huddled together and whispered.

The judge cleared his throat and motioned to the clerk. "I'll accept Miss Guthrie's documents."

She turned back to me. "Why would a grandfather demand uncles not to visit grieving children?"

My father met my eyes as if daring me to answer. What could I do? I was under oath and the truth was spelled out in the reports. "He insisted my brother and sister-in-law were murdered."

"Despite the police findings?"

"Yes."

Maggie cocked her head. "Would you say your father's actions were warranted?"

I rolled my lips in. She'd pushed a little too far. "I don't know."

"Would you say he was acting paranoid?"

Santiago's voice rang out. "I object. The witness isn't a trained professional."

"I withdraw the question." Maggie sighed. "Mr. Marchionni. Would you characterize our relationship for the court?"

I glanced from her to the judge and grinned. "Miss Guthrie and I are engaged to be married, and I can assure you, we will not miss another electric bill."

24

Maggie

"Where did all of this baby equipment come from? It looks like Babies R Us threw up in here." Shanna stood with her hands on her hips, surveying the cluttered living room.

"Most of it came from the attic." I eased Ella into the swing, pressed a few buttons, and gave the contraption a gentle nudge. "She's cranky today, but this will put her to sleep."

"I hate to admit it, but she's flippin' adorable." Shanna plopped down on the sofa. "Where's Prince Charming?"

"Work." I hovered near Ella until her eyes drooped.

Shanna had called to say she was dropping by an hour after we'd walked out of the courthouse. I still hadn't processed everything that had happened.

"I know that look. What's wrong? How did it go today?"

I sat beside her. "Good, I think. They tried to make Gabe out to be some sort of pervert for allowing Chloe and Ryan to sleep in his bed."

Shanna's brows disappeared behind her bangs. "Those assholes. He's their son."

I waved her off. "He set them straight. Told the judge about the kids missing their parents. Explained away my money trouble by saying we were engaged. I think the case will be dismissed. We won't know for a week or so."

My phone rang for the seventh or eighth time in the previous hour. I glanced at the screen and turned it to silent.

"Then why are you moping?"

I shrugged. Had I really expected Gabe to say his father was nuts on the stand? "I'm not. I'm just stressed."

"Uh huh." She shook my shoulder. "We don't have to talk about it now, but I'll get it out of you sooner or later."

I thought back to the argument Gabe and I had the night before. "Do you think I'm too controlling?"

"Controlling? You?" Shanna scoffed.

"I'm serious."

"You've always known what you wanted in life."

I rested my head on the back of the couch and stared at the ceiling. "That sounds like a nice way of telling me I'm a control freak."

Shanna tossed a pillow at me. "Enough of the melodrama. What's up?"

I turned my head in her direction. "Gabe told me he dumped me because he didn't fit into my plan."

"Bullshit." She glanced at the baby as if to make sure the infant wouldn't repeat after her. "He dumped you because he's a *jackass*."

"Maybe." I'd never really understood why he'd broken things off, which is why I'd assumed he'd met someone else. Now that we'd finally discussed his reasons, I *almost* would have preferred he cheated. Him being a jerk was easier to swallow than me being neurotic.

"Even if he felt that way, why not talk to you about it instead of ignoring your calls?"

Nothing the man did made much sense. Trying to figure it out worked as well as bubble wrap on a hand grenade. I pushed my wounded feelings and doubts about my relationship with Gabe down deep enough I'd need an excavator to find them. "You didn't come here to talk about my OCD. What did you want to tell me?"

My phone vibrated on the table.

Shanna narrowed her eyes. "Speaking of OCD. Since when do you not answer your cell?"

"I've been getting a ton of prank calls."

"Seriously?"

"They started shortly after Gabe moved in. I'm thinking it's one of his groupies." My blood ran cold. "Oh my God. I'm so stupid. Why didn't I think of this sooner?"

"What?"

"Chantal." I ran through everything I knew about the woman. It made perfect sense. "She called the house the other day. She's the one harassing me."

Shanna watched me for a long moment. "It wouldn't surprise me, but you need to know for sure. I can trace the calls, but I'll need you to come into the office."

Her offer tempted me, but I didn't have the energy to contemplate the implications. They were calls. Scary calls, but they weren't actual threats. Were they?

The next time it vibrated, Shanna grabbed it before I could stop her.

"Hello." She turned and narrowed her eyes. "Hi Justin. This is Shanna, Maggie's friend."

I wrestled the phone from her. "Hello?"

"It was rude of you to hang up on me the other day. You should know I've contacted an attorney." He sounded far too smug for a guy who'd cheated on his wife.

"You can't sue someone for hanging up."

"Not that, you stupid bitch. I'm suing Marchionni. Unless, of course, you two pay up—"

I disconnected and stared at the phone.

"Is he serious?" Shanna rolled her eyes.

"You heard that?"

She nodded. "We need to add him to the list of possible prank callers."

"There's no point. It's not Justin. The prank calls are coming from a woman."

"Regardless, we should have them traced. In the meantime, give Gabe a heads-up."

"Yeah. I will." I cleared the emotion from my throat, but I couldn't stop my brain from spinning like a roulette wheel. *Is this what it would be like to marry into the Marchionni family? How did Rebecca handle it?* "What was so urgent you needed to see me today?"

Shanna grinned. "I found the B.M."

"B.M.?"

"Baby Mama."

I cringed, not knowing which nickname I found more troubling.

Shanna pulled a thin manila folder from her bag. "She's a performer on a cruise ship out of New Orleans."

I opened it as a shot of adrenaline coursed through me.

I'd crossed a line that I couldn't uncross. Nevertheless, I flipped through the pages of typical private investigator documents. The driving and criminal records were unremarkable—although the grainy DMV photo confirmed my suspicions. The woman was gorgeous. More concerning, she looked familiar.

"What is it?" Shanna leaned closer to see what had caught my eye.

"It's hard to tell from this, but I think I've seen her somewhere."

"I'll dig up a better image. I'm sure the cruise line has promo material or employee badges."

"Maybe it's best you don't." I turned my attention back to the file. The credit report and bankruptcy filing surprised me, but the next piece of paper made my stomach turn. "She's married?"

"Was married." Shanna lowered her voice. "Her husband committed suicide about eighteen months ago."

I did some fast math. I blew out a breath. Not that it mattered in the grand scheme of things, but the idea of Gabe sleeping with a married woman made my skin crawl. "Before she got pregnant. Gabe said they dated a few times. You don't think the suicide had anything to do with him?"

"There's more." Shanna perked up. "On a whim, I cross checked the Marchionni files with Chantal's."

"I know Papa Joe suspected her of having something to do with the accident."

"Right, and I think I know why. I got a hit on B.M.'s husband."

I had trouble keeping up with Shanna, but I thought I

had the gist of it. "What does Chantal's husband have to do with the Marchionnis?"

"Martin Sinclair accused Papa Joe of sabotaging his business in order to force him to sell. A month later, Marchionni Corporation closed on his property, and Martin killed himself." Shanna sounded like she had hit the Lotto.

"Wait." I pressed my hand to my stomach to calm the churning.

Shanna didn't wait. She barreled on. "It gets better. Two months later, Chantal filed for bankruptcy."

I put the pieces together, but they didn't add up. "Why did Chantal file bankruptcy? Wouldn't the cash from the sale..."

"Looks like it wasn't enough." Shanna shrugged. "Or maybe they screwed her over?"

"Either way, why would Chantal get involved with a Marchionni after that?" Something told me I didn't want to know the answer. I stood and paced. "Her husband dies, somehow leaving her broke, and she files bankruptcy. Then she hooks up with Gabe and gets pregnant. Is this all part of a bigger plan?"

"Maybe she wanted proof of wrongdoing and thought Gabe was an easy target?"

"Or she's after his money, like Justin." I sank onto the sofa. "I'm going to be sick."

Shanna put her hand on my shoulder. "I'm sorry. I know this is a lot to take in."

"I need to talk to Gabe. He doesn't know she used him."

"Are you sure?"

"I'm not sure of anything, but something isn't right."

"This could end badly for Gabe. Chantal obviously

needs money, which Gabe has warehouses of. Has he filed anything to establish legal paternity?" Shanna chewed her lower lip.

"I don't know."

"Find out." She stood. "I have to run, but I'll check in tomorrow."

"Thanks." I couldn't tear my gaze away from Ella. No matter how this all came to be, the baby didn't deserve to be treated like a bargaining chip.

By the afternoon, I'd worked myself into such a funk I couldn't unravel the tangle of thoughts wadded up in my head.

Needing cake and needing it bad, I went straight for the kitchen. The store-bought variety never calmed my nerves. In times like these, only my grandmother's double fudge delight recipe would do the trick.

Zach came home from school first. He took one look at the contents of the counter and went to the pantry for the powdered sugar and cocoa. "Bad day?"

I wiped my eyes on the back of my hand. "I've had better. Are you okay with what happened in court today?"

"Yeah, I guess." He grinned, but I had a feeling he'd done it for my benefit.

"Need extra Xbox time?" While I had a million questions, I refused to put him in the middle of the fight between me and his grandparents.

"I'll grease and flour the pans." Zach didn't ask for an explanation, though I knew he worried.

"Thanks." I rested my hand on his shoulder and supervised as he scooped out the shortening with a paper towel.

Since I'd become his guardian, he'd developed a fear

something would happen to me. The therapists said not to worry. Kids grieving their parents often became protective of their caregivers. That was all fine and well, but I suspected since he was the oldest and a boy, he thought of himself as the man of the house.

Gabe came through the door with Ryan slung over one shoulder, his laptop bag on the other, and Chloe trailing behind him. He glanced between me and Zach. "Is Ella sleeping?"

I stuck my head in the fridge to hide my ugly-cry face. "She's in her swing."

"Everything okay? Are you coming down with something?"

I frowned. Of course, he'd comment on my puffy eyes and red nose. "Allergies."

"You look awful, take something for it." He set Ryan down. "Any word from the court?"

"Nope." I pressed my lips into a thin line and stared. We needed to talk, but not with so many little ears present.

"I referred a Mr. Trudeau to my lawyer today."

"He called me this morning."

"Don't take his calls. Santiago is handling it." Gabe nodded toward the stairs. "I promised to play with the munchkins."

"One less thing to worry about, I guess." I turned my attention back to the cake batter and ignored his irritated sigh. "Have fun."

Zach and I worked side by side, our silent labor inter-rupted by giggles and monster noises drifting down from the playroom. It would have been lovely to believe a happy ending waited at the end of the tunnel, but every day my doubts increased.

My phone buzzed in my pocket. "Hello?"

"Hi Maggie, this is Jessie. Can you come in tonight? One of the girls called in sick and I'm in a jam."

I glanced at the clock. "I can be there in an hour."

"We're slammed. Don't tell my cousin I said this, but the hotter you look, the hotter the tips."

"Good to know." I hung up and turned to Zach. "I have to work tonight."

"Okay." He gave me a look I couldn't interpret. Sympathy? Frustration? Anger?

"Are you okay with me being out in the evenings?"

"Yeah, it's nice having a guy around."

I forced another smile. "Take the cake out when the timer goes off. You remember how to make the frosting?"

Zach nodded and surprised me with a quick hug. "I love you, Aunt Maggie."

"I love you too."

25

Gabe

Chloe grinned and drew in a deep breath. "Aunt Maggie's baking."

I pressed pause on the video game and sniffed. Sure enough, the sweet scent of a chocolate cake filled the entire second floor. "My favorite. Must be a special day."

Chloe rolled her eyes. "It's not a birthday, so she's sad."

I tried to wrap my brain around Chloe's words. "Cakes aren't for sad days."

Ryan climbed onto my back for either a pony ride or round two of wrestling. "Cakes are for all days!"

Chloe gave the two of us a patient smile. "Aunt Maggie makes cakes on birthdays *and* when she's cranky or sad."

"Huh. Girls are weird." I pulled Ryan around, pinned him to the ground and tickled him until he squealed for mercy.

"I'm not weird." Chloe launched herself at us and peeled me away from her baby brother.

Zach came upstairs and watched the wrestling match

with a wry expression. "I hate to break up the party, but you should go talk to Maggie before she goes."

I pulled both munchkins off me and stood. "Where's she going?"

"To work. At the bar. *Your* bar." Zach stared. He'd perfected the teenage ability to call adults stupid without saying a word.

"I'm on it." I took the stairs two at a time, crossed the house, and glanced in Maggie's room. Not finding her, I went into the master and knocked on the bathroom door.

"Come in."

I hesitated, wondering if she realized it was me. She'd been almost hostile since I'd come home. "Maggie, it's me."

"Come in." She added more irritation to the two syllables.

"Zach told me you're going into work?" I walked in and stopped in my tracks.

"Jessie called. I figured you knew." She leaned over the sink putting on mascara with her mouth hanging open and both eyes open wide.

She's adorable.

My gaze fell to her ass. Bent over the counter, she looked better than the cake smelled. I took a step forward and set my hand on her hip. "You could be late."

She glared at my reflection. "I'm still upset with you."

"Is that why you were crying earlier?" I caressed her shoulder.

She turned and sidestepped me. "I'm in a hurry. We'll talk about it later."

I folded my arms and rested my hip against the vanity and considered the situation. Even though her words were less than friendly, she hadn't flinched when I'd touched her. The hurt look in her eyes concerned me, but she hadn't asked me to leave the room. The woman didn't seem to know what she wanted.

"Talk to me now." I followed her into her bedroom.

Maggie opened her closet and riffled through shirt after shirt. "Jessie suggested I dress sexy. What do you think?"

I think I'll have a little chat with Jessie. "Jeans and a T-shirt are fine. Sneakers or comfortable boots."

She pulled out a red, silky number that looked more like a bathing suit than a top. Before I could tell her not to wear the scrap of material, she whipped her shirt and bra off. My heart stopped beating when all my blood went south—a situation that didn't improve when she shimmied into the red halter top.

"Maggie." I spoke in a tone more warning than conversation.

"Gabe." She mimicked my voice.

I wrapped my hands around her arms, pulled her against me, and kissed her smart mouth.

She tensed but didn't pull away.

I coaxed her lips open with my tongue and grabbed two handfuls of her hair. Tugging hard enough to elicit a soft moan, I nibbled a line down her neck.

Maggie whispered, "I'm going to be late."

"I don't care." I cupped her face and forced her to meet my gaze. "What has you so upset?"

"I've had a really bad day, but I can't get into it right now."

The hitch in her voice made my heart clench. "I've got you. Talk to me."

"Tonight, after work."

I rested my forehead against hers. "On one condition."

"What's that?" She smiled at me for the first time in days.

"We have sex after. No matter what."

She furrowed her brow. "What if you're not happy with what I have to say?"

I kissed the corner of her mouth. "Then I'll be happy afterward."

Ella cried in the living room, and I took a step toward the door. "I'll get her. And I want you home as soon as it slows down."

Maggie tilted her head. "Won't I get fired for not finishing closing duties?"

"Only if you wear that red top."

Twenty minutes later, I kissed her goodbye. She'd changed into a T-shirt. It fit tighter than I would have preferred for work, but I took the high road and kept my mouth shut.

Never in my wildest dreams would I have imagined this would be my life. Sure, I'd always wanted a houseful of kids, a wife, and a picket fence, but when I'd imagined my future it'd always included a stay-at-home wife, a nanny, visits to the country club, and time on the golf course. I'd thought I wanted a marriage like my parents had, until now.

Maggie would never agree to give up her career, and I wouldn't expect her to. Though having some help around the house would be nice, but the woman refused to hire a nanny.

No matter how shitty my day, Ella's bath time always cheered me up. Her jerky splashes and sweet cooing noises washed away my stress better than single malt scotch.

"Let's get you dressed." I released the water from the mini-tub and wrapped her up before heading to the master bedroom.

Determined to be free of her hooded towel, Ella wiggled in my arms. She'd plumped up over the previous three weeks and had started to develop a personality.

I laid her on the changing table and tickled her tummy. Still damp and smelling like soap, she kicked her legs. I sang a couple of verses of a Louis Armstrong song while wrangling her into her PJs. The more I sang, the more she kicked as if determined to keep me from closing the snaps and ending our special time.

"Be still." Laughing, I glanced at her face.

Ella's eyes met mine, and she smiled her first, big, bright, toothless, baby smile.

Right then and there, I fell in love. Before that moment I'd protected and cared for her, but this...this was something different.

Ella had carved herself a hole in my heart that nothing, and no one, except she could fill. My daughter had wrapped me around her tiny finger with a smile.

I reached in my pocket for my phone. I had to call and tell Maggie what had happened. Better yet, I'd take a picture and text it to her.

I made faces at Ella, played peek-a-boo, even blew on her tummy, but nothing I did made her smile. Giving up, I picked her up and started humming again.

She freaking smiled.

"You like my singing?" I laid her on the bed and readied my cell. Before I could snap the picture, the dog started barking and Zach called my name.

I carried Ella down the hall and immediately wanted to turn around and lock myself in the bedroom.

The damned dog scarfed bits of cake from the floor, while Zach, also on the floor, tried to pull her back.

Determined to finish her dessert, Cocoa inhaled and gagged at the same time like a malfunctioning vacuum cleaner.

"What happened?" I set Ella in her port-a-crib, grabbed the dog's collar, and pulled her out of the kitchen.

She might have been a chocolate lab but eating that much chocolate cake would give her the runs.

"Cocoa got under my feet. I twisted my ankle." Zach held his lower calf.

Chloe and Ryan appeared at the bottom of the stairs and took in the show.

"Let me take a look at it." Ignoring the fact that Cocoa had followed me back into the kitchen, I knelt beside Zach.

"No. It's fine."

"Don't be silly, let me see." I reached for his foot, and he moved away.

"Don't touch it…" His reaction reminded me he was still a kid.

I lowered my voice. "I can look at it now, or we can call Maggie home, and I can take you to the ER for someone else to look at it."

"No," Zach cried out. "I don't need to go to the hospital."

I reached for his foot again. This time he let him take a

look. "It's not too swollen. Ice it. If it gets worse, we should get it checked out."

"I'm on it." Chloe filled a baggie with ice. Unfortunately, she spilled half of it on the floor.

"I'm on it, too!" Ryan tossed the cubes into the sink one at a time.

Cocoa retched in the living room, and we all moved at once. I went for the damned dog. Cocoa dodged, ran to the corner, and puked. Chloe ran for the bathroom. Zach scrambled to his feet and set Ryan on the couch.

"Go ice your ankle. I got this." I pulled the dog out the back door.

Zach hobbled into the living room and sat beside his brother.

Fearing the sight of vomit had made her sick, I hurried to the bathroom to check on Chloe. "You okay?"

"Yep." The girl practiced her dance moves in the mirror.

In the time it took me to get back into the living room, the dog had come back inside and left another mess. To be honest, I had no idea which end the pile of brown goo had come out of.

Adding insult to injury, Ryan had escaped the couch and was sitting in the middle of the kitchen floor eating chocolate frosting out of the bowl—along with the idiot dog.

I would have cried, but I'd been raised to believe that guys didn't shed tears, they yelled. "For Christ's sake, nobody move!"

Ella let loose a scream that hit the same pitch as a knife scrapping a plate.

"You get her. I'll take Ryan." Zach limped to the kitchen

and yanked the bowl away from his brother. This sent the boy into a full-blown tantrum.

"You need to ice your ankle." I shouted over the din.

"I will, but right now you're seriously outnumbered."

"Okay. You throw Ryan in the bathtub and stay with him. I'll settle Ella and clean up after the dog." I dragged Cocoa out back and made sure to turn the lock near the top of the door—out of Ryan's reach.

Holding Ryan at arm's length to avoid being slimed, Zach hobbled down the hall.

"This is between you and me. Man to man. The girls don't need to know."

"Gotcha." Zach called from the bathroom.

"The girls don't need to know what?" Chloe looked at her chocolate-covered brother and squealed.

"Maggie's cake's ruined. We'll make a new one." Zach motioned to the screaming baby. "Go give Ella her pacifier.

"Boys are weird." Chloe shrugged and skipped around the piles of chocolate vomit toward the port-a-crib.

I pulled my hair into a ponytail and went to the utility room to fill the mop bucket. I'd never have thought this would be my life, but I wouldn't trade any of it.

Except I'd exchange the damned dog with a nanny.

26

Maggie

PEOPLE PACKED EVERY INCH OF THE BAR, MOST OF whom shouted their orders. By now, I could mix most drinks without engaging my brain, which was good because all I could think about were the files I'd hidden in my room, and court.

I doubted Gabe knew about Chantal's connection to the Marchionni Corporation. If he had, he wouldn't have started a relationship with her. Would he? I didn't know the woman, but I feared Chantal would use Ella to extort money from him. I needed to ask the man some tough questions—if we could find five minutes alone together.

"Maggie, go on break." Jessie called from the other end of the bar.

The crowd had thinned somewhat, but not enough for one person to handle orders. "You sure?"

"Go." Two longnecks dangling from each hand, Jessie winked. "Before I change my mind."

In the breakroom, I sank into one chair and propped my aching feet onto another. Opting for fashion over function turned out to be a bad idea. Likewise, tight T-shirt had increased my tips, but I'd had more male attention than I could handle.

I pulled my phone from my back pocket. No texts or missed calls.

It should have been a good thing. Gabe could take care of the kids without my help, but it bothered me. The first couple of months after my sister died had been horrible, and not just because of our grief. The kids had tested me at every turn. More days than not, I'd considered handing them over to Evelyn and running for the hills. The idea Gabe could waltz in and run things without a hiccup made me more than a little jealous.

Deep in the throes of an aching-feet-failure-as-a-mom pity-party, I didn't hear anyone come in.

A male voice spoke behind me. "Maggie?"

I yelped and turned to find another of the Marchionni boys at the door.

Leo was as luscious as Gabe, though taller and thinner. He had the same green eyes as his brothers, but he wore his dark hair short, accentuating the sharp angles of his face.

"Hi, Leo."

"Did Jessie call you in?" He looked somewhere between confused and amused.

"Yeah, but I'm on break." I pulled my feet off the chair.

He took it as an invitation and sat. "Rumor has it you're going to be my new sister-in-law."

"So I hear."

"Never thought I'd see the day." He chuckled and ran his hand over the back of his neck—a habit he shared with his older brother.

"I hear tales of women from the surrounding parishes organizing to take me down." I wrinkled my nose. "He was a bit of a ladies' man."

"Besides the debacle with Chantal, not really. After you, he put everything he had into this bar."

"Oh..." The need to remove my foot from my mouth overtook me.

Leo seemed to sense my discomfort and flashed me the patented Marchionni grin. "It's good to see him happy again. He's like a changed man."

"You see a difference in him?" I probably shouldn't have asked, but they were close. If anyone could give me some insight into Gabe's psyche, it was Leo.

"Yeah. I would have chalked it up to getting some, but he's a man in love. All he talks about are you and the kids." Leo's smile faltered. "Nothing personal, but he's a better man than I am. No way could I walk into a ready-made family."

I laughed and stood. "He's a better man than I am, too."

"You guys are good together."

"Thanks." I still had my doubts, but overall, I agreed.

He stood and drew me into a hug.

A little voice inside my head reminded me that I had a story to write. I needed to ask about the business, about the family secrets, about something other than Gabe.

Leo released me. "I should let you get back to work."

"Do you think he'll be happy taking over for your father?" Not the most eloquent question, but it went straight to the point.

"I do. He's going to be a family man now, priorities shift."

"Can he do it? I mean, can he be as ruthless as Papa Joe?"

Leo squeezed my shoulder. "Hell yeah. Do you remember what a dump this place used to be? He worked his ass off to save it."

"But running a bar and running a company the size of Marchionni Corp are two different things. People come here because they love Gabe. Your father's not exactly known as a *nice* guy."

He leaned closer and lowered his voice. "Don't let Gabe's good looks fool you. He's as much a shark as Papa Joe."

I shuddered on the inside but kept my plastic smile in place. "I worry it'll change him."

"It may, but he has you to keep him honest." Leo headed for the door. "I have some stuff to do in the office. Catch you later."

I made my way down the hall. The ache in my feet paled in comparison to the ache in my gut. Could the same guy who'd built blanket forts with Ryan run a multi-billion-dollar company? A multi-billion-dollar company that might or might not be a front for the mob?

Absorbed in my thoughts, I collided with a wall of a man. "Excuse me."

"No problem, gorgeous." The guy looked me over as if I were a dessert tray. "That's some frown. Let me buy you a drink."

"I'm working, but thanks."

"In that case, I'll have a gin and tonic, hold the tonic." He took a step closer, and I took two steps behind the bar.

Feeling more secure with a physical barrier between me

and the big guy, I poured him a gin on the rocks, added a lime wedge, and set his glass on the bar.

"What time do you get off?" He set a twenty on the bar.

"Back off, Wayne. She's engaged." Jessie crowded in beside me.

"No ring. Whoever the yahoo is, he must be a loser." Wayne smirked. "I'd put a rock the size of a robin's egg on that pretty finger."

Jessie grinned at me. "Watch out for Wayne. He's one of New Orleans's finest."

A shot of adrenaline coursed through me. I had absolutely no reason to fear a police officer, or did I? Hadn't Gabe paid one off? "You're a cop?"

"A detective. Yes, ma'am. Lying to me is a felony. Are you really betrothed?" The grin never leaving his face, he sipped his drink.

"This isn't a Jane Austen novel, and yes, she's really engaged to Gabe." Jessie's perpetual smile brightened.

He coughed gin out his nose *and* mouth.

I moved down the bar and took another order while he cleared the ninety-proof, top-shelf liquor from his nasal passages.

"Tell me how Gabe locked you down without a ring?"

"They've been busy," Jessie said.

"I bet they have..." Wayne wiggled his brows.

I groaned. "Jessie, don't help."

She chuckled and took another order.

I wanted to crawl under a rock. Not only did he laugh, the commotion had drawn the attention of several patrons.

"Congratulations." Wayne shoved his paw across the bar. "I'm Detective Wayne O'Malley."

"Maggie Guthrie." I shook his hand.

His expression changed from congenial to knocked for six. "Any relation to Rebecca Guthrie-Marchionni?"

"My sister."

The detective frowned and looked down at the contents of his drink.

The change in his mood piqued my curiosity. "Did you know her?"

"I worked the accident investigation."

I held onto the edge of the bar to keep from toppling over. "Can I ask you a question, privately?"

He glanced between me and Jessie as if weighing his options, or maybe he thought she'd save him. Hard to tell.

I moved from behind the bar and rested my hand on his arm. "Please."

He nodded once and pushed to his feet. Any remaining warmth bled from his eyes. He squared his shoulders, stiffened his spine, and raised his chin. Heck, he even walked differently. Had I not witnessed the change in him, I would have thought the laughing guy and the detective were two different people.

The new version scared the crap out of me. I didn't know if I wanted to ask the questions, let alone hear the answers, but I followed him outside.

Wayne folded his arms and settled the weight of his stare on me. "What can I do for you?"

I debated beating around the bush but decided to get straight to it. "Do you believe my sister's death was an accident?"

He drew a deep breath and exhaled with a faint wheeze. "That's what the final report says."

"That's not what I asked you." I decided to try a different tactic. I lowered my gaze, slumped my shoulders, and softened my voice. "Please, I need to know. I'm about to marry into this family. I have to know if the kids and I are in danger."

"You have kids?" His voice rose in volume and pitch. I'd evidently hit a nerve.

Fidgeting with my hands, I nodded. "I have custody of Joe and Rebecca's three."

Wayne sucked air through his teeth, looked up at the sky, and cursed under his breath. "Is it true Gabe's taking over for Papa Joe?"

I nodded because I didn't trust my voice to come out normal. I'd gone from playing a victim to feeling like one.

"The Marchionnis have a way of pissing off people. I don't think there's imminent danger but caution never hurt anyone."

"People like Martin Sinclair?"

Wayne's eyes grew larger before he could sink back behind his detective mask.

"Did he have anything to do with what happened to my sister?"

"Martin Sinclair died before the collision."

"What about his wife? Was she questioned?"

"I'm not at liberty to say." Wayne motioned to me. "You're good. Batted those lashes and I fell for it."

I shrugged one shoulder. "Wouldn't you do whatever you had to do to protect the people you love?"

Oddly enough, he glanced back toward the bar. "Yeah. I would."

"I'll ask you again, do you think it was an accident?"

He turned back to me. "My gut tells me no, but my superiors put a hell of a lot of pressure on us to close the case."

I'd read as much in the report, but I appreciated his honesty. "Did Papa Joe pressure the department?"

He blew out a breath. "You're killing me. Let's just say, pressure comes from all sides in high profile cases."

My head spun. I felt like I'd walked into made for television melodrama. "Are they mafia?"

"Honey, if you have to ask me that, you shouldn't marry Gabe."

I hugged myself and bent forward a few inches. It'd all happened so fast. I loved him, but was that enough?

Wayne laid his hand on my shoulder. "Don't fall apart on me now."

Am I raising the next generation of mafia? Am I engaged to the next freaking *Godfather*? I righted myself and met his gaze. "I'm afraid of what I don't know."

Wayne glanced up the street and lowered his voice again. "What they call themselves doesn't matter. You don't get the level of power and influence the Marchionnis have without pissing people off and breaking a few laws. Take my advice—leave the *accident* alone. Nothing good will come of poking around in this."

"Maybe you're right."

His head remained still, but his gaze darted to the side.

Unlike the detective, I turned and locked eyes with *the* guy in the leather jacket. I pressed my hand to my chest and took a step behind Wayne. "I think that man's following me."

The detective nodded. "Wouldn't surprise me. He's on

the Marchionni payroll. The question is, why are they having you tailed?"

My grandmother used to have these seizures where she'd stare off into space, like she'd vacated her body. I had one of those right there in the middle of the French Quarter. One minute I was talking to Wayne, the next everything stopped. No sound, no sight, nothing except me and blinding fear.

"Maggie?" the detective called to me, but he seemed a million miles away. "Miss Guthrie? Are you okay?"

I snapped back into the present. "I need to get out of here."

"I'll drive you home." He narrowed his eyes at Mr. Leather Jacket.

The guy held his arms up as if to say *busted* and walked away.

"I can call a ride share."

"I'm not letting you out of my sight in your current state of mind." Wayne led me back into the bar, said something to Jessie, and followed me to the office. "Maggie, listen. Gabe's a good guy. Give him a chance to answer your questions before you go into hiding, but you have to ask him."

"I will." I couldn't help but wonder if he would have said the same thing if I'd told him my fiancé had a child with Martin Sinclair's wife.

27

Gabe

A VIBRATION IN MY PANTS WOKE ME. I EASED ELLA from my chest to the couch and pulled my phone from my pocket. "Hey, Leo, what's up? How are the poodles?"

"The dogs are fine. We have a different problem." My brother's voice came through along with music, chatter, and laughter.

"One sec." I scooted Ella away from the edge and put a throw pillow beside her to keep her in place. Dumb move, but I didn't plan to go far. "What problem?"

"There are several. One of the guys I put on Maggie was made tonight."

My stomach lurched. "How and by who?"

"Wayne O'Malley, while he was having an *emotional* conversation with Maggie."

"What the fuck do you mean emotional?" I inhaled and exhaled to the count of five and slid into business mode. I could handle this if I treated it like any other work crisis. This involved an employee, not the woman I planned to marry.

"Your girl was upset. Crying maybe." He paused and made a sound suspiciously close to a laugh. "Come on, man. You didn't think I meant they were together-together?"

"Go on." Some of the tension eased from my shoulders. The situation was bad, but it could have been worse. I wouldn't end up in prison for killing the cop who put his hands on my woman.

"Wayne told Jessie Maggie was sick, and he was driving her home. They left a couple of minutes ago."

That son of a bitch. Maybe I'd go to prison after all. "Anything else? Do you know what they discussed?"

"No clue, but earlier tonight she asked me about you taking over the business." The background noise quieted, but Leo kept his voice down. "What did you tell her about your job description?"

"Not much, but she's smart." *Smart enough to have a copy of the police records from Joe and Rebecca's accident.* "I'll handle it."

"Touch base in the morning."

I disconnected the call. Depending on where the detective had parked, I figured I had ten, maybe fifteen minutes until Maggie arrived home. If I hustled, I could get a shower. The conversation would be hard enough without me smelling like chocolate-covered dog vomit.

After settling Ella in her crib, I stripped and went into the bathroom.

A car door shut out front. A few seconds later, I heard Maggie greeting Cocoa in the front of the house.

I had two choices slide back into my filthy jeans or have the talk with Maggie naked. I chose option number two.

After five minutes and no sign of her, I regretted my decision. *Is she waiting for me to get out?*

She came into the bathroom at the exact moment I'd decided to go find her. "Hi. I really need to talk to you."

"I heard you come in." I cracked open the shower door and gave her a quick once over. She still wore makeup, so probably not crying. She'd smiled a little, so probably not pissed. Scratch that—she'd changed from her work clothes into a silky bathrobe. *Definitely* not pissed.

"Sorry it took me so long. Ryan wanted water. Then I had to wait for him to pee, tuck him in again, and speak to Chloe about her dream about unicorns. This led to a debate on whether they would throw up rainbows or chocolate cake."

I covered my cringe with a laugh. "I can see your unicorn dream, and raise you talking to a teenaged boy about a girl."

Maggie dropped the robe, stepped into the shower, and wrapped her arms around me.

My God, she's gorgeous. I caressed her from her shoulders to her bare ass "You're naked."

"I never shower with clothes on. What did Zach say? What girl?"

"He has a crush on a tuba player named Sam. Wanted to know if I thought he should buy her roses for after the band concert." I tilted her head under the water, grabbed the shampoo, and massaged it into her scalp.

"What did you tell him?"

"I told him to send her flowers at home. That way none of his knucklehead friends would tease him. If she shoots him down, it shouldn't be in public."

"Good advice." She closed her eyes and let the water sluice over her head.

I angled her beneath the spray and rinsed her hair. "Thanks. Now, about you being in my shower..."

"It's my shower." Maggie drew a shaky breath, and I knew she'd had enough small talk.

I leaned down and brushed my lips across hers. "What did you want to talk about?"

Maggie hung her head.

"What is it?" I lifted her chin.

"Why did your father insist Joe and Rebecca's accident wasn't an accident?"

"A deal went bad. The owner made threats against Joe and my dad."

"Did they stop after the accident?" Maggie rested her hands on my chest.

Be it her touch, or my need to come clean with her, I decided then and there to tell her everything. "The threats stopped before the accident because the guy offed himself."

Her hand flew to her mouth.

I nodded and continued. "But Pops was still convinced it was the dead guy's people. The cops couldn't prove anything."

"Is that why you held back on me in court? You don't think Papa Joe's paranoid at all, do you?"

"Paranoid, no. Cautious, yes."

Maggie shivered. "I talked to a detective tonight. Wayne O'Malley."

"I know him. Decent guy."

"He asked if I was related to Rebecca, and the conversation went from there." She pulled back and looked into my eyes. "Should I be worried? I mean, will someone try to kill you or me and the kids? I'm getting all these threatening calls"

"What?" A lightbulb came on in the back of my mind. "The prank calls?"

"Do you think they could be coming from Chantal?"

Her question hit me like a throat punch. My daughter's mother harassed me via telephone, why not Maggie? "It's a distinct possibility. I have people at Marchionni Corp who can trace them."

Nodding, she murmured, "They're just calls, right?"

I have no idea, but I intend to find out. I pulled her tighter and kissed the top of her head. "We deal with some *interesting* people, but you don't need to worry. I had Leo put security on you."

Her mouth fell open. "It was you? Why?"

"After the engagement announcement, I didn't want to take any chances—"

"My God, you scared the hell out of me. I thought your parents were having me tailed." She smacked my arm.

"Ow. Easy there, slugger."

"I don't want people following me."

"Mags—"

"We'll talk about that later. I have more important questions right now." She avoided making eye contact.

It surprised me that she seemed more nervous than upset. *What the hell does she know?* "Wayne told you something else?"

"No, not Wayne." Maggie chewed her lower lip. "I did some checking up on Chantal."

I coughed from the second verbal throat punch in as many minutes. "Why?"

"Because I'm worried about you and Ella. Did you know she was married?"

Blindsided and more than a little pissed, I stepped out of the shower. "She's widowed."

Maggie started to follow me out of the shower but stopped when I turned to face her. "Gabe, she—"

"You had no business poking into this."

"I'm sorry, but I disagree. If you and that sweet little girl in there are going to be part of my life, I need to know what's going on." She dipped her chin.

I needed a few minutes to calm the fuck down before I said something stupid. "Let's finish this in your room. I don't want to wake Ella."

"All right."

I checked on my daughter, pulled on a pair of PJ pants, and second-guessed myself from every angle. I needed to tell her about Chantal, but first I wanted to know what she'd found, where she'd dug it up, and why. *Had Leo's guy misread her signals, or was there something else going on with her and Wayne?*

I crawled into her bed and stared at the ceiling. If we had to argue, I preferred to do it horizontally.

Maggie came into the room and stretched out beside me —*in nothing except her robe.* This woman knew how to surprise the shit out of me, piss me off, and turn me on all at the same time.

She snuggled against my side. "Promise me you'll file paperwork to establish legal paternity as soon as possible."

"It's already in the works." I kissed her forehead. "I put

security on you because the situation with Chantal is getting out of hand."

"How so?" She propped herself up on her elbow.

"She wants money before she signs the custody papers."

"There's something you need to know." She sucked in a breath. "Chantal was married to Martin Sinclair."

Tonight was a night of surprises, and I fucking hate surprises. "I know."

"Oh." Maggie rolled to her back. "Of course, you knew."

"She's not responsible for the accident."

"How do you know?" Her voice trembled.

"Because I was with her that night." I held my breath and waited for her to explode.

"Your relationship with her... It's in the past, right?"

Boom. Another surprise. She didn't lose her shit. "Yeah, of course."

"Then it isn't any of my business. As long as you know the score, which you obviously do, and she isn't a psychopath out to hurt my family... She isn't, is she?"

"Physically, no she's not the type."

"Then why do I need security?" Maggie turned my head and forced me to look her in the eye.

"She threatened to tell you about the situation with Martin and my family." I'd chosen my words carefully. Chantal had implied more, and yes, I needed to tell Maggie about the family business, but she'd had enough to process for one night. We both had.

"If she's not a physical threat, I want you to call off the security guards. I don't like the idea of people following me around."

"Done."

"Any word from the attorney about Justin Trudeau?"

"After a conversation with Santiago, he's decided it's a bad idea to sue."

"Because his wife would find out he was seeing other people?"

"Probably." I nuzzled into her chest. "I'll never let anything happen to you."

"I know, but—"

"No buts and no more snooping."

"Gabe—"

This time, I surprised her by pinning her to the bed and kissing her stupid.

28

Maggie

WHILE THE CONVERSATION HAD GONE BETTER THAN I'D hoped, I still had questions—earth shattering questions. Despite what Wayne said, labels did matter. A shrewd businessman and a member of the millennial version of the mafia were two entirely different things.

Are you a mobster? Simple as that. Why can't I spit out the words? Because if he tells me what I already know, I'll have to do something about it. This'll end, and I don't want it to. Not yet. Maybe not ever.

"Maggie, stop thinking and start kissing." Gabe nipped my earlobe.

Before I had a chance to do as he asked, he moved down and drew my nipple into his mouth. I must have gasped, because he met my eyes and ran his tongue over the hardened flesh.

"Still thinking?" He flashed me a grin hot enough to melt my lingering doubts.

"I can't remember. Did I give you that file of receipts?"

"Maggie..." Leaving a moist trail of kisses in his wake, Gabe worked his way down my body. "How about now?"

"Uh huh. Thinking about the grocery list."

He settled between my thighs and buried his face between my legs. No teasing, no warning, no nothing except his tongue and lips and teeth.

"Oh God." I dug my heels into the mattress and raised my hips.

He slid his hands under my butt and lifted my lower body from the bed. I had no choice but to give in. The position made it impossible for me to move.

Gabe added fingers into the mix, and it took all my strength not to cry out. The man played my body like he played the guitar—practice and skill and passion. I closed my eyes and counted backward from ten. Somewhere between eight and seven, the orgasm crashed over me, but he wasn't finished.

"Stop. Stop. Stop. I can't." I twisted and turned until he let me go.

Gabe slid out of his flannel pants and climbed up my body until his face hovered above mine. "Still want me to stop?"

"No." I slid my hand down his chest and wrapped my hand around his length. "I want this."

He growled and lowered his mouth to mine, but otherwise, remained still. While I felt as if I'd spontaneously combust, he seemed content to kiss me silly. The more I tried to speed things along, the more he teased.

I curled my free hand in his long hair and tugged until he broke the kiss. "I need you inside me now."

Gabe fished around in the nightstand and came up with

an empty box. "Shit. Hang on. I have one in my wallet."

Talk about a buzz kill. I pulled the sheet to my chin and tried really hard not to think. Unfortunately, it didn't work.

He returned and waved the foil packet like a victory flag. "Add condoms to your grocery list."

"You'd better check the expiration date on that thing." I was only half teasing. He and Leo had both said he hadn't dated anyone since Chantal.

He flipped the light on, studied the wrapper, and grinned. "It's still good."

"But you're not." I licked my lips and motioned to his less-than-ready appendage. "Come here, let me help you."

As if by magic, the mere suggestion of a blow job hardened his cock before he'd slid between the sheets.

"You were saying?" Suited up and ready to go, he crawled on top of me.

The world seemed to hinge on my next breath, his next move. We stayed still for a heartbeat. In torturous slow motion, he pushed his hips forward and sank deep inside me.

I clutched his shoulders and bit my lip to keep the moan building in my throat from escaping. I felt him everywhere —his soapy scent, his still damp hair, his hard chest, and soft hands. It was overwhelming. *He* was overwhelming.

I couldn't focus on my pleasure and look at him at the same time. I closed my eyes and turned my head.

"Look at me," he whispered.

My breath caught when I met his gaze. Gabe Marchionni, one of the strongest men I knew, had tears in his eyes.

This time he looked away.

Rather than telling him I understood, that I was in this with him, that he was my first and my last love, I wrapped my hand around the back of his head and pulled his face to mine.

"I love you." Gabe nuzzled against my cheek, thrust a few more times, and released a shuddered breath. "I'll never let anything happen to you."

"I love you, too." My voice cracked. We'd said the words before, but this time I felt them in my soul. *Heaven help me, I can't imagine my life without him.*

Our bodies still connected, he rolled us to the side and cocooned me in his arms. For the first time in a long while, I felt cherished.

Ryan opened the bedroom door. "Aunt Maggie. I need you."

My heart jumped into my throat. I scrambled to make sure all of the important parts were covered. "What's the matter?"

Gabe mumbled something about locking the door.

"I had a bad dream. Read me a story." He rubbed his eyes.

"I'd love to. Go pick out a book and get in bed. I'll be right there."

The boy nodded and shuffled back into the hall.

I waited to make sure he'd gone and slid into my robe. "Stay here. I'll be back in ten minutes."

"Make it five." Gabe rolled over and hugged my pillow. If I had to place bets, I'd wager he'd be fast asleep before I made it to Ryan's room.

The boy sat in his bed with his favorite book in his lap. I eased in beside him and read about a little bird that lost his way home. When I'd finished, I leaned over to kiss the top of his head and smelled chocolate.

I sniffed again. "Why do you smell like cake?"

"Because I ate the icing." He squirmed away, but I pulled him close.

"How much did you eat?"

"Cocoa and I ate it all," Ryan whispered. "Then she threw up all over."

I bit my lip to keep from laughing. "Oh my. Then what happened?"

"Zach hurt his ankle, but he still made me take a bath." Ryan folded his arms and stuck out his lower lip.

I poked his side until he giggled. "I don't think you got it all off. Did you use body wash?"

"There isn't any, and Zach wouldn't let me use the shell soaps."

The pieces of the puzzle clicked into place. "Which tub did you use?"

"The one with the fancy towels." He yawned.

I stood and pulled his Spiderman comforter to his shoulders. "Goodnight, sweetheart."

"G'night."

The closer I came to the bathroom, the greater my sense of doom. I opened the door and the aroma of chocolate almost knocked me over. It looked like Willy Wonka had set up shop. Brown goo covered the floor and walls and tub. No amount of bleach would save the pretty white guest towels.

I smiled and closed the door. Mr. Wonderful didn't have things as under control as he wanted me to believe. He didn't do a better job at parenting than I did. He *faked* it better.

29

Gabe

THREE WEEKS HAD PASSED SINCE THE LAST TIME I'D heard from Chantal. Her radio silence should have been a good thing, but I didn't trust it. She still hadn't signed the damned papers. While I didn't want to believe Chantal had tricked me into knocking her up to extort money, it made sense. One thing I knew for sure, women like Chantal didn't give up easily.

In four days, the clock would run out on whatever game she was playing—four freaking days until the judge ruled on my petition for full custody of Ella.

"Maggie, we're late for work." I'd paced a rut in the kitchen floor waiting for her.

"Sorry, I was working on my novel and lost track of time." She handed Ella to Hildie, who I'd begged to come help with the kids.

Hildie smiled, but I didn't. Maggie looked like hell. Her skin seemed paler or maybe it was the dark circled under her eyes. She'd lost the little bounce in her step—even her hair seemed to slouch. With Mardi Gras season in full swing, we'd worked long hours and the days between now and Fat Tuesday would be even crazier.

"Why don't you take the night off?" I pressed my hand to her forehead, but she batted it away.

"I'm fine. Let's go."

"You might want to change your shirt." I motioned to the spit-up on her shoulder

Maggie groaned. "Dang it."

Hildie said, "I always think it smells like week old alfredo sauce."

Maggie choked out a laugh and went back down the hall to change.

I texted Jessie to let her know we were running late.

"Okay, I'm ready." Maggie returned to the kitchen wearing a long-sleeved T-shirt with the bar logo.

We kissed the kids and headed for the car.

"Are you sure you aren't coming down with something?"

"Gabe, seriously, I'm fine." She checked her reflection and sighed. "You're giving me a complex."

"I worry. Sue me." I turned off the highway and navigated through the Quarter. "I spoke to Santiago today. The judge still hasn't made a final ruling on your case."

Her eyes went all sort of watery.

"Babe, don't cry. It'll work out in our favor."

"I hope so."

"We're going to be busy tonight. I'll be behind the bar with you and Jessie."

"Okay." She gazed at my mouth and licked her lips.

"Don't look at me like that or we'll never make it inside." I pulled into a spot in the alley behind the building.

"Maybe that's my evil plan." She hopped out of the car before I could reply.

"We aren't that late." I moved behind her and slid my hand under the front of her shirt as she punched the code into the keypad.

"Five minutes won't hurt anything..."

I pushed her through the door with every intention of bending her over my desk. Unfortunately, it wasn't technically my desk anymore.

Leo popped his head out of the office. "Gabe, got a sec?"

"Piss off, will you." I loved my brother, but I fucking hated the situation. This was my bar. I'd worked my ass off to turn it around. I didn't want to run my father's business. I wanted Maggie and the kids and a life that didn't involve guns, money laundering, or murder.

My brother and Maggie stared.

I pressed my back against the wall and hung my head. This wasn't Leo's fault. My brother didn't want to manage the bar any more than I wanted to take over for my father. It was up to me to atone for decades of sins. "Sorry, man. I didn't mean to snap at you."

"Don't worry about it." He ducked back into the office.

Maggie kissed my cheek and handed me her purse. "We aren't blind. We can see losing the bar is tearing you apart. Talk to your father."

"What's done is done." I watched her walk down the hall before heading into the office to lock up her bag and talk to Leo.

She hadn't asked anything else about the family business, and I hadn't volunteered any information. Not yet. I'd planned to, but things were going too good to screw them up. Besides, I'd rather wait until I knew for sure I could break my brothers and me free of the Cosa Nostra once and for all.

Leo glanced up when I came into the office. "Nice handbag. Is that a Kate Spade?"

"It's Maggie's, and I'm not in the mood to listen to you bust my balls about carrying her purse."

He raised his hands in surrender. "Who am I to judge? I spent hours this morning searching websites for poodle puppies."

Of all the words I'd heard come out of my brother's mouth, those were the most bizarre. "Tell me you're kidding."

"What can I say. The little fluff balls grew on me."

I pinched the bridge of my nose to stave off an oncoming headache. "The accountant is all settled into his new digs?"

Leo nodded. "I get why you did it, but the risk..."

"All's well that ends well."

Maggie's phone rang for the fourth or fifth time since we'd left the house. My curiosity got the better of me, and I pulled the cell from the outside pocket.

Leo's eyes rounded. "I'd reconsider whatever it is your considering, bro."

I smirked and answered. "Marchionni."

The caller disconnected.

My pulse sped as I scrolled through her call history. "She's got fifty-six voice mails from a blocked number."

Leo motioned to the drawer. "Put the phone down and step away from the desk. You're entering dangerous territory."

"She said she's been getting threatening prank calls." I pressed play on a random message. Halfway through the obscenities, I hit delete and played another. This one made my blood boil. "Some asshat's leaving death threats."

Leo snatched the phone from me and pressed it to his ear. He listened, scowled, and listened again. "Jesus."

"I'll have someone in the office trace the calls and find the psycho." And then I'd see how the caller enjoyed real threats. The silver lining, if I could call it that, the female caller didn't sound like Chantal.

"Speaking of psychos, any word from your baby momma?"

I dragged my hand over my face. "Nothing."

He nodded and drummed his fingers. "Listen. What Maggie said in the hall was right. I've been talking to Enzo. You have a family now. It makes more sense for him to work with Pops. He's hungry for it and has less to lose if things go south."

"Thanks, bro. I appreciate it, but I'm up to my balls in it now. Besides, Enzo's more likely to keep us *in* than get us *out*." I loved him for making the suggestion, but I couldn't shirk my responsibilities. With Joe gone, I was the oldest. This was my cross to bear—a cross I intended to throw into the wood chipper at the first opportunity.

He pressed his lips together and nodded. "I've been going over the books. Tell me again why you don't take credit cards."

I gave him what I hoped was a patient stare.

He shrugged. "I'm just saying. It's all about customer service."

I lowered my voice. "Our largest customers are in Sicily."

He furrowed his brow, but the freaking lightbulb came on over his head. "Right. It's harder to launder money with a paper trail."

Once again, my blood pressure shot through the roof. "How do you not know that? You run a Marchionni Corp-owned business. Am I the only one up to my ass in illegal shit?"

Leo grimaced. "It's impossible to run a restaurant on a cash basis, but it takes a lot of food and *other* products to run a restaurant. We get more than our fair share of deliveries, if you know what I mean."

"I gotcha." My stomach turned. I understood all too well. New Orleans was a port city and easily accessible to Central and South America. Leo and Enzo were importing a lot more than fruit and vegetables. "I better get out there. The girls are probably swamped."

"Sure thing." Leo turned his attention back to the computer.

Less than an hour later people packed into every nook and cranny of the place. Maggie, Jessie, and I struggled to keep up, but I loved every second of it. Almost every second of it. I could do without Detective Wayne O'Malley growing roots on the stool in front of Maggie's workstation.

Wayne motioned to her, then tapped his watch, signaling he wanted to close his tab.

"Leaving already?" Maggie cleared his empty glass.

"Yeah, I have an early day tomorrow." He set a twenty on the bar.

"I'll get your change."

"Keep it." Wayne turned and disappeared into the crowd.

"I don't like the way he looks at you." I punched an order into the computer.

"Who?" She cocked a brow.

"That detective."

Maggie grinned and shook her head. "He isn't looking at me."

Then who the hell is he looking at? Before I could sort it out, a busty redhead waved cash in my face. "What can I get you?"

She said something, but I didn't catch it.

"Come again?"

The woman planted her elbows on the bar and leaned close enough I could count the freckles on her breasts—not that I was looking. "Jack and coke."

Maggie rolled her eyes and moved to the next customer.

I nodded and took the redhead's money, but she grabbed my hand and damned near pulled me across the bar top.

"What time do you get off?"

Drunk women hitting on bartenders was an occupational hazard. I'd learned early on it was best not to shoot them down outright. Instead, I laughed and shook my head. "Not until dawn."

"I could get you off right now." She slurred her words.

"Your fiancé is about ready to kick your ass," Jessie whispered in my ear.

I glanced past her to Maggie and wished I hadn't. The look she gave me could have frozen all nine layers of Hell.

The redhead wrote something on a napkin, kissed it, and pressed it into my hand. "Call me."

Maggie tossed a rag on the counter. "I need to go on break."

"Shit." I tossed the napkin in the trash and turned to follow her.

"Let her go." Jessie laughed.

"You're enjoying this?"

"Oh yeah, it's about time you met your match."

Ten minutes later, Maggie returned dressed like my cousin. Actually, I'd bet my right nut she'd rummaged through the spare clothes Jessie kept in back. Not that any of that mattered—not when she looked smokin' in a room full of drunk guys.

The short denim skirt barely covered her ass, and she tied the *Got Beads?* tank top in a knot to show off her midriff. Not only was she showing serious skin, she'd applied makeup. The look would have seemed slutty, but the little temptress had woven her hair into twin French braids. Fuck me, she looked like a cross between a rocker-Barbie and a schoolgirl.

Thank Christ she didn't change out of her combat boots.

On second thought, the shit-kickers look hot. Too dammed hot.

She smirked, returned to her station, and got to work.

"Maggie."

She ignored me. Smiling, she tucked a twenty into her bra and poured a drink.

I pulled her to the side. "What are you doing?"

"Working on the kids' college funds."

She's paying me back for the redhead. "I don't like it."

She twirled a braid around her finger. "You don't like it?"

I freaking died. How in the hell did she expect me to work with a raging hard-on? "No. You look...distracting."

"Then don't look at me." She turned and took another order.

Oh, hell no. I wasn't about to let her get the last laugh. She might have changed her clothes, but this was Maggie. *My Maggie.* She was more comfortable in a pew than on a pole.

I scooted past her and grabbed her ass. I don't mean a pinch. I mean I slid my hands under the denim and took two handfuls.

She yelped and turned to me as if dumbstruck.

"Get back to work." I motioned to the waiting customers.

Closing time had come and gone. Stressed, and exhausted, I wanted to go home. Unfortunately, everyone else wanted to hang around the empty bar and gab about my life.

I sat between Leo and Maggie and watched with rapt fascination as she attempted to open a locked set of handcuffs with a bobby pin.

He whispered, "She's doing field research for her book."

Maggie shoved the pin into the lock, twisted it, and frowned. "The entire situation with the bar is ridiculous."

"Right?" Dahlia huffed. As Leo's *friend*, I figured she'd heard her fair share of my brother's bitching. "I don't understand why Papa Joe insists that Leo run this place. He has his hands full with the restaurant."

Dahlia was a looker—jet black hair, pale skin, and a body like a supermodel. What the hell was Leo waiting for? They seemed into each other from day one, and that was almost ten years ago.

"Do you guys always do what Papa Joe tells you to do?" Maggie glanced between me and Leo.

I pinched her leg under the table. This conversation didn't need to happen in front of witnesses. Besides, I was more interested in going home and trying out the handcuffs.

"Almost always." Jessie unclipped her hair and gave her head a quick shake. Growing up, she'd spent so much time at my folks that I thought of her more like a kid sister than a cousin.

Maggie perked up. "Jessie, you ran the place before. Have you thought about taking over for Gabe?"

"Women in this family only work until they have babies, if they work at all."

"That's ridiculous." She glanced at me as if for confirmation.

"Pops is old school. So is Jessie's father."

"So... Maggie. If the whole writing thing doesn't work out, you could become a dominatrix or maybe join the police academy?" Jessie winked, easing the tension at the table.

"Like hell." I jabbed my index finger into Jessie's ribs.

Maggie rolled her eyes. "He's right. I would stink at both. This is research. My main character is shackled and has to escape. It's much harder than I'd hoped."

"Let's practice at home...in bed."

The woman stunned the hell out of me by looking from my face to my cock and back again.

I took her hand and pulled her to her feet. "Time to go."

Dahlia sipped her wine. "Maggie, you have to get dressed for the gala with us. The guys can't see us before the big reveal. It's a tradition."

Son of a bitch. I'd forgotten to tell her about the party.

"Mardi Gras Gala? Aren't we working?" She glanced at me.

I'd screwed up. Big time.

"No way. We're all expected to be at the gala. Gabe closes early that night." Jessie gave me a dirty look. "You didn't tell her?"

The gala was one of the largest social events of the year, hosted by none other than my father. "We've been busy."

Dahlia gave me an equally dirty look and turned to Maggie. "Have you ordered your gown?"

"I'm not much of a gala person." She tossed the unlocked cuffs on the table.

"Nonsense. I even scored a ticket for Shanna. You have to come. It won't be the same without you." Dahlia glanced between me and Maggie.

"I might be able to squeeze into one of Rebecca's old dresses." She chewed her lower lip.

"Oh no you won't. I'm going to take you shopping. Face it, Maggie. People know you two are engaged, they will expect to see you on his arm looking good." Dahlia turned to Leo. "I'd murder you in your sleep if you forgot to tell me about something like this."

Maggie sighed. "It's no big deal. I doubt we can get a sitter on Fat Tuesday anyway."

I squeezed her hand, thankful she didn't seem too upset. She'd said *we*. "Ready to get home?"

She nodded, but I had the feeling I had some serious explaining to do.

The ride home sucked. I didn't know what to say, so I drove while she stared out the window.

Apologize before this gets out of hand. "I'm sorry. I should have asked you. I assumed you'd say no. I know how you feel about my folks."

"I...don't know what this is between us."

The muscle in my jaw tensed. I thought we'd gotten past the point of running for safety every time one of us stepped on the other's feelings. "What do you want it to be?"

"Part of me wants it all. The church, the white picket fence, the happily ever after."

"And part of you doesn't?" My chest tightened. Having this conversation behind the wheel was asking for trouble. I slowed and pulled into an empty parking lot.

She shifted to face me. "I'm scared history will repeat itself."

"So am I, but I'm willing to give it a shot." I slid my fingers between hers and kissed the back of her hand.

"Me too." She waved her hand. "I'm tired, and moody, and ready for a shower."

A bolt of electricity zipped through me. Hope. This woman had just handed me a gift-wrapped package of hope that we'd make it. "Will you go to the gala with me?"

"No, but I'll meet you there."

"What? Why?"

"You heard Dahlia. You have to pick me out of the crowd or something."

"Honey, I'd recognize you anywhere, but I'll play along." I leaned across the console.

She met me in the middle.

I chuckled. I couldn't help it. She looked so damned cute with eyes half closed and lips parted and those freaking braids. "Did you want something?"

"I want you."

I cupped her face. "If all you're going to do is use me for sex, we may as well be married."

Maggie licked her lips. "Married people don't have sex,"

I cocked one brow and did my best imitation of The Rock. "We will."

"Everyone thinks that—then they get married and the well dries up."

"I, for one, plan to test this theory, every night for the rest of my life." I couldn't stand to be wrong, nor could I stand another second ticking by before I kissed her smart mouth.

30

Maggie

Though Fat Tuesday was days away, my early afternoon shift had dragged on and on and on. I sat behind the bar and reread the final draft of the Bourbon Street Bad Boys articles. While I didn't have a firm deadline, Marlena had hoped to have it last week. However, I hadn't had a clue what I would write until the conversation with Dahlia and Leo two nights ago.

I shifted my weight in an effort to relieve the ache in my lower back. Tired from too little sleep and too much Gabe, I'd stopped for coffee on my way in, but it had made me queasy—weird considering I practically lived on the stuff.

I hit send on the email and closed my laptop. I'd gone way off the script from the proposal, but I was proud of my work. I only hoped Gabe liked it, too.

The same blonde I'd caught in the breakroom weeks ago slid onto a stool. "Maggie, right?"

"That's me." I smiled, though it always freaked me out a little when the patrons knew my name.

"I thought it was you. You don't remember me. How

could you? I mean it's been a year. I'm Lindsey. A friend of Rebecca's. We met at the funeral."

Why is she just now introducing herself? "You've been in here quite a bit..."

"Yes, but I wasn't sure you were the same person. I saw the announcement in the paper. Congratulations."

"Thanks." My voice came out breathy. I'd decided to pick my battles with Evelyn. While I didn't appreciate her putting my personal business in the newspaper, she was Gabe's mom.

"I read in the paper that you're engaged to Joe's brother." She tilted her head to the side as if studying my reaction.

Nope, not discussing my life with someone I hardly know. "Corona with lime?"

"Not this early. Diet Coke, please." Lindsey put her elbows on the bar. "How are the kids? I bet they're getting big."

I filled a glass with ice and soda and set it in front of her. "They're doing great."

"If you don't mind me asking, are you okay? I saw him put his hands on you the other night."

Gabe and I'd worked every night for two weeks straight. I had no idea what she referred to. "When?"

"A couple nights ago. You'd changed clothes. He seemed angry..."

"Oh, no. We were goofing around." I forced a smile unable to imagine my sister befriending someone so awkward.

"I only ask because I do advocacy for abused women." She sipped her drink.

I laughed before I could stop myself. "I'm fine, really."

"When's the wedding?"

"We haven't set a date." Hoping she'd stop the interrogation if I looked busy, I went into the back and returned with a bag of limes.

The blonde motioned to my hand. "You don't have a ring?"

"Not yet." I slammed the knife through the fruit. "How did you know my sister?"

"Oh, we met at Chloe's preschool. Rebecca and I visited while the girls had playdates."

That makes sense. You can't choose mom friends like you do friend-friends. "Does your daughter go to Chloe's school?"

"Oh, no. We can't afford Sacred Heart." She seemed offended by the thought.

"I can't either. Her grandparents insisted."

"Do you have a picture of Chloe? I'd like to share it with Ainsley."

"I left my phone in the back. Why don't you text a picture of your daughter, and I'll respond with one of Chloe? I'm sure she'd get a kick out of seeing her photo."

Lindsey hesitated. "You're a mother now. You should have your phone on you at all times. Let's go get it."

Before I could sort out the weird request, Dahlia and Shanna arrived. Both women dressed to the nines, I took one look at them and groaned. "I totally forgot we were supposed to go shopping today."

"You're going." Dahlia made sitting at a barstool look graceful.

I'm not ashamed to admit I envied her long legs.

Shanna wore a smirk, and a little black dress. "Did you bring a change of clothes?"

I shook my head. "I forgot all about it this morning. Can we do this another day?"

"You'll be lucky to find an off-the-rack gown as it is. The gala's this weekend. I ordered my dress six months ago. Face it, honey, it's today or never." Dahlia glanced at Shanna as if expecting her to agree.

"She's right. This late everything will be picked over." Lindsey smiled, seemingly unaware she'd butted into their conversation.

Shanna glanced from Lindsey to me with a what-the-hell expression.

Dahlia didn't seem bothered—that or she had better manners. "Hi. I don't think we've met. I'm Dahlia."

"Lindsey. Nice to meet you."

"I name-dropped us into an appointment at Harold Clarke," Shanna said, ignoring the other conversation.

"Whose name did you drop?" I put the cut lime wedges in a container and stuffed it into the mini fridge.

"Yours of course, and I happened to mention your fiancé."

Perfect. As a general rule, I hated shopping. Nothing fits the way it should when you're short and busty. "Give me a few minutes to clean up."

In the time it took me to freshen up, Lindsey had wrangled an invitation to go shopping with us. I found it weird. Judging by Shanna's expression and constant eye rolling, she agreed. Dahlia, on the other hand, seemed too excited to care.

We arrived at the dress shop five minutes past our

appointment time, but I didn't think our tardiness had caused the salesperson's sour expression.

The woman glanced from my beat-up boots to my messy bun and frowned. It reminded me of the scene from *Pretty Woman*, except I'd brought friends and...well...I wasn't a prostitute.

Shanna did the talking while I browsed the dresses on display. A pit formed in my stomach, a pit that threatened to swallow me from the inside out. Generally speaking, if the menu didn't have prices, I couldn't afford the food. I assumed dress shops operated under the same principle.

"Ladies?" An older woman motioned for us to follow her into a sitting area near the dressing rooms. She turned to Dahlia and smiled. "You must be Mary Margaret."

Oh, God, can this get any more embarrassing? I raised my hand. "I'm Maggie."

The woman's smile faltered. "What size are you, dear?"

Yes, it could get more embarrassing. "A twelve."

The woman tittered. "Why don't we take some measurements? You don't look like a size twelve, though it's hard to say in those baggy clothes."

I followed her behind one of the drapes like an obedient puppy. "I just got off work."

"Please, call me Clair, and don't worry about it. We'll get you taken care of. I understand you need a couple of cocktail dresses, as well as the formal?"

"No, just the formal."

"Oh? I spoke to Mr. Marchionni this afternoon. He said to assure you that he would take care of everything." Clair smiled, and I swear I saw dollar signs in her eyes. "His instructions were clear."

My heart fell to my knees. Which Mr. Marchionni had agreed to pay for my dresses? It had to be Papa Joe, because I couldn't imagine Gabe caring what I wore. "Okay."

"I'll be right back." Clair left me sitting in the dressing room wearing a lavender silk robe and chewing on my bottom lip.

Shanna and Dahlia talked in hushed tones outside.

I poked my head out of the drapes. "What are you guys talking about?"

"You, of course." Dahlia laughed.

Lindsey glanced at the other two and nodded with a bright smile, too bright.

I did my best not to think about her. I hated to be mean, but the woman gave me the creeps. "Shanna, did you know they called Papa Joe and asked about payment?"

Shanna hitched a shoulder. "They called Gabe."

My mouth fell open.

"He wants you to pick out a dress for tonight, too," Dahlia said.

"What's tonight?" I knew I hadn't forgotten plans with Gabe. We didn't date, we played house.

Before they could answer, Clair returned with an armful of dresses.

I must have turned eight shades of red when Clair stayed in the dressing room. While I appreciated the assistance with zippers and such, I wished I hadn't left home wearing a ratty old bra and Hello Kitty panties.

First, I tried on a sleek, black sheath dress with a deep V-neck. It. Was. Awful. Half my bra hung out and my boobs looked deflated.

"Let me get you something that will help." Clair stepped out of the room.

I stared in the mirror, imagining what my mother would say about this dress. Nadine would *not* approve.

Clair returned with a strapless bra and proceeded to help me into it. It fit perfectly, no binding in the back and no boob spillage over the cups. When I pulled the dress up again, it looked like a different garment altogether.

"Wow." I leaned closer to the mirror, then turned sideways. My tummy had flattened, waist narrowed, and my breasts...holy moly. The stress diet was working.

"Would you like to show your friends?"

Heck yes! "Sure." I followed the woman out into the sitting area.

Dahlia clapped and Shanna gasped. "Oh, Maggie, that's gorgeous."

"It's simple, but stunning." Dahlia motioned for me to turn.

Watching my reflection in the mirror, I spun in a slow circle. "I'll take this one."

Another woman rolled a rack of five or six gowns outside her dressing room. I took one look at them and the room tilted. Cocktail dresses were one thing—formal wear made me want to run for the door.

"You look frightened. We'll do this one at a time, dear." Clair patted my shoulder.

I tried all six gowns on but none of them fit—too short, too long, too boobish, too matronly. It was a disaster.

Clair hung the last reject on its hanger. "Excuse me a moment. I have some things in back that you may like."

While the saleswoman hurried to a different part of the

store, I popped my head out to talk to my friends. "Where's Lindsey?"

"She had to go," Shanna said. "Seriously, Maggie. Hasn't anyone ever told you not to pick up strays?"

"She's harmless," Dahlia said.

"She's weird," Shanna replied.

No sense in arguing with the truth. "I agree she's odd."

Clair returned, and I went back into the dressing room.

"I think I have the perfect dress for you, but I have some questions first." Her smile lit her eyes.

"All right." I stared at the garment bag, praying this one would do the trick.

"We don't want to put you in something that's the same shape as your wedding gown. Have you chosen one yet?"

I reached for the wall for support. The mere mention of wedding dresses made my already queasy stomach lurch.

"Would you humor me and agree to wear a mermaid fit for your wedding? With your hourglass figure, it would be breathtaking."

"Can I wear a strapless with my bust size?"

"Not all mermaids are strapless. I envision you in a halter neckline, mermaid bottom, very old Hollywood."

"That sounds perfect." Years before, I'd spent days poring over bridal magazines with my sister. I knew the lingo well enough to picture the dress.

"Good. Next question." Clair hesitated as if nervous to ask. "Would you consider lightening your hair to a paler shade of blonde?"

I glanced at the mirror at my dark blonde hair. I'd never colored it. "Do you think it would look better?"

"It would brighten your complexion and bring out your eyes."

"Sure. Why not."

"I'll call my guy. He's the best. Do you have time to do it this afternoon? You'll want it done as soon as possible. I wouldn't suggest waiting until the day before the gala."

"Let me ask." I pulled the curtain aside. "Do I have time to get my hair done today?"

"Yes, for all three of us. Shanna has to get the red out of her hair or she'll look like a Christmas tree in her green dress," Dahlia said.

I turned back to Clair. "Would you ask if the salon has time for three appointments?"

"Let me make a call." Clair seemed too excited. She walked to the other salesperson and whispered something to her. When she returned, she rubbed her hands together and grinned.

The next time I came out of the dressing room, I practically floated on a cloud of filmy fabric. "This is the one."

The dress draped in a Grecian style that left my shoulders bare and gathered at my wrists in woven silver bangles. The matching belt made my waist look tiny, yet didn't feel confining. Best of all, the color gradually faded from silvery white to the same robin's egg blue as my eyes.

Clair handed me a delicate metal mask in the same silver as the belt and bracelets. One large white plume sprang from the side of the mask, sparkling with tiny crystals.

"Oh, Maggie..." Shanna brought her hands to her mouth.

"No, no, you can't wear that, or you'll upstage me." Dahlia grinned.

I stared at myself in the mirror, speechless.

Clair knelt to check the hem. "Once she lightens her hair, with her pale skin and blue eyes, she will look like a Nordic Queen."

Shanna and Dahlia stood and admired the gown up close.

I couldn't tear my gaze from the mirror. "Do you think Gabe will like it?"

"Yes, it's perfect." Shanna embraced me.

"Careful, if I didn't know better, I'd think you'd softened toward Gabe."

She wrinkled her nose. "I have to like the big jerk. He makes you happy."

"I have one more for her to try on." Clair helped me down from the platform.

"This is the one. I don't think you can top it." I followed her into the dressing room.

She pulled a silk scarf from her pocket. "I don't want you to see yourself until I'm finished."

Part of me wanted to get the heck out of there, but she'd piqued my curiosity. I sat while she tied the scarf over my eyes.

Nearly blind, I had no choice but to allow Clair to put me into the next dress. The woman fastened something on my head, and I knew—she'd put me in a wedding gown.

I trembled as Clair led me to the platform. Behind me, my friends gasped and whispered.

Clair untied the scarf.

I almost fainted. I wore the dress Clair had described as

old Hollywood glam. The sapphires and diamonds around my neck probably cost more than a house. The silky fabric shimmered in the light, hugging every curve. I turned to see the back of the gown and fell in love. It dipped low with pearl buttons running from my lower back to the end of the fluted skirt. No lace, no fussy embroidery, just ruching across the bodice hips and thighs.

"What do you think?" Clair tilted her head.

"I... I..." I burst into tears.

Clair's mouth moved wordlessly before she managed to speak. "It's all right, dear. A lot of women cry the first time."

31

Gabe

AT SEVEN O'CLOCK SHARP, A LIMO STOPPED IN FRONT OF the salon. I'd waited my entire life for tonight, and I wanted it to be perfect. I'd shaved and dusted off my favorite Armani suit for the occasion. Hell, I'd enlisted the help of a saleswoman to convince Maggie to buy a cocktail dress.

I opened the glass door. No matter how beautiful the salon, they all smelled the same, like chemicals and incense. Both made my nose twitch.

Shanna and Dahlia smiled, and the guy standing beside them looked like he'd eat me alive given half the chance, but I didn't see Maggie.

I took several steps forward before my brain clicked in and zeroed in on the platinum blonde bombshell in the tight black dress. Until that moment, I would have thought it impossible for her to look more beautiful, but she blew me away.

Maggie took a step forward and smiled.

My pulse beat a cadence loud enough to drown out the

chatter around me. I dipped my chin to hide my grin and held my hand out toward her.

Her smile went straight to my heart. She took several quick steps, glanced over her shoulder at her friends, and slowed her pace.

The little devil. I bet they'd coached her on how to walk in stilettos.

I motioned for her to turn.

Maggie stopped and spun in a slow circle. "Do you like my hair? The sales lady at the dress shop suggested I lighten it for the gala. Is it too much for a mother of four?"

"You look amazing, and who says mothers of four can't be sexy?" I needed to get her to dinner fast or I'd throw the plan out the window and take her straight to the hotel. I set my hand on the small of her back and guided her to the limo.

"Where are we going?" She slid across the leather seat.

"I'd like to take you home and peel that dress off." I traced a line from her knee to her inner thigh.

Maggie grabbed my hand. "Later. I'm starved. Wherever we're going, I hope food is involved."

I knocked once on the glass separating us from the driver, and the limo pulled from the curb. I couldn't stop touching her. "I love the dress. Did you find something for the gala?"

"Yes, but..." Maggie lowered her eyes. "I spent a lot of money today."

"I don't mind." I hooked my finger under her chin and brushed my lips across hers. "It's worth every penny to see you happy."

"I let the salespeople talk me into a few things I don't really need."

"Maggie, stop worrying. I wouldn't have given them permission to charge me if I didn't want to spoil you. Where are your bags?"

"Shanna's taking them to her place. We're getting dressed for the gala there."

"You should get dressed at home, with me."

"I want to surprise you." The limo came to a stop, and she peeked out the dark glass at a wrought iron gate. "Where are we?"

"You're not the only one who's full of surprises." My voice cracked like that of a fourteen-year-old kid. I had to get a hold of my nerves before I ended up making a fool of myself.

I stepped out of the car before the driver came around. Music floated over the brick walls, and the aroma of our dinner made my stomach growl—loud.

Maggie took my hand. "Seems I'm not the only one who skipped lunch."

"I've been busy today." *Lame, Gabe. Real Lame.* "You took my breath away in the salon. I barely recognized you."

Her cheeks turned a pretty shade of pink. "Thanks."

"Full disclosure, I asked Clair to talk you into going to the salon."

"Why?" Maggie's mouth fell open.

"Because I wanted you to feel beautiful." I ran my thumb over her lower lip. "There's nothing wrong with taking a little time to yourself."

She blushed again and glanced out the window. "Where are we?"

"Enzo uses this for special events." I led her through the gate and into a private courtyard.

A fountain bubbled in the center of the space and various types of flowers and trees lined the perimeter. A single table with a white cloth sat under a canopy of twinkling lights. Enzo's people had outdone themselves.

I pulled out her chair. Once she sat, I nodded to the musicians. The soulful blues music quieted to a conversational volume. *Perfect. So far, so damned good.*

"You did all of this for me?" She glanced from the pale pink roses on the table to the candles burning throughout the garden.

"Yes." I hoped what I lacked in words, I'd made up for in effort. I needed her to know she was the most precious thing on this earth to me.

"Thank you. I'm overwhelmed."

"We don't get out much. I wanted to make tonight special." I pulled a piece of paper from my jacket and handed it to her.

"What's this?"

The ink had barely had time to dry on the court order. "It's temporary for six months, then Ella's legally mine."

Maggie squealed, jumped from her chair, and hugged me. "That's awesome."

One down, two to go... I kissed her lips but pulled away before things crossed from PG to rated R. "Dinner first. We have plenty of time for that later."

"What time did you tell your mother we'd pick up the kids?" Maggie eased into her chair.

"Ten in the morning. We have a room at the Monteleone."

The look in her eyes made my cock sit up and take notice. I'd never make it through dinner at this rate.

A waiter came forward and filled our wine glasses, while another poured water. When they finished, another came forward and presented the first course. "Dungeness Crab Gratinée."

God, bless Enzo. I nodded my approval. *Food now, sex later.* "Did you enjoy your day?"

"Not as much as you did." Grinning, she sipped her wine.

"Everything all right at the bar?" *What am I doing?* I had important things to discuss with her, and here I was making small talk.

"Busy for an afternoon."

"It's that time of year. Thanks again for covering the shift."

"I met a strange woman. She said she knew Rebecca from Chloe's preschool. She's been in a few times. She ended up coming shopping with us tonight."

"Did you recognize her?" I sat back in my chair.

"No. She seemed, awkward. Not the kind of woman Rebecca would have befriended."

"Be careful. Your name's been in the paper and you can learn a lot about a person online. I hate to say it, but the bar brings out the crazies. It's not a good idea to let bar patrons into your personal life. Including shopping trips."

Maggie nodded and looked away.

"The harassing calls you've been getting... I had someone in IT security put a tracker on your phone."

Her mouth fell open. "What? How?"

"I borrowed it one morning while you were writing. I

don't pretend to know how it all works, but the guy was able to trace the calls. Do you know anyone who works at the Hilton on St. Charles Avenue?"

"No."

Pleasantly surprised she hadn't taken my head off for stealing her phone, I eased forward and drew her hand. "We've contacted the general manager for a list of employees. We'll find out who's doing this and put an end to it."

"Thank you. Between the calls, the woman at the bar, and dress shopping, I'm a wreck." She pulled away and pushed her food around on her plate. "What else did you do today? Besides get one step closer to keeping Ella forever?"

"I visited my father and went over some contracts. Though my mind wasn't in it." I took a bite, but while delicious, the buttery crab hit my stomach hard. I needed to steer the conversation to happier topics quick or I'd blow the entire night.

"What were you thinking about? Ella?"

"You. Tonight. Us."

The waiters returned with fresh glasses and a new bottle of wine. I lifted my glass, swirled it, smelled it, and took a sip, before nodding to the sommelier. He filled Maggie's glass, and another staff person served the main course of broccoli agnolotti and striped bass with braised Cipollini onions.

Maggie sipped her wine and smiled. "Are you feeling better about the job?"

"Yes and no. It's not as much fun as the bar, but the hours are good, and it forces me to use my brain."

"So, you're not just a pretty face?" She laughed and took a bite of her fish.

"I've been told I'm pretty good in the sack, too." I met her gaze and neither of us looked away. The staring contest ended with Maggie lowering her eyes and me chuckling. I loved this woman.

Maggie cleared her throat. "Why not let Jessie take over? She's more than capable."

"If it were up to me, I'd make her managing partner and keep a piece for myself. Unfortunately, that isn't how my father does business."

"Your father's retiring."

"And when he does, things will change. Until then, I'll deal." I pulled a second envelope from my pocket. "For you."

She unfolded the handwritten letter and pressed her hand to her chest. "Is this legal?"

"Santiago filed it along with a motion to dismiss my parents' case against you."

She blinked back tears. "Your mother wrote this...about me? Did you ask her to?"

Evelyn Marchionni hated two things, protestants and admitting she was wrong, but she'd done just that. "It was her idea. She's impressed with the way you accepted Ella as if she were your own. Not to mention, she's thrilled you civilized me."

Maggie started to speak, but my phone interrupted her. "You should answer."

I turned the sound off and slid it back into my pocket. "Not tonight."

I managed to get a couple of bites of my fish down before my cell vibrated again.

She raised a brow.

"Ignore it. Please, enjoy your dinner."

The third time it rang, Maggie sighed. "At least check voicemail. Something could be wrong with the kids."

"You're right." I scrolled through my call log, and the phone buzzed in my hand. This time my father was on the line. "Hey, Pops. Everything okay?"

"No, everything is not okay. I received a call from Scott at the *Picayune*. There's an article about the family coming out in the paper tomorrow."

I stood and walked away from the table. "You mean about the business?"

"I mean exactly what I said. *Someone* wrote an expose on the *family*."

Son of a bitch. Why tonight? I drew a breath but couldn't stop shaking. My father had ordered the execution of an employee over breakroom gossip. What would he do to a journalist who'd dared to investigate the family? "How bad is it?"

"I haven't read it, but he said it's personal. He agreed to squash it and find out who the hell's been poking around, but it's going to cost us."

"I'm in the middle of something. Can this wait until morning?"

He went into a coughing fit that had the hairs on the back of my neck standing on end. When he came back on the line, he could barely speak. "Could the Guthrie girl have done this?"

"No. It wasn't her."

"Be here at ten in the morning." He disconnected.

I glanced back to Maggie. *She couldn't have? Could she?*

"Everything okay?" She started to rise.

I motioned for her to sit and returned to my chair. "Problem with work. Nothing that can't wait until tomorrow."

"Are you sure?"

"Positive." I signaled for the staff to clear our plates. *I needed to get this done before anything else blew up tonight.*

One refilled their wine, while the other whisked the dishes away. Once they left the courtyard, I reached for her hand.

Maggie furrowed her brow. "You're trembling."

"I'm okay."

"You're not yourself tonight. What's wrong?"

I kissed her knuckles. "There are some things I need to say to you."

32

Maggie

I'D FINISHED THE ARTICLE, PULLED A SHIFT AT THE BAR, went dress shopping, had a makeover, and received some amazing news, but I was exhausted. More so, I was worried about Gabe.

He stared at me with the oddest expression. If I didn't know him so well, I'd have thought he had a case of the nerves. His stiff posture differed from his typical laid-back style. Maybe it was the clothes. After all, I sat straighter in the dress than I would in jeans.

No. It's not the suit. Something's wrong.

He kissed the back of my hand. "There are some things I need to say to you."

I nodded, confused and somewhat frightened. I'd never seen this side of him. Sure, he'd been melancholy and intro-spective when he'd first showed up on my doorstep, but I blamed that on becoming an instant father. He'd gone back to his normal self within a couple of weeks.

"You probably already figured out that my family is old fashioned. My brothers and I may be wild, but we honor our parents. We tease each other mercilessly, but we don't betray or disrespect our own."

My throat tightened. *He found out about the article.* No matter how I'd spun it, the Marchionnis would see airing family secrets as the ultimate betrayal. "Gabe, I'm—"

"Let me finish, please."

I nodded again, but I couldn't look him in the eye.

"My parents have been married for fifty-four years. We don't do divorce. We have big families, we work hard, play hard, and love with everything we have. When I found out about Ella, I thought of you. Not because I wanted a place to dump my problems. Because I wanted to share my daughter with you. It killed me to stay away from you after Joe and Rebecca died. Knowing you were close, and I couldn't see you was torture."

I couldn't take it anymore. I had to tell him the truth. "Gabe, there's something you need to know."

He released my hand.

"I wrote an article about your family."

He recoiled as if I'd struck him.

My brain worked faster than my mouth. I had to explain, to tell him what I'd written, to make him understand why I'd done it. "It isn't what you think. It's a personal piece."

"I know." He spoke in a shaky whisper.

"How do you know?" I leaned back in my chair to put some distance between us.

"That's what the phone calls were about. My father's contact at the *Picayune* gave him a heads-up." He ran his hand over the back of his neck and shook his head. "What have you done?"

"My job. I did my job. What do you mean, a heads-up? What guy?"

He set his elbows on the table and steepled his fingers. "Think about it. How many news articles have you seen published about my family or our business?"

"None." My mouth went dry. *None, because Papa Joe paid people to kill the stories before they went public.* The part of me that believed in freedom of speech and freedom of the press balked, but damn it, this was Gabe and my principles would wait. "What I wrote, it wasn't about Marchionni Corporation or the mob or any..."

His brows rose.

I'd said too much, or maybe I'd said enough at the wrong time. Either way, I needed a rewind button. "I mean... Has he read the article? I think you're both overreacting. It's about a first generation of Italian immigrants walking the line between—"

"It's going to kill him when he finds out it was you." He rolled his lips in and closed his eyes. "Fuck, Maggie."

"You're not listening to me. It's not that bad. It's more of a human-interest piece than an exposé, and I wrote under a pen name." A little voice inside me screamed to ask him about the mafia outright. I knew the answer but knowing and understanding the implications were two different things.

"I need a drink." He signaled to the servers.

One came forward with a bottle of wine. Another waiter brought two plates, which I assumed were dessert.

"Just the wine for now. Scotch if you can get it," Gabe said to the waiter.

The man hesitated and turned, but not before I spotted the chocolate truffles.

I not only wanted them, I needed them with every fiber of my being. Chocolate would give me courage... "Actually, I would like dessert now."

The waiter looked between us.

"Later." Gabe motioned for the man to go.

"Don't be ridiculous. Leave them on the table. No sense in making him walk back and forth."

The waiter gave in and set a plate in front of me.

I popped one into my mouth.

Gabe groaned, sank back into his chair, and covered his face with his arm.

I froze mid-chew.

"This isn't how tonight was supposed to go."

"While we're on the subject of your father, I need to ask you—" I glanced at the dessert plate and blinked. Nestled between the truffles was the biggest diamond I'd ever seen. My world tilted. "Gabe?"

"Yeah. I know."

The courtyard, the new dress, the music, the private dinner. *His speech!* I'd ruined his proposal. "Oh my God."

Gabe dropped his hand from his eyes and smiled.

"This is for real? You're asking me for real?" Feeling lightheaded, I pushed my chair back and bent forward. It may not have been ladylike to put my head between my knees, but I did it anyway.

Gabe knelt in front of me. "Mary Margaret Guthrie, I've been in love with you from the moment I first saw you. I love your smile, your laugh, your goofy glasses and ratty pajamas."

Please stop talking. "I don't..." I shook my head.

"I haven't asked yet." He curled his finger under my chin and lifted until I met his gaze. "Will you marry me?"

I wanted to say yes more than anything, but it wasn't just me. I had children to consider. I had to know the truth. "Are the Marchionnis a mafia family?"

His expression darkened. "Does it matter?"

"It doesn't change the fact that I love you, but I can't accept your proposal until I know what you're asking me to marry into."

He turned his head, nodded, and looked back to me. "We are part of the Cosa Nostra, but I'm working on changing that, and your article has complicated things tremendously."

A million questions danced through my head. *Was he a criminal? What kind? Could he quit? Would it put him, or our family, in danger?* "Could we go home and talk about this?"

"Sweetheart, there are things I can never share with you, but I will tell you as much as I can."

Would that be enough for me? "Did Rebecca know?"

"Yes."

I ran through everything I knew about my sister, her marriage, her husband, their life and came up with even more questions. "I need time to sort this out."

"I understand." He kissed my cheek, stood, and walked toward the gate.

"Wait." I shot to my feet but had to grab the table to stay upright. "Where are you going?"

"I need to take a walk. The driver will take you home

when you're ready." Shoulders slumped and head down, he looked defeated.

I wanted to go to him, to apologize, to tell him I'd marry him tonight, but I couldn't do any of those things. "Wait. Please, come home with me."

He stopped walking but kept his back to me. "Mags, I'm not giving up on us, but right now... I need to handle the situation with the article before my father finds out you wrote it."

"If you both would read it—"

"He won't care what it says. The fact you wrote it is a betrayal."

To him or to you? "You forgot the ring." My voice trembled.

"Keep it until you decide." Gabe slipped through the gate, leaving me alone with the wait staff and the weight of the world.

I knew what I had to do.

I slipped the ring on my finger, wrapped the remainder of the truffles in a napkin, and headed for the limo. After giving the driver the address to the Marchionni mansion in the Garden District, I sent Evelyn an email with my article attached.

Gabe's mother had been a pain in my butt since my sister died, but no one could accuse her of not wanting the best for her sons.

The car came to a stop in front of the imposing Greek revival house, and my nerves kicked into high gear. *What if she hadn't received the email? Should I have sent a text? Called?*

Deciding to wait until morning, I knocked on the glass

to get the driver's attention. Unfortunately, the front door opened before he lowered the glass.

Evelyn Marchionni stood on the front steps with several sheets of paper clenched in her hand. Even from the distance, I could tell the woman glared.

I opened the door but hesitated.

"Stay in the car."

For a split second, I thought she'd refused to see me, but rather than going back inside, she joined me in the limo.

"This will never see the light of day." She shook the copy of my article at me. "Do you understand?"

"I do." Journalistic integrity, paychecks, and my pride be damned. I would have done anything to take it back if that meant I didn't have to see the hurt and disappointment in Gabe's eyes.

Her expression softened a smidge. "Is it true? They don't want the life we've made for them?"

"I can't presume to speak for the others, but Gabe is struggling." I lowered my voice in hopes of keeping the tension in the car to a minimum. We were two women having a conversation about a man we loved.

Evelyn glanced out the window and drew a deep breath. "My parents held the deed to our house until they died. Joe's father left the business to him in his will. This is how things have always been done."

"Your sons know this and respect you and Mr. Marchionni too much to put up a fuss about it, but—"

"They don't like it."

"No, they don't." I took a moment to gather my thoughts. "The guys were raised in the States. They have the best of both worlds. Sicilian values and American work ethics. Gabe busted his butt to make his bar successful. Handing it over to Leo..."

"He will make the Marchionni Corporation just as successful." She raised her chin.

"You're right. He will." I chose my next words carefully. "He will do what's asked of him. He'll live where you tell him to live. Work where you tell him to work, and marry who you tell him to marry, but at what cost?"

She stared as if daring me to say more.

Rather than go at her with both barrels, I went for a softer approach. "What was Mr. Marchionni like when he was young?"

Evelyn cracked a half-smile. "A lot like Gabe. Handsome, driven, and tender-hearted."

Her candor surprised me to the point I pushed the *subject-that-shall-not-be-mentioned*. "I don't want the *family business* to harden Gabe the way it did Papa Joe."

Her eyes widened before she could smooth her expression. "Boys grow up and become men. It is a fact of life."

"Gabe *is* a man. A successful man in his own right, as are Enzo, Leo, and the rest." I drew a deep breath. "As I wrote in the article, Gabe has one foot in the old world and one in the modern world. It's tearing him apart."

She sighed. "I see."

"Your sons should be allowed to run their own lives. Own their homes. Choose their careers, even if that means they don't want to be a part of the family business."

She straightened her spine and folded the papers in half —a sure sign the conversation had come to an end. "You are a naïve girl who doesn't understand the world."

"Maybe, but I know you don't want to bury another son. Can you honestly tell me Gabe will be safe?"

She dipped her chin and made the sign of the cross. "It won't come to that."

"Even if it doesn't, do you want to visit your sons in prison? It's not like it used to be. Everything we do leaves a digital footprint. Law enforcement already suspects they're involved in organized crime. How long until one of them is caught?"

Tears filled her eyes.

I reached for her hand. "He'll honor his father's wishes to take over the company, but he *will* run it the way he sees fit, including breaking ties with organized crime."

Evelyn's shoulders slumped, and for the first time since I'd met her, she looked her age. "I pray we will all live to see the day."

"I have faith in your son."

33

Maggie

DALIA AND I SAT AT SHANNA'S KITCHEN TABLE, WHICH had been turned into a makeshift salon. Piles of makeup, hair accessories and styling tools lay in disarray on every level surface in the small space.

"Let me get this straight. He hired a wait staff, took you to a private courtyard, wined and dined you, then you went home alone?" Dahlia shook her head.

"Pretty much." I sighed, trying to be still while Stephen pinned a curl in place.

"Forget that. I'm pissed Papa Joe killed your article. What ever happened to free speech?" Shanna's mouth moved, but the rest of her remained still as her stylist glued a thick row of false lashes in place.

I had mixed feelings about the violation of my constitutional rights. In truth, I'd written the article for an audience of two, Evelyn and Joe Marchionni. "I don't care about the article. I need to set things right with Gabe."

Dahlia sighed. "I still don't understand what happened. What did you argue about?"

I couldn't exactly tell them the details of the conversation, and I had to give them something or Shanna would keep digging. I went with the next obvious explanation. "I told him I had Chantal investigated."

"This Chantal woman had a husband who killed himself because the Marchionni Corporation took his business out from under him?" Stephen made a clucking sound with his tongue, as he wound a chunk of my hair around the curling iron.

"Pretty much, though we don't know for sure why he killed himself." I turned my head a fraction, and Stephen yanked my hair. "Ouch."

"Beauty is pain. Be still." He jabbed a bobby pin into my scalp.

"So what? He slept with a married woman?" Stephen took a step back admiring his work.

"Not unless the relationship lasted longer than he says." Shanna sprayed enough hair spray to mortar a brick wall.

"I don't care if he slept with a married woman. I mean, he isn't the one who broke a vow, right?" I glanced between them.

"Right." Stephen grinned and moved in front of me to put the finishing touches on my makeup. "Spoken like a woman in love defending her man."

"Wrong," Shanna added.

"You're actually going to marry him?" Shanna asked, incredulously.

"Of course she is," Dalia said, opening her eyes wide to free her natural lashes from the glue.

"If he'll have me." I glanced at the diamond on my finger.

"Honey, stop worrying about it. You're going to kiss and have hot, make up sex." Stephen grinned.

"Easier said than done." I surveyed my reflection, hardly recognizing myself. The new shade of blonde and a heavy amount of makeup made my eyes look bluer. Stephen had darkened my eyebrows and used a pale pink shimmer on my lips. I held the silver mask in place, surprised that it didn't get in the way of my mile-long lashes.

Looking rather proud of himself, he folded his arms. "Time to get dressed, princess. We can't have you late to the ball."

THE LIMO INCHED UP THE STREET LEADING TO THE Marchionni's mansion. Unlike the last time I'd visited, this time I had an invitation.

I'd spoken to Evelyn several times since our chat in the limo. While she still insisted the old-world ways were best, she conceded on several points, including allowing her sons to handle their finances.

I wasn't naïve enough to believe she could talk Papa Joe into renouncing his ties to the mafia, but I trusted her to do what was right for family—and that gave me hope.

I peeked out the window at the costumed people milling about the portico. It reminded me of a scene straight out of Venice, minus the canals, of course.

My throat tightened, and my vision blurred at the thought of Gabe. I hadn't seen him or Ella in several days, not since the night I'd ruined his proposal. I missed him more with each passing second.

Shanna gave my hand a squeeze. "If I can do this, so can you. You know how much I hate these society things."

Dahlia rolled her eyes. "You always say that, but I didn't hear you complaining when I got your ticket, or when we were getting dressed.

"Fine. I like the events, but I could do without the people...except you two. Maggie is as poor as I am, and you can't help it your father is an oilman turned governor." Shanna turned from Dahlia to me. "You got this."

I nodded.

"Cheer up, Mags. A lot of women cry their first time," Dahlia whispered, and the two traitors burst out laughing.

"I'm never going to live that down, am I?"

"Not a chance." Dahlia snickered.

"Let's put our masks on and pretend we're movie stars." Shanna winked and tied her mask behind her head.

Dahlia stared out the window, likely searching for Leo. "Ready, ladies?"

"As I'm ever going to be." I twisted the engagement ring.

Dahlia climbed from the limo as if she rode in limos every day. Her easy grace made me feel even more awkward.

For the umpteenth time that day, I wished Gabe was by my side. He had a way of calming my nerves and making me feel beautiful.

Shanna stepped from the limo and joined Dahlia beside the car.

I drew a quick breath and set one foot on the driveway. Taking my time, I arranged the layers of silk chiffon before I stood. "Here goes nothing."

The breeze picked up sending my hair and soft blue and white fabric swirling around me. From the corner of my eye, I noticed Gabe. He stared but I couldn't decipher his expression.

I took a step forward and stumbled on the uneven cobble stone.

Shanna caught my elbow before I embarrassed myself. "Did you see him?"

"Yes, but he disappeared again."

"He might have been called away. Leo swears he isn't angry with you." Dahlia moved to my other side.

We walked into the large courtyard behind the portico. A band played in the distance, and waiters with trays of champagne and hors d'oeuvres milled among the new arrivals.

"There's Leo. I'll get the scoop." Dahlia lifted her skirts and hurried off.

"One down, one to go," Shanna said under her breath.

I motioned to the couple, who were whispering like schoolgirls. "I don't know why they don't admit they're in love and put each other out of their misery."

"Pot, kettle." Shanna smirked.

"That's what I'm here to do." I hooked my arm in Shanna's and walked through the crowd toward the sound of music.

The first Marchionni to approach was Enzo. Dressed in a dark tux, white shirt and deep green tie, he looked like he belonged with Shanna. Even the blues and greens in his mask complemented her peacock feathers. He nodded in my direction, but his eyes remained focused on my bestie.

He leaned close and whispered, "Would you care to dance?"

"Oh, I see how it is. Not even a hello, Enzo?" I lifted my mask.

He did a double take. "Maggie? Wow. I didn't recognize you. You look fabulous."

I twirled, showing off the costume. "Thanks. So do you. Have you met Shanna?"

Enzo smiled behind his half mask. "I have now."

"Shanna, this is Enzo Marchionni. Be careful. He's almost as smooth as his brother."

"Please, dance with me, *bella*." He offered his hand.

And just like that, Shanna seemed to fall under his spell. "I'd love to."

I couldn't help but smile as they walked to the dance floor. In all the years we'd been friends, I'd never seen Shanna blush—until now.

Once the crowd swallowed the couple, I turned and almost toppled over a waiter carrying a single glass of champagne. "Excuse me."

"This is for you from the gentleman." He nodded toward the drink.

"Thank you. Which gentleman?"

The waiter gazed over the crowd. "My apologies, miss, but I don't see him."

"Thank you." I took the glass and walked away.

Sipping champagne, I glanced over the crowd and met Gabe's father's gaze. *Crap. The last person I want to speak to.*

I made my way toward the dessert table to avoid the

elder Marchionni. A couple of chocolate treats would ease my nerves.

"Maggie?" Papa Joe kissed my hand. "You're a vision tonight."

All of the Marchionni men were handsome, including Papa Joe. He had the same green eyes as the boys, but his hair had turned silver.

"Thank you, Mr. Marchionni." I took a large gulp of champagne and made a show of looking around. I had no idea if Evelyn had told him I'd written the article, or about our conversation.

"Please, call me Joe. It's almost time for Chloe to perform. You're seated with the family."

"Of course." I knew that she and Gabe had been planning a private recital, but I had no idea what they had in store. I couldn't imagine putting Chloe on stage in front of so many people. My stomach knotted with worry at the thought.

Papa Joe led me to a table front and center of the stage. A half a second later, Gabe and Zach walked toward the stairs, carrying guitars.

Nadine and Evelyn joined us, both women staring at me openmouthed. I probably wore the same expression. As far as I knew, they couldn't stand each other, but to see them now, you'd think they were old friends.

My mother nodded to me. "Mary Margaret, you look..."

"Gorgeous. You look absolutely gorgeous." Evelyn patted my hand.

I might have been petty, but I reveled in my mother's stunned-stupid reaction. The makeover had done wonders for my confidence—not even Nadine could ruin it.

My mother leaned close and whispered, "I'm hurt I had to read about your engagement in the paper."

I cringed. She deserved to have heard it from me, but things had gone sideways after the announcement was published. Not to mention, I didn't want her negativity muddying the already dirty water. "I should have called, but I wasn't sure you'd approve."

She managed to frown without actually moving her lips. "Why would you think that?"

"Men like Gabe marry girls that look like Rebecca."

For the first time in as long as I could remember, my mother seemed flustered. She pressed her hand to her chest and bowed her head. "I only meant to spare you pain."

Before I could respond, the lights dimmed. Gabe half-sat on a stool, his acoustic guitar settled onto one thigh. Zach stood at the microphone, glancing around. The band behind them quieted and a single spotlight centered on the teen.

"For those of you who don't know me, my name's Zachary Marchionni. A year ago, my parents died in a car accident. My little sister and I would like to dedicate this performance to them."

Zach moved to the stool beside Gabe and the spotlight widened to include a larger portion of the stage. Gabe and Zach began to play the first few notes. The wall behind the stage lit with family photos of Rebecca, Joe, and the kids.

Each image struck me like a throat punch. I couldn't look. Instead, I focused on my guys.

The crowd gasped when Chloe took the stage. She wore a soft pink tutu, trimmed in deeper shades of pinks and purples. Two fluffy wings rested on her back.

Gabe strummed the rhythm and Zach played melody. It was gorgeous, but I almost fainted when Gabe leaned closer to the microphone and sang Clapton's, "Tears from Heaven."

Chloe completed several pique' turns, glided across the stage, and dipped into a plié without missing a step. Her performance was fluid and graceful, even when she spun in a series of slow pirouettes. I'd never been so proud of her, but I would have loved it if she'd stomped across the stage doing the chicken dance.

I didn't as much as blink, until all three took their bows and made their exits.

Evelyn and Nadine both blotted their eyes with tissues. Even Papa Joe looked misty-eyed. I swallowed the lump in my throat and fought to hold back tears of my own.

The guests cheered until the trio returned to the stage and took another bow. Then Chloe ran down the stairs and straight into my arms—which was when I lost my battle and choked out a sob.

"Did you see me? Did you like it?" Chloe grinned, her cheeks red from dancing.

"You did great. I loved it."

Zach dragged the toe of his shoe across the ground. His cheeks were red too, but not from physical activity.

I drew him into a quick hug. "You're getting really good. I'm so proud of you."

He grinned and shrugged. "Gabe's been helping me."

Zach surprised everyone when he offered his hand to his sister. "Would you care to dance?"

Chloe squealed and pulled him to the dance floor.

I watched them for a moment, but I needed to find Gabe and bury myself in his arms.

Papa Joe stood. "Would you dance with an old man?"

"I'd love to." I finished my champagne in one gulp and set the glass aside.

He set his hand on the small of my back and led me to the dance floor. The gesture reminded me of Gabe. *He had to see me at the table. He must be avoiding me.*

Papa Joe took my hand, placed his other on my hip, and led me in a slow waltz across the dance floor. His cancer hadn't stolen his charisma. He had an old-world grace that reminded me of classic movies and gentler times, although few would call Giuseppe Marchionni Sr. gentle. The contrast between the family man and the business tycoon confused me. *Is Gabe the same?*

"How are my grandchildren?" He smiled behind his simple mask.

"They're great. Growing up too fast and keeping me on my toes, but I wouldn't change a thing."

"I want you to know that I think you're doing a terrific job raising them. You're good for my son, too."

"Thank you."

A shadow passed over his expression. "I read the article you wrote."

Blood roared in my ears. "Mr. Marchionni...Joe... You have to know I—"

"It's given me a lot to consider." He spun me in a circle and drew me closer. "But I trust there will be no more stories about the family?"

A little lightheaded, I held tighter to keep myself upright. "No. As a matter of fact, I finished my novel. I'm expecting an advance from the publisher within a week or two."

"That's wonderful news. Another female spy thriller?"

How did he know what I wrote? "Yes, with the same heroine."

Papa Joe chuckled. "You seem surprised I read your books."

"I just never pictured you as my demographic."

"I'm more than the business, Maggie." He lowered his voice. "The greatest gift you can give Gabe is to always remind him he's a father, a husband, and a man—not simply a title and a job."

I nodded. Between the sentiment and the champagne, I didn't trust my voice.

Something behind me caught his attention, and he stopped dancing.

"May I cut in?" Gabe brushed his hand over my bare shoulder.

The sound of his voice caused flutters in my belly and my hands to tremble. I turned and smiled through the blur of unshed tears.

"Of course. Thank you for the dance, my dear." Joe leaned forward and kissed my cheek before turning me over to his son.

Without a word, Gabe slid his hand into mine and spun me in a slow circle. The sight of him threatened to buckle my knees. His red leather mask had thin black brows painted over its slanted eyes. Between the mask and his pointy goatee, he looked like one heck of a sexy devil.

"Stop staring at me like that." His lips curled into an evil grin that intensified the effect of the mask.

"Like what?"

"Like you're thinking about my tongue between your thighs."

Emboldened by his comment, I whispered, "How'd you know?"

"Because I know you." He chuckled and dipped me backward.

Once upright again, I pressed my cheek to his shoulder. "I wish we could rewind and start over."

"I don't. Every moment good and bad brought us to where we are right now." He drew me tighter and swayed to the music. "But I've missed you."

I pulled back to look into his eyes. "Gabe, I..."

He placed his finger on my lips and smiled, though it didn't reach his eyes. "I'm sorry I walked out on you after dinner. I needed to think. I've pushed too hard for this marriage. You're right. It's too fast. I'll back off."

My throat tightened. "Are you moving out?"

"Is that what you want?" He stopped dancing.

"No. That's the last thing I want."

He pulled me close and kissed the top of my head.

"Gabe, I don't want—" I missed a step and swayed against him. My vision blurred and this time it had nothing to do with my feelings for him. "Can we sit? I'm feeling ill."

Gabe tucked me against his side and led me from the dance floor.

The room began to spin, and I slumped against him. "Something's wrong."

He bent down and lifted me into his arms. "When did you eat last?"

Did I eat today? I couldn't remember, in fact I couldn't

hold onto a thought long enough for anything to make sense. My limbs grew heavier by the moment, as if my bones had disintegrated into Jell-O.

Gabe set me on one of Evelyn's oversized loveseats and untied my mask. "Stay here. I'll be right back."

I started to stand, but he put his hand on my shoulder.

"Maggie, I mean it. Don't move. I'll be right back."

34

Gabe

CATERERS AND WAIT STAFF CROWDED THE KITCHEN, making it difficult for anyone not on the payroll to enter the room. I surveyed the trays of food waiting to be served, looking for something with protein and not too rich. Dinner selections consisted of jambalaya, shrimp creole, greens swimming in bacon, Étouffée, and other traditional Cajun dishes. Nothing I could feed Maggie in her condition.

Jessie pushed her way toward me. "Is Maggie all right? I saw you carry her inside."

"She didn't eat much today and with the champagne, she's dizzy." I snatched a dinner roll from a tray and opened the drawer.

"Gabe," Jessie shouted.

"What?" I turned with the roll in one hand and the knife in the other.

"Did you do something stupid again? She seemed fine until she talked to you."

"How can I cause her to be dizzy?" I stuffed a piece of cheese into the roll and pushed my way out of the kitchen.

Jessie followed. "Stop for a second, will you?"

"I need to get this to Mags."

She grabbed my arm. "Have you seen Chantal DuBois lately?"

I jerked free. "No, why?"

"There's a woman who keeps showing up at the bar when Maggie's working."

"What woman? Jess, I don't have time for this right now."

"I think it's Chantal. Her hair's blonde and she's chubbier..."

"I haven't heard from her in weeks. She didn't even show up for our court date." I headed toward the parlor.

Maggie's mask sat on the loveseat where I'd left it, but she'd vanished. My first thought was the powder room. I knocked. When no one answered, I opened the door. Empty.

I pulled my cell from my pocket and dialed Maggie. No answer, but her ringtone played nearby. I hit redial and followed the ringing to her purse under the loveseat.

I tore the mask from my face and called Enzo. "Hey, have you seen Maggie?"

"Yeah, man she's looking smoking hot tonight. I'm *busy*. Can this wait?"

"Enzo, listen. She isn't feeling well. She's not where I left her, but her purse is here."

"Hang on." Mumbling came over the line as if he'd covered the phone with his hand. "I'm with Shanna. She said Maggie was fine earlier today. We'll help search for her."

I strode back toward the kitchen in hopes of finding

Jessie. I caught a glimpse of her bright red gown outside, but lost sight of her by the time I made it to the door. *Why do women keep disappearing on me tonight?*

My mother came out of nowhere and set her hand on my arm. "Is everything okay?"

"Have you seen Maggie?"

"Not since you carried her inside. What's going on?"

I ran my hands over my head. "She isn't feeling well. I need to find her, Ma. Something's wrong."

She pursed her lips. "Did you pick a fight?"

"No, I did not pick a fight."

"She probably rejoined the party. Relax, she'll turn up when your father announces the engagement."

"There's no engagement. I called it off. She needs more time before we force her down the aisle."

"Nonsense." Evelyn handed me an envelope. "She's a little naïve, but she loves you. If you don't believe me, read the article she wrote about you."

I shoved it in my jacket pocket and walked away before I said something I'd regret. I spotted my father in the center of a semicircle of young women. "Sorry to steal him away, but I need a quick word."

Papa Joe flashed the women an award-winning smile and turned to me. "What's wrong?"

"I can't find Maggie, and Ma told me you're planning to announce our engagement?"

Joe laughed and slapped me on the back. "She'll turn up when I call her name."

I lowered my voice. "There is no engagement. I need to find her."

"She was wearing your ring earlier. What did you do?"

She was? "Nothing. Why does everyone in this family think I did something to Maggie?" I sighed, scanning the crowd. "She's ill. End of story."

Joe opened his mouth, closed it, and shook his head. Before he could say anything else, I walked away.

Shanna stopped me on the way back to the house. "Have you found her?"

"No." I noted her swollen lips and wrinkled gown. *Fucking Enzo.* "Careful with my brother. He's... It's complicated with him."

Chloe ran to me and hugged my leg, her smile fading when she saw my expression. "What's wrong?"

I brushed my hand over her cheek. "Sweetheart, have you seen Aunt Maggie?"

"Ladies and Gentlemen, may I have your attention." Papa Joe's voice rang out over the crowd.

Me and everyone else turned our attention toward the stage.

"It seems my son has lost his fiancé. Mary Margaret Guthrie, would you please return to the parlor to claim him?" Joe chuckled and the crowd joined in.

Holding my breath, I scanned the crowd for any movement toward the main house.

After a few moments, my father made the same announcement, but Maggie still didn't materialize.

Shanna tugged on my jacket. "Did you two have another argument?"

"No. I left her for five minutes to get her something to eat. When I returned she was gone." I lifted Maggie's silver purse in front of Shanna's face. "She left this behind."

"Maybe she went home," Shanna mumbled.

I nodded, though I doubted Maggie would have left without her purse or without telling anyone. With each passing moment my gut clenched tighter. Coupled with the frustration burning a hole through my chest, I felt as if I'd would come out of my skin if I didn't find her.

I held my phone to my ear and forced myself to loosen my grip before I cracked the case. "Hildie, this is Gabe. Is Maggie there?"

"No, she isn't. Is everything all right."

Frowning at Shanna, I shook my head. "Call me the moment she comes home."

An hour later, we'd searched the entire house and called the police. The party guests began to leave when the squad cars arrived.

Detective Wayne O'Malley had been at the party when Maggie went missing. He pulled me into an empty guest room and closed the door behind him. "Did the two of you have an argument?"

"No." I folded my arms across my chest, rather defensive after answering the same question so many times in one night.

"Look, I'm trying to help."

"We were dancing, and she said she felt faint. I brought her inside and went to get her some food. When I came back, she was gone." I sank into a chair. From the moment she went missing, I'd been hit with questions like machine gun fire.

"And you found her purse near where you left her?"

"I called her cell and heard it ringing." I ran my hand through my hair again. At this rate, I'd be bald by morning.

"I sent an unmarked car to her house in case she turns up."

"I checked in with the sitter a while ago. She wasn't there. How could she disappear?" I stared at Wayne, trying to decide if I wanted to punch the man in the face or cry on his shoulder.

"What about security cameras?"

"My folks...don't usually bother with them during events like this. Too many people in and out..." I stumbled over my words. It's not like I could tell a detective my father turned them off to provide the less savory guests privacy.

"Is there anyone you can think of who would want to harm her?" Wayne maintained a professional tone, though his eyes gave away his concern.

"Jessie said something about my daughter's mother hanging around Maggie at the bar." I balled my hands into fists. *I promised her I'd protect her. If anyone hurt her, I'd make them pay.*

"What's her name and address? Do you have a current picture?" Wayne pulled out his phone.

"No photo. She's about five-eight, long dark hair, though the woman Jess saw is blonde. If it's even the same woman. Last I heard from Chantal she'd left town."

"Name?"

"Chantal DuBois. 921 Dauphine, Apartment A. She works for one of the cruise lines. I haven't seen her in almost three months, since she dropped my daughter off on my doorstep."

Wayne winced and typed into his phone. "Anything else?"

"She's been trying to extort money from me since she got the paternity results."

"Child support?"

"No, she doesn't want the baby. She wants money."

He glanced at me as if he had something to say but shook his head and rubbed his jaw.

"Chantal was married to one of my brother Joe's business associates. The deal went south, and the guy offed himself."

"Martin Sinclair?" Wayne's eyes widened a fraction.

"That's the one."

35

Maggie

"Maggie, are you okay?"

The jackhammer in my head caused the softly spoken words to sound as if broadcasted through a concert sized speaker. I tried to sit up, but the room began to spin.

"Oh, my goodness. Here, let me get you home. My car's right out front." Denise Trudeau forced me upright.

Who invited her of all people? I shook my head and the slight motion caused my stomach to lurch.

Someone lifted me to my feet and another person pressed against my side. *A man, Gabe? No too short and bald. Justin?*

Voices whispering, then talking, reassuring that they would take me home. They said I'd had too much to drink. Passed out. It felt as if half of the world moved as fast as a carnival ride, while the other oozed in slow motion.

I had the sensation of movement.

This isn't right. Foggy and confused, I tried to sort out what happened. "Put me down. Where's Gabe?"

Something smashed against the back of my head. It took

a moment for my brain to register pain before everything went black.

———

Gabe

"They left in a dark colored sedan, Toyota, I think." The young valet looked between Wayne, me, and the gathering of uniformed police officers.

"Is this the woman who was passed out?" Wayne held Shanna's cell phone to the guy's face, a picture of Maggie in her gown on the screen.

"Definitely. I remember the dress. I thought she looked like a Valkyrie or something."

"You let these people put an unconscious woman into a car?" My anger and fear narrowed to a single point, the valet.

"They said she had too much to drink," he murmured.

Wayne took a moment to scroll through the pictures on Shanna's phone and showed the valet a photo with Chantal in the background. "Is this the woman who took her?"

The kid shook his head, then hesitated and shrugged. "No. She had red hair."

"Could she have been wearing a wig?"

"Maybe, I don't know."

"Did you get a look at the man?" I stared at the image and my blood ran cold. It had been taken in the dress shop.

"Short and stocky. He wore a black mask. The cheap kind, like you get at the French Market."

"Don't you guys write down license plates?" It took

every ounce of my willpower not to slam the kid into the wall.

"Yes, and the color, make, and model, but we toss the ticket when they pick up the car."

Wayne motioned to one of the uniformed cops. "Go through these. Look for an older, dark colored sedan."

"I'm going to Chantal's." I turned to walk inside, but Wayne grabbed my arm.

"You need to stay put. We have people there now. If this is a ransom situation, they will likely call your cell. Let's go find out why Shanna has a picture of your baby mama on her phone."

Shanna sat on a sofa in the den. Her makeup smeared down her cheeks. Evelyn, Nadine, and Dahlia sat on the opposite couch. The women looked up when they entered the room. I met my mother's gaze and shook my head.

"Where's my daughter?" Nadine stood, placing herself in my personal space.

I set my hands on her shoulders. "The police are looking for her."

"What did you do to her? What did you do?" Nadine crumpled into a heap on the couch.

Wayne squatted in front of Shanna. "Why do you have a photo of Chantal DuBois on your phone?"

"What?" The color drained from her face. "*That's* Chantal?"

My frustration threatened to pour out of my mouth, but I forced myself to keep my voice at a reasonable volume. "Yes. Now answer the question."

"We didn't know who she was. She said her name was Lindsey. She's the one Jessie said has been hanging around the bar. I'd seen pictures of Chantal, but she looks so different now." She glanced between the detective and me.

I remembered Maggie mentioning a tag-a-long the night of the proposal. *I should have listened.* "Where did you see pictures of Chantal?"

"Maggie asked me to do some digging right after you moved in. She was worried about you and Ella."

Wayne nodded. "What did you find? Anything you can tell us might help find Maggie."

Cringing, I prayed she wouldn't say anything to add gasoline to the inferno brewing in the room.

"She works for the cruise line. Has an apartment on Dauphine. Widow of Martin Sinclair and filed bankruptcy after he died. Maggie worried that she would try to use Ella to extort money." Shanna wiped her eyes on a tired looking handkerchief.

"Does your father know?" My mother speared me with a glare. Evelyn was wicked smart. Too smart. Though Shanna hadn't come right out and said it, my mom had put the pieces together. She knew I'd knocked up the enemy.

"I don't know." I'd half expected Santiago to tell them. Cowardly, but I couldn't figure out how to tell them without starting the apocalypse.

Evelyn turned her head as if she couldn't stand the sight of me.

Nadine mumbled something under her breath.

Shanna took her hand. "They'll find her."

Wayne and I locked eyes. He made a slight motion with his head, and I followed him outside.

"This is looking more like a ransom situation than a jealous former lover," Wayne said.

"Whatever they want, I'll pay it." I sat on the edge of a concrete planter and hung my head.

"That generally isn't a wise strategy. If they get the money and run, there's no guarantee you'll get Maggie back, or that they won't try something like this in the future." Wayne's radio chirped and he walked a few feet away to answer.

I stood and went back inside. I needed to talk to my brothers.

36

Maggie

My head bounced against something hard several times and gasoline fumes assaulted my already turbulent stomach. I forced myself to focus on my surroundings—a moving car?

Oh my God. I'm in a trunk.

A scream bubbled from deep in my gut, but fear seized my lungs making it difficult to get a breath. The air felt thin, too thin to *breathe*.

I pushed the trunk door with bound hands, but it didn't budge.

Calm down and think.

I felt along the lock for the safety release. My fingers pressed against a wire, but the latch itself had been removed.

Pushing my fear down deep, I focused on the situation. I was in a locked trunk, hands bound in front of me. Legs free. *I can do this.*

I managed to pull a bobby pin from my hair. It fell beside my cheek. I removed another one, but it was hard to hold onto it with my hands cuffed, in a moving car, while shaking in fear.

Holding the third pin tight, I bit off the rubber tip and scraped the end of the pin across the body of the cuffs. Once the tip entered the lock, I bent it to a ninety-degree angle.

Halfway there. I wedged the curved end into the hole and twisted in the opposite direction, forming a dip before the first bend. I put the pin in my mouth and used my tongue to test the shape.

The car slowed and I gasped, nearly swallowing the damned pin. My heart raced as unwelcome thoughts filled my mind. If they stopped, if my kidnappers came for me now, I'd be defenseless. Closing my eyes tight in the dark space, I worked the bobby pin into the lock.

The car lurched forward, and I dropped the pin.

Minutes, seconds, or hours ticked by. Time became too dangerous a concept to consider. *Are these my last moments alive?*

The longer they drove, the better my chances of getting out of the cuffs, but the longer they drove the farther away from home I'd be. Time was not my friend.

The lock opened with an audible click.

One hand free, the cuffs dangled from my other wrist. No sense in wasting time picking the other side. Plus, if they stopped, I could slip my free hand into the loose cuff to make it look like I was still bound.

I felt along the trunk door near the lock, where the safety latch should have been. I found the release wire and wedged my bracelet between the wire and the metal. Turning my wrist side to side, I wrangled the wire loose.

The trunk door presented another problem. The kidnappers would see if it flew open.

I ran my fingers over the latch in search of a groove or hole to hold onto when I pulled the release cord. I found a hole large enough to push the end of the open handcuff into. Yanking to test the hold, I grabbed the wire with my free hand.

Keeping the tension on the handcuff and the trunk door, I yanked down on the cord and flexed my other arm at the same time. The latched released, but thankfully, the door only opened an inch.

It worked!

I pushed on the metal above my head. The trunk opened enough for me to taste freedom. Unfortunately, we were traveling at a good speed, too fast for me to jump.

Gabe

I rounded the corner into my parents' living room and stopped dead in my tracks. Chantal fucking DuBois stood next to the fireplace with Shanna.

"Where the hell is she?" I had the woman a foot off the ground and pinned to the wall before I'd realized I'd moved.

"Stop it. She doesn't know anything." Shanna tugged my arm, but no way in hell would I let Chantal go before I got some answers.

"Why are you here?" I shook her hard enough that her head thudded against the wall.

"To talk to you."

I knew better than to trust her tears. I'd seen them before. They meant shit. "Talk."

Shanna sighed. "Gabe, put her down."

I released her but refused to step back. *Fuck her personal space.*

Chantal straightened her shirt. "I swear, I don't know what happened to Maggie."

"This is the second time your name's come up when someone I love is in trouble."

She turned her head and nodded.

"If you didn't have anything to do with this, why have you been following Maggie?" I studied her reactions for any hint she was lying. A waste of time, but it gave me something to do that wouldn't land me in jail for assault and battery.

"I went a little nuts when I saw the engagement announcement—"

"No fucking kidding." I balled my hands. "You threatened her."

"I know and I'm sorry." She drew a deep breath. "I was okay leaving Gabriella with you. You're rich with a huge family. I knew she would be loved, but I didn't know anything about Maggie."

What the hell is she talking about? "Don't tell me you actually care about *Ella*."

Chantal hung her head. "I can see why you'd think that, but I carried her inside my body for nine months. I tried to love her when she was born, but all I could see was you in her."

I stepped back to keep my balance. I knew she'd played me the entire time we'd dated, but I had no idea how much she hated me. "Did you get pregnant on purpose?"

"Yes, because I saw a child as a way to get back what your family stole from me." Her bluntness surprised me.

"Tell him why you followed Maggie." Shanna stepped closer to me.

"I wanted to make sure the woman raising my daughter was a good person." Her voice cracked.

Something didn't add up. I ran through everything I knew about her situation and everything she'd said. "Why tell me this tonight?"

She drew a breath and delivered a bomb. "I came to confront your father. I found the original documents from the sale of mine and Martin's bar. I've contacted an attorney and plan to go public with the information. Your family will be ruined."

"And you're here to give me one last chance to pay you off?"

She gave me a sad smile. "That or to warn you to distance yourself from your father so Maggie and Ella don't get caught in the crosshairs."

I sank onto the loveseat. I had no idea what had happened between her late husband and my father, but I'd pay any amount to protect Ella, Maggie, and my mother from scandal. "I'll give you the money, but I expect you to sign a statement that the problems with the contract have been rectified."

"Agreed." She reached for me but seemed to think the better of it. "This can wait a week or two. Make sure Maggie's all right first."

"Thank you."

The front door opened, and my heart stopped.

Hildie rounded the corner with Ella in her carrier and Ryan by her side. "Any word?"

"No." I glanced at Chantal, half-expecting her to make a break for the baby, but the woman turned to face the wall.

"I thought it best if we were all under the same roof." Hildie took in the scene as if she knew exactly what she'd walked in on. "I'll take the little ones upstairs and put them to bed."

"Thank you." I stood but had no idea what to do next.

Shanna cleared her throat. "I'll walk Chantal out and catch Detective O'Malley up to speed."

"I'll be in the study."

The two hours Maggie had been missing felt like days. It was a strange feeling, needing to do everything in my power to find her, and being powerless to lift a finger.

I wandered through the house in search of my father. If I couldn't help Maggie, I could damned sure get some answers.

"Why haven't they found her yet?" Zach's voice echoed down the hall.

"They will." I set my hands on his shoulders.

He reared back and punched me in the chest a few times. "I told you if you hurt her— If anything happened to her— You're supposed to protect your women."

"I'm sorry." Feeling as helpless as the kid, I wrapped my arms around Zach's shoulders.

"She has to be okay."

My phone buzzed. A call from a blocked number. "Go get your uncles."

Zach nodded and took off down the hall.

"Marchionni."

"I have something of yours." The man sounded as if he worked to disguise his voice.

Heart pounding, I forced my voice to remain detached. "I'm listening."

"One hundred thousand in cash and another five million transferred into my account. You'll receive a text with the wiring instructions. I'll contact you with the location of the exchange once I have confirmation of the transaction."

"You hurt her and I will rain hell—"

The caller disconnected.

I turned as my brothers and father entered the study. "Five-million-dollar wire transfer and a hundred thousand in cash tonight."

"Take the money out of my trust fund. I know my mom and dad left money for us. Take it and get Maggie back," Zach said from behind the men.

I hadn't realized the kid had returned, but I couldn't do anything about that now.

We had a bigger problem. One look at my father's face and I knew he wouldn't give up the money without a fight.

"Zach, please. Go wait with your grandmother." My father's voice echoed through the room.

"No. Gabe said men take care of their women. I'm staying." Zach closed the door behind him and folded his arms.

"We have the cash. I say we pay it. Once Maggie's safe, we track them down and take them out." This from Enzo, who wouldn't know how to censor himself around kids if his life depended on it.

My father said, "No. We pay the hundred thousand

ransom and have the guys in IT send a fake wire transfer for the rest."

I pinched the bridge of my nose. "And if something goes wrong and they catch on?"

He narrowed his eyes. "I've been at this a long time. No one ever catches on until they show up at the bank. By then, we'll have the girl back."

"We're paying them." I squared my shoulders and stared the old man down. "So help me God, if you say one more word about it, I'll walk out of this house and this family."

Leo, Dante, and Marco stood and moved to my sides—a symbolic closing of ranks.

My father stammered. "You four think you can survive on your own? You have no idea what it means to work for a living."

With that a miracle happened, Enzo pushed to his feet and stood alongside us.

Leo said, "What's it going to be? Are you willing to lose the rest of your sons over chump change?"

"Pay the fucking money!" My father stood but swayed and sank back into his chair. The coughing started with a clearing of his throat and ended with him hooked up to his oxygen tank.

37

Maggie

THE CAR SLOWED, STOPPED, AND MOVED FORWARD again. A few minutes later, it slowed and stopped. I cracked the trunk open and headlights blinded me. We were stuck in traffic.

Now or never.

I slid the end of the cuff out of the hole and threw the trunk open. Waving my arms and screaming at the top of my lungs, I almost fell out. The sudden movement sent a wave of nausea through me, but I held down the bile by force of will and adrenaline.

The driver in the truck behind us opened his door and ran toward me. Pinned in by traffic, my kidnappers hit the gas and the brakes and the gas again—but they had nowhere to go.

I tumbled from the trunk with my legs tangled in the long layers of my dress. Skin peeled from my hands and knees stung, but I didn't care. I had to get away before Justin and Denise grabbed me again,

Shouting, car doors, and heavy footfalls came from all

around me.

I scrambled to gain purchase on the asphalt. The sounds of metal slamming into metal and shattering glass filled my ears. My head exploded in pain and my legs refused to hold my weight, but I crawled toward the truck. A man knelt and pulled me to his chest. A woman pressed close and murmured words like *safe* and *you're okay*.

"It's all right." The man released me and motioned toward the car. "We got them."

It took my brain a minute to make sense of the scene. Several people had pinned Justin and Denise Trudeau to the ground.

"It's over?"

"Yes, ma'am."

I choked back a sob and crumbled against the stranger.

Gabe

Wayne came through the front door without knocking. "They found her. She's alive—only minor injuries."

My father let his head fall to his chest. "Thank God."

For the first time in my life, I watched my father cry. He had always been the rock of the family, the man that had held us together after my brother died. Perhaps the guilt of his decisions wore on him more than we imagined.

Zach sat beside his grandfather and draped his arm across the older man's shoulders—a kindness none of the grown men in the room seemed inclined to do.

I swallowed my emotions. "Where is she?"

"Baton Rouge General. She escaped." Wayne smiled.

"Who took her? Who was it?"

The detective glanced down at his phone. "Justin and Denise Trudeau. We don't know why they targeted her."

"Maggie dated him a few times. She didn't know he was married." I looked away. "He threatened to sue me after an altercation. I should have paid the son of a bitch."

"You're not in the state of mind to hear reason, but this wasn't your fault."

"You're right. I don't want to hear it."

Jessie and Evelyn came through the door next. Evelyn went straight to Joe, and Jessie surprised everyone by throwing her arms around Wayne. Right there in front of God and everyone, she kissed him on the mouth.

"Huh." For months, I'd thought Wayne hung around the bar to flirt with Maggie. Seemed I was wrong about a lot of things.

"I'll drive. There's something I need to talk to you about." Wayne jangled his keys.

Against my better judgement, I agreed and climbed into the detective's car.

Keeping his eyes on the road, Wayne cleared his throat. "I got a tip on your brother's accident."

As if I don't have enough on my mind? "From who?"

"A guy looking down the barrel of a life sentence. He claims his cellmate told him about a paid hit. He seems credible. He knows details about the accident that we never released to the public."

I hadn't realized I was tensing up until my teeth hurt.

"We're in the process of questioning the suspect." He sighed and drummed his fingers on the steering wheel. "I'm sorry to lay all this on you now, but I thought you'd want to know."

A paid hit. A paid hit. The words ricocheted in my skull like a low caliber bullet. "Did he mention any names?"

"Pietro Lazio." Wayne studied my reaction, but I gave him nothing.

"Keep me posted." I motioned to the speedometer. "You think you could risk a few traffic violations? I have somewhere to be."

He nodded and turned his attention to the road.

Pietro fucking Lazio. The head of another Sicilian mob family, my father's closest associate, and if my mother had her way, Enzo's future father-in-law. Why in Christ's name would Pietro order a hit on Joe Jr.?

An hour later, I burst through the doors of Baton Rouge General and went straight to the information desk. "I'm looking for Mary Margaret Guthrie."

The old woman behind the computer nodded, seemingly unfazed by my urgency. Her fingers couldn't have moved slower over the keyboard if she'd dropped dead.

I ran my hand over the back of my neck and tried counting backward from fifty to calm my nerves. About the time I reached twenty-two, she smiled.

"Are you family?"

"I'm her fiancé."

"And who's this?" the woman asked in her pleasant volunteer voice.

"I'm Detective O'Malley from New Orleans PD."

"She's in room 230, second floor—"

Before she'd finished giving directions, I headed for the stairs. We'd received the call that Maggie had been found almost two hours ago. Waiting for information after she went missing felt like the longest few hours of my life. Allowing the detective to drive me to Baton Rouge was worse. Besides the news about my brother, Wayne was perhaps the only person in the state of Louisiana who drove the speed limit.

I stopped outside the door and drew a breath. I needed to put on my game face before I went inside. I didn't know anything about her condition, other than she'd been drugged and bound in the trunk of a car. It'd do Maggie no good if I wept like a baby at first glance.

The door opened and a nurse came out of the room. She stopped and smiled.

That's a good sign, right? "I'm looking for Maggie Guthrie."

"This is her room. Are you family?"

"I'm her fiancé."

"Go ahead. She's expecting you." The nurse smiled again.

"Is she going to be all right?"

"Yes, Miss Guthrie and the baby are both doing fine. The doctor wants to run more tests. He may keep her until the poison she ingested clears her system. She's been through a lot."

The hall became white hot, and I grasped the door jamb. Nothing the woman said after the word *baby* registered in my brain. I considered the probability of there being two Maggie Guthrie's in the hospital.

"Are you okay?" The nurse set her hand on my shoulder.

Wayne stepped beside me. "He's fine. It's been a long night."

"And you are?" The nurse looked at Wayne as if she could tell his profession by his demeanor alone.

"I'm a friend."

"As long as you're not here to question her, you can go in." She hurried down the hall.

"Go ahead, I'll give you two some privacy." Wayne grinned.

A baby? Maggie's pregnant? I slipped into the room and stopped a few feet from her. I noted the bandages on her hands and the side of her head. She looked small in the center of the bed, with tubes running from her to various bags and machines.

She opened her eyes. "Hey."

"How are you feeling?" I sat on the edge of the bed.

"Better." She shifted her weight as if trying to sit.

"Here, let me." I pushed the button with the up arrow and raised the head of the bed.

"Where are the kids? Are they all right?" She reached for a Styrofoam cup.

I helped her guide the straw to her lips. Her busted and swollen lips. "They're with my folks. They wanted to come with me, but my mother convinced them to wait until you returned to New Orleans.

Maggie nodded and looked toward the window.

Her eyes brimmed with tears and what was left of my heart crumpled. She seemed so broken. I wanted—no, I needed—to know what she'd been through. How she'd got away. How she felt about carrying my child, but all of that would have to wait.

"Maggie?" I brushed my hand across her cheek.

She turned her head toward my touch and closed her eyes. "Hmm?"

"I love you. When I thought we might lose you..."

She nodded, but the slight movement seemed to cause her pain. "I love you too."

"I read your article. My mother gave it to me."

"And?"

"It was humbling to read how you see me and my situation."

"Did I get it right?" Her lopsided grin made my chest hurt.

"You more than got it right." The reality that I'd almost lost her made my voice tremble.

We'd have plenty of time to get into the specifics once she'd recovered, but given we were going to have another child, I needed to give her some peace of mind.

"I'll answer all your questions when you're out of here, but you should know I've done everything in my power to keep my bar—and my nose—clean. My brothers and I never wanted in, but we didn't have a choice. Now that I'm in charge, I'm going to get us out. I just have to be smart about it. Do you trust me?"

"I do." She reached for my hand and hesitated. "What you said before, about backing off the engagement."

Afraid to hurt her, I eased an inch or two closer and whispered, "I'm not going anywhere. I'll wait as long as it takes for you to be sure, but I'm not leaving unless you throw me out. Fair warning, I'll buy the house next door if that's what it takes to be near you."

"I'm sure." She lifted her hand and flashed the diamond

ring I'd given her. "I put it on the night in the courtyard and haven't taken it off since."

I cleared the emotion from my throat. "Then we have a wedding to plan as soon as they spring you from this joint."

"Sounds wonderful. I already have a dress." Her eyes drifted closed and popped back open like Ella when she fought to stay awake.

"Babe, you're exhausted. Get some sleep." I kissed the part of her forehead not covered with gauze. "I'll be right here when you wake up."

"I want to go home and sleep in our bed."

"I know, but the doctors want to make sure you and the baby are okay." As soon as the words came out my mouth I cringed.

She widened her eyes.

"Before you say it, remember I wanted to marry you before I knew about the baby."

Maggie grinned, but winced and touched her split lip. "How did you find out?"

"The nurse told me." I wiggled my brows. "We're going to need a bigger house."

"And a nanny."

"Thank Christ. It's about time you came to your senses."

38

Gabe

For the first, and hopefully the last, time in my life, I sat at the head of the Marchionni Corp conference table. I had to admit, the power oozing from the chair gave me a rush, but it was a trap.

My brothers and father had arrived before me. Though I'd told no one why I'd called them here, a nervous energy hung over the room like cigar smoke.

"What's with all the formality?" Enzo nodded to the clock. "I have to be at the restaurant by eleven."

"And I have to pick up Maggie in Baton Rouge."

He had the decency to look away.

I'd hated to leave her at the hospital, but the outcome of this meeting would set the course for our future. Besides, I hadn't left her alone. She had Shanna and her mother to keep an eye on her until I could return.

I pulled a file from my bag and handed the papers to Leo. "This is a legal filing Chantal DuBois plans to take to court and release to the media in a few days. I've made copies for each of you."

My father's spine stiffened.

"Can we get the Cliffs Notes version?" Enzo took his copies and passed the rest on to Marco.

"In short, the Marchionni Corporation screwed her out of half a million dollars on the sale of a bar she owned with her husband, Martin Sinclair. As a result of the fuckery, Sinclair killed himself. She plans to sue us for the half-mil, along with pain and suffering and anything else she can squeeze out of us." I withheld the fact that I'd come to an agreement with Chantal. I needed my father to come clean about what had really happened.

Leo turned to our dad. "What do you know about this?"

"Joe made the original deal with Sinclair for his half of the bar, but the wife refused to give up her half." He kept his expression smooth, but I had him by the balls and he knew it.

Enzo motioned for him to continue. "Any reason why?"

"The wife suspected us of running off their customers and reporting them for selling to minors."

Leo pinched the bridge of his nose. "This is how you acquire businesses?"

My father raised his chin and glared. "You don't get to judge when the money I've made put clothes on your back and paid for your college."

"Joe was involved?" My youngest brother, Dante paled. He'd worshiped Joe like others did rock stars.

"Your brother was a saint." My father smiled, but Dante looked away. "By the time the wife agreed to sell, we were in a rush. The contract had a clerical error. She didn't bother to read it before she signed." My father shrugged.

This is why Chantal hates this family? I ground my teeth. "Clerical error?"

"It gave us full ownership for half the cost."

The room grew still.

"Is that why Joe tried to quit the business?" Dante leaned forward and looked my father in the eye.

"Yes, one of the reasons."

"Joe wanted out?" This was news to me. I'd always thought of him as a younger version of our dad. Although, it gave Pietro Lazio a hell of a reason to want my brother dead.

My father shrugged. "He would have changed his mind."

Dante shook his head. "Not true. Joe promised me he'd get all of us out of this life."

I needed time to think about the implications of Dante's revelation, so I steered the conversation back to the matter at hand. "Why didn't you correct the contract?"

"I didn't know the bitch would go off the deep end and cause this much trouble." He looked at each of us as if to judge our worth.

"I will not run the corporation if this is what you expect of me. Martin Sinclair is dead, and I've already been a participant in another—" I clamped my mouth shut. This wasn't the time for me to give confession. Though I technically didn't have Artie Guzman's blood on my hands, I couldn't tell them the truth. Not with my father in the room.

Dante's mouth hung open. "You killed someone?"

Leo, God bless him, broke the silence. "What do you propose we do about Chantal's case against us?"

I cleared my throat. "I've already taken care of it. The

company will pay her the money owed to her, with interest. In exchange, she's agreed to sign documents stating the terms of the original contract have been met."

My father's eyes rounded. "You played us?"

"I learned from the best."

Enzo glared and shoved back from the table. "Thanks for wasting everyone's time."

I ignored him. There was another matter we needed to discuss. "You should know the police have a tip in Joe and Rebecca's death. Some inmate knows details that weren't released to the media."

My throat tightened. Each of my brothers had a visible reaction to the news, but my father hadn't flinched. I'd made the right decision in holding back details like the name of the person who allegedly ordered the hit.

Dante's voice trembled. "He's saying Joe was murdered?"

Keeping my gaze on my dad, I nodded. "Claims a former cell mate said he was paid to take him out."

Leo sucked air between his teeth. Dante wiped his cheeks. Enzo and Marco hung their heads. My father? He stared at me as if daring me to keep talking.

I kept talking. "You knew about this?"

He smirked. "How would I know about this?"

"When did you figure it out? Before or after you accused an innocent woman?"

Leo whispered, "Let it go for now."

Out of respect for my brothers, I dropped it, but my father and I would have a long conversation about the Lazio family. "I plan to start the process of separating our legitimate business holdings from the Cosa Nostra and all their known associates."

Enzo plopped back into his chair. "Can we afford that?"

"We may need to tighten our belts. I'm going to dump anything that isn't earning a profit without the mafia's cash flow."

"Is it safe?" Dante whispered.

Rather than outright lie to them, I nodded to my father. "What kind of blowback should we expect?"

"That will depend on how you go about this." He chuckled but it sounded hollow. "I'd tell you to go slow. Find a compromise you can live with, but you're like your older brother. Neither of you seem capable of taking your time."

I took a moment to let them digest the information. "If any of you disagree with my decision, now's the time to speak."

Enzo squirmed in his chair, but kept his mouth blessedly shut.

When no one spoke, I glanced back at my father. "Pops?"

"It seems I'm outvoted. Run the business as you see fit." Joe sat as a coughing fit stole his breath.

I waited until he quieted. "I hope you mean that."

39

Maggie

"Hi." I stretched and nuzzled into my own pillows. After a few nights in the hospital, I was beyond glad to be home.

Gabe pulled me close and kissed the tip of my nose. "Good morning, beautiful."

"I'll never take sleeping in my own bed for granted again." What I really meant was *I'd never take sleeping in my own bed next to him* for granted again. The man kicked off enough body heat to chase away the chill, not to mention he smelled good—really good like fresh cut lumber and spices and sex. "What time is it?"

"Eight-thirty." His graveled just-woke-up voice gave me all sorts of wicked ideas.

Between the days after the disastrous dinner in the courtyard and the two-night stay in the hospital, I was starving for a heaping helping of Gabe. "Do we have time to fool around before we meet the wedding planner?"

"Maggie." He'd used the same voice he normally reserved for misbehaving kids.

Lucky for me, I felt like being naughty. I brushed my fingers down his chest, to his navel, to the v-shaped muscles...

He took my bandaged hand and kissed my fingertips. "None of that."

"We aren't even married yet and our sex life is dead. I told you so."

"It isn't dead, just on hold."

I kissed the spot on his neck that drove him wild. "When will it be off hold?"

"Soon." He'd used the voice again, but his lips curled into a grin.

"How soon?" This time I caressed *my* chest.

His eyes darkened.

Almost have him. I let out a soft purr and toyed with my nipple.

"Not soon enough." Gabe swallowed and pulled the sheet to my chin. "We have an OB appointment next week. I don't think we should have sex until we know everything's okay."

"The doctor at the hospital gave the all clear. You heard the heartbeat. Are you seriously going to make me wait another week?"

He freaking nodded.

Pouting, I crawled on top of him. "How about a blowjob?"

His body tensed to the point it felt like I was laying on a concrete slab—a warm, sexy, concrete slab. "We could sixty-nine, if we're careful."

"Victory is mine!" I ducked beneath the covers.

The doorbell rang.

"You've got to be kidding me." I'd never understood the big deal about honeymoons until that moment. Between the kids and the soon to be mothers-in-law, morning sex never happened.

Gabe laughed, threw the covers off me, and headed for the door. "Get dressed."

I tugged on the sweats and T-shirt I'd left on the floor the previous evening and walked into the living room as Gabe welcomed Detective Wayne O'Malley into our home.

Wayne turned to me. "How are you feeling?"

"I'm okay. What's going on?" I motioned for him to sit and curled up in the corner of the couch. Though I didn't want to admit it to Gabe, I ached from head to toe—being drugged and kidnapped could do that to a girl.

Gabe set three bottles of water on the table and sat beside me.

Wayne leaned forward and put his elbows on his knees. "Justin and Denise Trudeau are being charged with abduction with intent to extort money, assault, and felony stalking."

The memory of the two of them being shoved into police cars sent a shiver down my spine. "Will they get bail?"

"It's unlikely." Wayne pressed his lips into a thin line. "I'll need an official statement when you're up for it."

"I'll bring her in tomorrow." Gabe released me and pushed to his feet. "We have a lawyer, but I'd appreciate it if you'd keep us up to speed."

"Will do." His expression hardened, and he glanced at Gabe as if asking permission.

He nodded. "Sweetheart, Wayne has some news about

Joe and Rebecca's accident."

My heart hammered against my ribcage. "Okay?"

"We have an informant who claims the accident was a paid hit."

The blood whooshing behind my ears made it difficult to hear the rest of what he had to say, but I caught enough of it to understand Papa Joe was right. My sister was murdered.

Leaning in, Gabe put his face in my line of vision. "Breathe, sweetheart."

I blew out a sigh. "I'm okay. I mean...I think I've always known. When will you make an arrest?"

Wayne glanced at Gabe, likely for back up.

"These things take time. For now, know that you and the kids are safe, and we will make the guy pay."

The darkness in his expression sent a shiver down my spine. "I believe you."

The detective stood. "Maggie, are you planning to go back to work? We miss you at the bar."

"No more bar work for her." Gabe gave my shoulder a little shake.

I started to argue but bit my tongue. I had plenty of other things to keep me busy. Besides, being on my feet for hours on end while pregnant would suck.

The detective rubbed his jaw. "Out of curiosity, how did you get out of the cuffs?"

"I practiced on a cheap pair as research for my latest novel. You'd be surprised what you can learn on the internet."

Wayne chuckled. "You should finish the series. The first books are fantastic."

"That's the plan. After my ordeal, I'm full of ideas."

"Can't wait to read them." He pantomimed taking off a hat. "Now that the professional part of the visit is over, can I give you a hug?"

To my surprise, Gabe moved over so I could stand.

The detective wrapped me in his enormous arms and whispered, "I'm glad you're okay."

"Me, too."

Gabe walked with Wayne to the door.

I glanced around the room and realized he'd been right when he'd said we'd need a larger house. Part of me hated to give up another piece of Rebecca, but we all deserved a fresh start.

Gabe sat beside me. "Are you all right?"

"Yes and no. I'm glad they are looking into Joe and Rebecca's deaths, but I'm not looking forward to opening old wounds."

"Maybe getting justice for them will help everyone heal."

"Maybe." I couldn't shake the feeling he knew more than he'd let on. "This has to do with the mafia, doesn't it?"

He closed his eyes and drew a deep breath. "Yes."

Hearing him admit it out loud scared the ever-loving hell out of me. "You're getting out, right?"

"Yes. I told my father and brothers the day I picked you up from the hospital. It may take longer than I like, but we will go legit as soon and as safely as possible."

"And you'll tell me what you can about the process?"

He took my hand and pressed my palm over his heart. "I'll tell you as much as I can. I swear it on our unborn baby's life."

"I trust you." I hated to bring up yet another serious topic, but it'd been bothering me for weeks. "Do you think Chantal got pregnant on purpose?"

"Did I forget to mention it when I told you about my conversation with her at the gala?"

I narrowed my eyes. "I'm pretty sure you did."

"She admitted it. As a matter of fact, I believe she's responsible for the bun in your oven, too."

My blood turned to ice. "What?"

He rested his head in his hand and ran his fingers over his forehead. "The rubber I had in my wallet came from a box she left at my place. I had Leo check. They all had holes in them."

My nose wrinkled. He had sex with me with another woman's condom? "That's just wrong."

He ignored my comment. "She was desperate to get the money my father stole from her."

"That's awful." I pressed my hand to my belly. Despite my feelings for her, I had Chantal to thank for two of the five children in my life.

"Speaking of which, it seems she was right about one thing. My father did swindle her out of half a million dollars. I'm setting things right. It won't bring her husband back, but it's the right thing to do."

That he wanted to do that for Chantal after everything she'd done gave me hope he'd stay true to his promise to break free of the mafia. I curled closer. "What are we going to tell Ella about her mother?"

"Eventually, we'll tell her the truth, but that's not something we need to worry about anytime soon." Gabe kissed the top of my head. "Are you sure you're up for wedding planning today?"

"I don't think your mom will let us wiggle out of it."

He flashed me a grin that was one part *let's rebel* and one part *I have an idea*. "Let's get married in the same church as my parents in Sicily. A small family only event."

"I love it, as long as Shanna, Dahlia, and Wayne are considered family."

Gabe groaned. "I'm never going to get rid of the detective, am I?"

"Not a chance. You do realize Jessie has a thing for him, right?"

"Yeah, she made that quite clear." He shuddered. "I'll call and tell both mothers we're canceling the wedding planner."

"Oh yeah, that's going to go over well." I was glad he'd volunteered for the task. I'd rather go downtown and give my statement about the kidnapping than face Nadine and Evelyn.

"You know they're arguing over which neighborhood we should live in."

"How about Florida? I hear the Keys are nice." I laughed. After everything we'd gone through, it felt good to think of the future.

"They'd follow us. I say we look for something near Loyola. You'll be close to campus next fall."

"I have to plan a wedding and give birth before I can think about applying to school. Plus, I may not get in."

"You'll get in."

I smiled, loving that his belief in me gave me more confidence in myself. I would get into the Master of Fine Arts program, write best-selling novels, raise five kids, and have an awesome marriage. I could do it all, especially with a man who loved and encouraged me every step of the way.

A car door slammed, and Evelyn Marchionni walked past our front windows.

"Crap, we waited too long to cancel." I had a moment of total panic. We weren't exactly dressed for company.

Evidently, Gabe didn't give a crap. He opened the door and gave the woman a shit-eating grin. "Good morning."

"Jesus, Mary, and Joseph, this is how you open the door?" Evelyn handed Ella to him and made a beeline for me. "How are you, dear?"

"I'm okay. A little sore." I forced a smile.

She sat and patted my still flat tummy. "You take care of yourself and my grandson."

"I'm staying off my feet and reducing stress." I nodded toward her son. "We've decided to get married in Sicily."

She gasped and pressed her hands to her chest. "In the church I married my Joe! We can have the reception at the family villa. It will be beautiful. I'll go and—"

Gabe raised a brow.

Evelyn glanced between us. "Would either of you mind if I handle the details? Some of the best vendors in Ragusa only speak Italian."

That she'd thought to ask meant the world to me. "That would be great, thank you."

"I should get started." She gave me a quick hug, her son a peck on the cheek, and all but ran for her car.

Standing in the door, Gabe waved, but rather than coming back inside, he frowned. "We have more company. Shanna's here. Looks like she's been crying."

"Really?" I leaped from the couch and regretted it immediately. My head swam, and my right knee felt as if someone had driven a hot poker through it.

Gabe slid his arms around me before I toppled into the coffee table. "Whoa, there!"

"Sorry." I plopped back down.

Red faced and puffy-eyed, Shanna came through the open door. "Where's Evelyn going? I thought we were planning a wedding?"

"We're getting married in Sicily." Gabe backed his way toward the kitchen.

"Cool. I'll catch you two later." She sighed and turned for the door.

"Uh-uh. No way. Not until you tell me why you're upset." I motioned for her to sit.

Sinking into a chair, she eyed Gabe. "Have you talked to Enzo lately?"

He muttered something under his breath and shook his head.

What in the world was wrong with him? "Shanna, what's going on?"

She dipped her chin.

I narrowed my eyes at my fiancé. Judging by his reaction, he had at least a vague idea of what had Shanna so upset. It seemed his promise to tell me what he could didn't extend to his brothers' personal lives.

"I'm going to check Ella's diaper." He grabbed the baby and hot-footed it out of the room.

Shanna waited until the bedroom door closed. "Enzo and I had a *moment* at the gala before Gabe told us you were missing. Now, he's ghosting me."

"That jerk." I didn't know Enzo as well as the other brothers, but he'd never struck me as the type to hit and run.

"It's ridiculous to get so upset over an *almost* one night stand, but we texted all day and talked on the phone for hours every night since the gala. I thought..." She wiped her eyes on the back of her hand.

"Maybe he's busy with work or something's come up?"

"I saw him with an Italian supermodel-type this morning. She was dripping in designer clothes and jewelry. They seemed *close*."

"Are you sure she was Italian?"

Shanna smirked. "I overheard them talking."

"Gabe?" I spoke loud enough for him to hear me from the back of the house.

He peeked around the corner as if afraid he'd catch a case of estrogen. "Yeah?"

"Do you have family visiting from Italy? A woman, tall, thin, fancy clothes, and friendly with Enzo?"

"Sounds like Nicolina Lazio." His jaw tensed. "Definitely not family."

Shanna's frown deepened.

I stared at him until he squirmed. "Who is she?"

He held his hand up. "Don't force me to break the bro-code."

I narrowed my eyes. "Spill it."

"They've dated on and off." He glanced back down the hall likely planning his retreat. "If it's any consolation, he's not interested in Nico."

"Thanks for clarifying, but I'm done worrying about it." Shanna sat straighter. "Your brother's an ass."

I didn't believe her for a second. She hadn't been so

worked up over a guy since high school. I'd get the truth out of her alone over a gallon of ice cream

"Tell me something I don't know." Gabe held Ella over his head, smiling at her like an idiot.

I watched in horror as the inevitable happened.

Ella giggled and cooed and spit up. A mixture of drool and soured formula fell in a straight line, into Gabe's open mouth. The man didn't miss a beat. He walked to the kitchen, rinsed, and spit.

My stomach lurched. "Gross."

He waved me off like it was nothing.

Shanna slapped her palm on her forehead. Laughing, she turned to me. "He doesn't act like a card-carrying member of the Bourbon Street Bad Boys Club."

I rested my hand on my tummy. "Some bad boys grow up and become good men."

THANK YOU FOR READING ABSINTHE MINDED. I hope you enjoyed Maggie and Gabe's story.

CURIOUS TO KNOW WHAT REALLY HAPPENED BETWEEN Shanna and Enzo? Will the Marchionni brothers break free from the mafia?

GET YOUR COPY OF HIGHBALL & CHAIN NOW TO find out. Here's a hint – it all goes sideways at the destination wedding in Italy.

Chapter 1

HIGHBALL AND CHAIN

Shanna

Cinderella never doubted her social skills. A new dress and glass shoes gave her all the self-confidence she needed to walk in and dance with the prince. Too bad I didn't have a fairy godmother or a pumpkin carriage to get me through my best friend's engagement party.

Who am I kidding? It's going to take a lot more than pixie dust to survive tonight.

I'd rather have a root canal than spend a night hobnobbing with New Orleans' rich and *in*famous. Then again, high society events and dentistry had a lot in common. Both were agony made *barely* tolerable by copious amounts of numbing agents.

Don't get me wrong, I was happy for the newly engaged couple. They'd managed to do the impossible, find love.

Me? I'd long since stopped believing in knights in shining armor riding in on white horses to save the day.

Heck, if my prince ever did arrive, he'd be a misogynist pig, and his noble steed would shit on my lawn.

Nope. I didn't believe in love and romance any more than I believed in fairy-tales. I'd learned to doubt men when my father left. My doubt had solidified into a cynical distrust when I started working for a private investigator.

I loved my job...most of the time. *Tonight? Not so much.*

Two hours hiding behind a planter in a hallway of the Bourbon Orleans Hotel could do that to a girl. If I didn't shoot some video of the mayor and his flavor of the week soon, I'd never make it to Maggie and Gabe's party on time.

Over the previous few days, I'd photographed the elected official with a blonde, a brunette, and a redhead— variety was the spice of life after all. Tonight's spice was an Amazonian woman with dark hair and legs that belonged in the WNBA.

Most of the good citizens of New Orleans knew their mayor was a cheating piece of crap, but I needed proof. So far, I'd filmed them exchanging documents and what I assumed were envelopes of cash. However, Mrs. Carter wasn't interested in her husband's dirty politics.

Pictures might be worth a thousand words, but for me, an incriminating video was a month's rent, and the difference between pasta at Antoine's and ramen noodles.

The mayor and the brunette exited their room without as much as a boob graze, but I took a couple of photos to document the time.

I hiked my bag higher and strolled down the hall. My boss had taught me the key to maintaining one's cover was to blend in, act like you belonged, and deny, deny, deny.

Alex was a top-notch private investigator, but he knew squat about being a female in a male profession.

As such, I took a slightly different approach. I stood out and acted like I didn't give a flying fig.

The couple stepped into the elevator. I picked up my pace and jammed a size eight Doc Marten in the closing doors. Once inside, I ignored their frowns and swiped right to activate my smartwatch spy camera. Aiming the lens at the couple, I pretended to scroll through my phone and prayed for him to break his freaking vows.

Jefferson Carter, father of three, and husband of twenty-six years, did not disappoint. He kissed the Amazon like he was trying to eat her face off. Seriously, I'd seen cows chewing cud with more finesse.

The recording rolled the entire time. *Gotcha, asshole.*

The elevator stopped, and we stepped out. The mayor and the woman turned right while I faked a left and ducked back once they were out of sight. Peeking around the corner, I eased my watch into position and continued to record them. Afterall, when proving infidelity, quantity often trumped quality.

The brunette's eyes went wide. "Hey! Stop!"

Busted.

Carter didn't scare me, but his playmate looked like she could pick me up and toss me out the window without chipping her nail polish. I made a break for the exit and didn't stop until I reached Royal Street. Heart pumping, thigh muscles screaming, I bent at the waist to catch my breath.

The bells of St. Louis Cathedral chimed seven times, reminding me I was late for Maggie and Gabe's party. The Marchionni-Guthrie nuptials would take place in Sicily, but the couple's mothers had strong-armed them into holding a pre-wedding event—a black-tie event. My jeans and T-shirt weren't going to cut it.

Lucky for me, I'd been a boy scout in a former life. *Always be prepared.*

I headed down Royal and ducked into Landry & Sons Antiques.

The owner, and one of my oldest friends, glanced up from his paperwork. "Shanna, what a surprise."

"Sarcasm doesn't become you, Jack." I pointed to the backroom without slowing my pace. He might or might not have groaned, not that I cared. I had places and people and all that jazz.

Five minutes later, I emerged from the stockroom in a vintage dress that would make Jackie Kennedy drool and a pair of second-hand Jimmy Choo knock-offs. "How do I look?"

He quirked a single brow and motioned for me to turn. "Wrinkled."

I smoothed the fabric over my hips. "It was in my bag all day."

Jack, bless his heart, walked to a jewelry case and pulled out a necklace. "Here. Put this on, and no one will notice the dress."

The thing looked like it cost more than my car. "I can't. What if I lose it?"

"It's insured." He motioned me closer. "A girl has to look the part, even if the girl lives on a dental floss budget."

I turned my back to him. "The term is shoe-string."

"Honey, in your case, it's more like thread." Jack

fastened the necklace and spun me around. "Gorgeous, but you're late."

"I know. I know. I was working." I zipped my backpack and hoisted it to my shoulder.

"Leave the bag." He pointed at my wrist. "And the watch."

"I can't. I don't have a purse and this dress doesn't have pockets." I batted my lashes. "And without my watch, how will I know how many steps I've taken?"

This time, Jack did groan. "One of these days, I'll make a girl out of you."

Laughing, I handed over my backpack and spy watch. "It's *woman*, and no thanks."

"Well, you're all woman tonight." His voice came out somewhere between strangled and breathy.

I turned and caught him checking out my ass. *That's new.* "Thanks, Jack."

"I have a gold brocade bag in back that will match the embroidery on your dress…"

I'd wasted another ten minutes, but Jack had hooked me up with an antique clutch and earrings.

"Thanks. You're the best." I planted a kiss on his cheek.

"So you keep saying." He looked me over as if I were one of his antiques. "Remember, be polite, smile a lot, and for God's sake, don't talk about religion or politics."

"Not a problem. I don't plan on talking to anyone except Maggie and Dahlia, and all we gab about is sex." I checked my reflection one last time. Thanks to the ballcap I'd worn on the stakeout, my hair stuck out at odd angles. I smoothed the short pieces in hopes of achieving an Audrey Hepburn vibe.

"Live a little. Branch out. Cozy up to one of the Marchionni brothers before they're all married off." He sounded like he'd swallowed something foul.

No-freaking-thank-you. "If you're so interested in the Marchionnis, you should come to the party as my plus one."

Jack lowered his brows. "Unless you're proposing a threesome, I'll have to pass."

"Now there's a mental picture I'll never be able to unsee."

In all honesty, Jackson Landry had it going on in the looks department, but he was like a brother to me. The thought of him getting busy with anyone, male or female or anything in between, gave me the heebie-jeebies. As for the Marchionnis, they could bump uglies with whoever they wanted as long as it wasn't me.

He wrapped his hands around my upper arms and waited until I met his gaze. "Seriously, Shoshanna, isn't it time you let someone in besides your cat?"

"Hey, don't you dare besmirch Mr. Boogerre. He's soft, round, and is happy as long as I feed him. He's the perfect man."

"Stop deflecting." Jack folded his arms. "There are men in this world who would never hurt you if you'd only give them a chance."

"I know, but if I set the bar any lower, I'll have to bury it." Best-guy-friend or not, I didn't have time for this conversation. "I *have* dated, and I've learned battery-operated-boyfriends are a better bet. Less disappointment."

"You're deflecting again."

"Bye, Jack." I shook my head and exited the shop.

I didn't hate men or anything. I just didn't have much

luck playing the dating lottery. I'd shared few magical hours with Enzo Marchionni, a card-carrying member of the Bourbon Street Bad Boys Club. After which, I'd spent my nights on the phone and my days texting with him. For a brief shining moment, I'd thought we had a connection.

Enzo asked me to dinner, but he'd canceled and ghosted me like a bad Tinder hook-up. A few days later, I'd caught him with an Italian super-model type.

Fool me once and I'll never give you the chance to do it again.

Heels clicking on the uneven sidewalk, I hurried toward *Enzo's*, as in Lorenzo Marchionni, AKA the *Ghoster*. It made sense he'd host his older brother's engagement extravaganza, but I'd rather have eaten out of trash cans than set foot in his restaurant.

The things we do for our friends.

I'd agreed to be Maggie's maid of honor the second she'd asked. A few moments later, I'd realized my duties would entail seeing a lot of Enzo and rubbing elbows with NOLA society. Not that my friends and I belonged to the upper crust, or lower for that matter. We lived in the middle of the pie between the chunks of chicken and peas.

I rounded the corner and groaned. It looked like a luxury car dealership had exploded in front of the restaurant. As I'd predicted, the engagement party was the social event of the season.

Squaring my shoulders, I weaved my way through the cars and guests.

Maggie, the bride-to-be, climbed out of a limo. "Shanna! Perfect timing."

I gave her a quick hug and found myself one breath

away from a wardrobe malfunction. "Strapless dresses weren't invented for women with B-minus cup sizes."

"You look gorgeous." She looped her arm with mine.

I took in her flowy pale blue dress and matching heels. "Thanks. So do you. Where's Gabe?"

"Something came up at work. He's meeting me here." Maggie squared her shoulders and raised her chin. She might have tried for calm, cool, and collected, but I knew better. The woman was as nervous as a cat in a dog yard.

I squeezed her hand. "You got this."

"I'll feel better once I'm inside."

"Morning sickness?"

"More like morning, noon, and night sickness."

"Are you going to survive a transatlantic flight tomorrow?" I hated to think of her spending the trip from New Orleans to Sicily in an airplane bathroom, even if said bathroom was on a private jet.

"We're flying at night. I plan to sleep unless this little one has other ideas." She rubbed her slightly bulging belly.

After two months of listening to Maggie describe the early stages of her pregnancy, I had absolutely no desire to experience motherhood. "You had to know this baby would be a pain in your butt. Look at its father."

"Be nice." Laughing, Maggie slapped my arm. "And relax. You might actually enjoy yourself tonight."

"I doubt it. I'm not comfortable around these people. All of this wealth makes me break out in hives."

She lowered her voice to a conspirator's whisper. "They aren't *all* bad."

"So you keep telling me."

Maggie was right. They weren't all bad. I'd changed my

mind about her fiancé, Gabe, after he'd proven himself to be a stand-up kinda guy. Though he'd broken her heart years before, he'd proved that some bad boys can morph into good men. I mean seriously, it took a spine of steel to raise five kids, three of whom were not his.

Too bad his younger brother hasn't emerged from his cocoon as a hot, successful, butterfly with a heart of gold.

The moment we walked inside, people swarmed the bride-to-be. I took the opportunity to slink away and find the bar. No way could I get through the night without alcohol.

"Shanna." The man's voice made my toes curl and my hands ball into fists.

I turned ready to give Enzo Marchionni the brush off of his lifetime but stopped short. Enzo hadn't said my name, Gabe had. Great, not only did the brothers all look alike—evidently they sounded alike, too.

The groom-to-be took a step back and raised his hands. "Easy tiger."

"Sorry, thought you were someone else. Aren't you supposed to be at work?"

"I've been dealing with a situation."

I turned my attention to the bartender. "I'll have a Sazerac."

"Make it two."

"Should you be drinking Absinthe?" I noted the tension in his jaw and his rigid posture. "Don't tell me you're nervous."

"About the wedding no." Gabe dragged his hand over his mouth and chin. "I need a favor. A big one, but you can't say anything to Maggie until after the party."

"Unless it has something to do with a gift or the super-secret honeymoon plans—"

"It's far more serious than that." He lowered his voice. "Possibly life and death."

I gave him a *yeah-right* look. Did he really expect me to keep secrets from my best friend since high school? "Go on."

He glanced over the crowd as if he'd changed his mind, sucked in a breath, and whispered, "Someone poisoned the minestrone."

Before I could make sense of what he'd said, I spotted the Amazonian I'd photographed with Mayor Carter.

The woman met my gaze. "You!"

I grabbed Gabe's arm and pulled him toward the kitchen. "Let's go investigate your poisoned soup."

Chapter 2
HIGHBALL AND CHAIN

Enzo

THIS IS MADNESS. I STOOD IN THE CENTER OF THE kitchen surrounded by absolute chaos, and I loved every second of it. While I could do without the contaminated soup, there was no place I'd rather be than in my restaurant in complete control. I was the Sorcerer's Apprentice waving a baton to command flood waters of his own making.

Head bowed, I listened to my assistant manager run through the revised menu for the evening. Not only had someone sabotaged the soup, the incident had sent the kitchen staff into panic mode.

I stopped her before she launched into alternative soup options. "Substitutions will take too long. We go with what we have."

Her eyes widened and the color drained from her face. "But sir..."

"What am I missing?" I'd hired Hazel before the restaurant opened its doors. I trusted her implicitly. If she was worried, I had a problem.

"We planned for soup *or* salad. We don't have enough greens and fruit prepped to serve all two-hundred and fifty guests."

Son of a bitch. I had too much riding on this party to let something as inconsequential as pears and gorgonzola screw it up. I drew a deep breath and forced myself to speak at a normal volume. "Tell the prep crew I'll pay bonuses if they get it done in the next fifteen minutes."

"Yes, sir." Hazel spun around and ran directly into an enormous rack of pre-plated salads.

I witnessed the catastrophe in slow motion. Pears, field greens, and heavy stoneware dishes crashed onto the tile—along with Hazel.

She clutched her arm to her chest and went as white as my chef's coat.

"Are you all right?" I knelt before her and picked chunks of cheese from her hair.

"My wrist." She looked down and swayed to the side.

I caught her before she managed to do any additional harm to herself. A quick glance at the unnatural angle of her hand told me she'd broken something. My vision went blurry, but I refused to pass out in front of my staff. Instead, I averted my gaze, pulled her closer, and shouted, "Someone call 9-1-1."

"I don't need an ambulance." Her voice shook.

I disagreed. No way in hell would I allow her to suffer. *What's one more screw up in my family's eyes?* "I'll drive you. Can you make it to my car?"

"What about the party?" Hazel shook her head.

It killed me to imagine my father's disapproval if the dinner went sideways, but Hazel's health had to take priority. "Your wellbeing is more important."

"I appreciate the offer, but someone else should drive me."

"I'll take her." Tara, one of my long-time servers, stepped forward.

Helping Hazel to her feet, I said, "Thank you. Please stay with her and keep me informed. She has my personal cell number. I'll pay you double-time for the entire night, but please stay with her."

"You don't have to do that." Tara dipped her chin and stared at me through her lashes. "Should I expect you at the hospital later?"

My brain short-circuited. She'd worked for me for years without a hint of flirting. I made a mental note to keep an eye on the situation. If it continued, I'd have to fire her. *What the hell else can go wrong tonight?* "I'll be tied up here for hours. Just call me when she's out."

"I'll be fine, Enzo. Stop worrying and focus on the food." Hazel shambled toward the service exit. Her slow, unsteady gait concerned me. Normally, my assistant manager had two speeds—fast and Mach 5.

I waited until the back door closed and frowned at the ruined salads. "Everyone, listen up. We're skipping the *antipasti* and going straight to the first course."

The sous chef called out, "You heard the boss. Serve the pasta with pesto and Pecorino-Romano."

I walked into the cooler to check the desserts. The cold, sugar-tinged air felt good against my face, and reminded me of Shanna. I should never have canceled our date. Better yet, I should have manned-up and told her the truth.

Right, because every woman dreams of a man telling her he's enamored with her, but the relationship can go nowhere.

Grinning like a kid at a candy buffet, a busboy poked his head inside the cooler. "Enzo, someone's asking for you at the service door."

I figured his goofy expression meant the person asking for me was female, likely a hot female. It wasn't unusual for patrons to ask to see the chef. Maybe Shanna had decided to leave the party and check in? The mere thought made my pulse race. I hadn't been so ass over teakettle for a woman since high school—another reason I should put her out of my mind.

If it was only that simple.

"It's the second woman I've let in tonight." The kid shook his head. "Must be good to be the king."

I ignored his comment. The last thing I needed were my employees thinking I had a revolving bedroom door. "In the future, don't let anyone in the kitchen unaccompanied. In case you missed it, someone poisoned the soup."

His eyes widened. "I didn't think about that. She was tall, with long dark hair, Italian accent. I figured you knew her."

"Regardless, we don't allow guests in the kitchen." I nodded to the service door. "Tell whoever is waiting I will be right up."

The kid hung his head and turned to leave. Before he reached the exit, the door swung open and the last person I expected, or wanted, to see strode in.

"Enzo!" Nicolina air-kissed both cheeks and wrinkled her nose. "You are so sweaty."

What the hell is she doing here? The last time I'd laid eyes on her, she'd given me the finger and a nice view of her ass before slamming the door. "I work in a kitchen, Nico. What do you expect?"

"I expect you to smile when you see me." She flipped her long dark hair over her shoulder.

I would smile, but I was certain it'd come across as a snarl. "Why are you here? I'm in the middle of work."

"I came to surprise you. I've missed you." She ran her hand over my cheek.

Missed me? I'd all but packed her bags and put her on a plane back to Paris when she'd shown up unannounced after the gala. "Nothing's changed."

Nico pushed her lower lip out. "None of that matters. It's your brother's engagement party. You shouldn't be working. Come, join me."

"I can't. We're short-staffed. I need tonight to be perfect." Or as perfect as it could be after the rocky start.

She folded her arms. "Still trying to please your father?"

I ignored the jab. "I have to get back to work."

"I came all the way from Paris and you can't find time for me?"

"You should have called."

"So you've said, but I'm here now." Her tone grated my ears.

"I'll join you for a drink after dessert is served." I ducked into the prep area before she could argue.

Why here? Why tonight? We'd known each other since we were kids. At my mother's urging, we'd gone out on a few dates years before. The time we'd spent together had sucked to the point I'd told her I didn't want to see her anymore. Nico, being Nico, disagreed.

She followed me. "Don't be ridiculous. We should be seen together."

"I don't see why." I had to get rid of her so I could focus. Stinking of onions and garlic and sweat, I threw my arm around her designer clad shoulder. "We're friends, nothing more. Which of us is being ridiculous?"

She pushed me away. "You're filthy. Get cleaned up before we see your parents."

"There is no *we*, and I've already seen my folks tonight. In case you missed it, Gabe just got engaged. I'm not getting sucked into *that* conversation with my mother. Again."

Nicolina grabbed my chef's coat and yanked me closer. "You're not getting any younger. Maybe it's time you started thinking about settling down."

Here we go again. I hated to hurt her, but I'd already made myself clear on the matter. "We've had this conversation. I *am* settled down. I'm happily married to my restaurant."

Nico lowered her voice to a purr. "You need someone to take care of you. To remind you what it is to laugh and enjoy life."

"I laugh."

Her words puzzled me. She'd never shown any desire to *take care* of anyone except herself.

"Honestly, Enzo. Why do you work so hard? It's not like it's *your* restaurant. It belongs to your father. Why doesn't he hire someone to run it?"

"My name is on the sign." I jerked free of her. "It's mine in every way that matters."

"When will you learn? Nothing you do will make your father proud." She had the audacity to bat her lashes after she'd verbally kicked me in the balls.

Nico might have known me well enough to play me like a keyboard, but she'd forgotten familiarity went both ways.

"When will you learn to stop causing drama to get your father's attention?"

"I have learned. I've grown up since we dated. I'm living my own life. Isn't it about time you did the same?"

I'd heard enough. *Time to cut to the chase.* "Why are you here?"

"Is it so hard to believe that I missed you?"

"Yeah, it is."

She threw her hands up. "Your mother called and told me about Gabe's engagement. It got me thinking about you. About us."

I nodded. This I could understand. Women tended to freak out when someone got married, pregnant, engaged—it started their clocks ticking or some shit. What I didn't understand was why my mother had called her of all people. "Nico..."

She slid her arms around me and pressed her face to my chest. "I've loved you since I was ten years old."

"Listen." I kept my hands at my sides. "We've tried."

"I was little more than a child."

And you're still acting like one. "I don't mean to hurt you, but I'm not interested."

"I don't believe you." She narrowed her eyes. "Unless there's someone else?"

Shanna danced across my mind. I should have called her. Had I reached out, I suspected I'd have a different answer to Nicolina's question. "There's no one else."

"I'll stay for a week. Spend time with you. See how things go?"

I scanned the ceiling. *God, if you're listening. I could use some divine intervention.* "You think we can stand each other for a week straight?"

Likely sensing she'd won the argument, Nicolina grabbed my face. "We can if we spend most of it in bed."

A sharp intake of breath caught my attention. I turned to find Shanna and Gabe staring—neither seemed amused.

Certain I looked as guilty as I felt, I took a step back. I couldn't stop staring. Shanna's unassuming beauty stole my breath. With very little make-up, a pixie-cut, and an embroidered dress, she reminded me of a heroine from one of the old black and white movies my mother loved so much.

"Nico, good to see you. When did you get into town?" My brother stepped forward and kissed her cheeks.

If she responded, I didn't hear her over the whoosh of blood rushing behind my ears.

Shanna swallowed hard and shifted her weight from one foot to the other.

I searched for something to say to her. Something that wouldn't set Nico off.

"Gabe said someone poisoned the soup?" She scanned the busy kitchen. "Have you called the police?"

Nico whipped her head toward Shanna like a shark scenting blood in the water.

"I'd rather not involve the cops tonight and ruin the party." I motioned for her to follow me.

Thank Christ, Gabe used his common sense and distracted Nico with wedding talk.

"Was anyone injured?" Shanna glanced from me to the bowl of minestrone I'd set aside.

"No. It smells horrendous. I doubt anyone would have put it in their mouths." I couldn't stop staring.

Why the fuck didn't I call her? Because she scared the ever-loving-shit out of me. I'd never connected with a woman so deeply in such a short amount of time. I didn't need a crystal ball to tell me it'd end with both of us in pain. She didn't strike me as the kind of woman who'd settle for a fling, and I couldn't give her more.

She smirked. "If no one was injured, there's not really a problem."

I panicked and babbled like an idiot to keep her with me a few more minutes. "The assistant manager slipped and fell. I sent her to the emergency room to get checked out. She's fine. Probably a broken wrist, but fine. Unrelated to the soup, of course. She tripped over the salads."

"Did someone poison the vinaigrette, too?" Shanna smiled and my world tilted.

"No." I pressed my lips together to force myself into silence.

She sniffed the container of soup and jerked back. "It smells like nail polish remover, which makes zero sense."

"How so?"

"If the culprit wanted to make people sick, they would have used something odorless. This seems more like sabotage. You have no idea who did this?"

"No. One of my bussers mentioned a woman stopped in

to see me earlier. He let her in the kitchen, but she didn't stick around to speak to me."

"I see." She glanced back to Gabe and Nico. "There's nothing else I can do. You should file a police report."

The last thing I needed was cops poking around. Scratch that. The last thing I needed was cops alerting the health department about my acetone soup. I shook my head and focused on the bigger problem—Shanna, and what she'd overheard. "Can we talk? Alone?"

"Did you lose my number?"

I tilted my head. "No."

She patted my cheek. "You should."

Chapter 3
HIGHBALL AND CHAIN

Shanna

THE PLANE NEARED THE GROUND AND MY STOMACH knotted, but it had nothing to do with the change in altitude. I hadn't heard from Enzo Marchionni since the case of the tainted soup at the engagement party. Soon, I'd come face-to-face with the *Ghoster*.

Two months of maid of honor duty hadn't lessened the sting of my epic walk of shame. The fact that he hadn't bothered to return my call or texts pissed me off. Though, I supposed I deserved it.

What kind of woman has an almost-one-night stand with her best friend's fiancé's brother?

The plane bounced a couple of times as the wheels made contact with the runway. Before I could catch my breath, the pilot hit the brakes. I tightened every muscle in my body to resist the forward pull.

Dahlia patted my hand. "Relax. That was the last landing until it's time to go home."

The thought of repeating the trip in reverse made my already-aching head worse. After two connections and a total of twenty hours traveling, I wanted a hot meal, a shower, and a warm bed. "Thanks for the reminder."

She ignored my comment.

Peering out the window, I said, "I thought the airport was bigger?"

"You're probably thinking Palermo. Comiso is tiny, but closer to the villa."

"Right." I ground my teeth. Despite the fact the plane had stopped, no one stood.

Dahlia rummaged through her bag. "I still don't understand why Maggie insisted on having the ceremony in Sicily. So what if the press covered the wedding? One of us should be married in St. Louis Cathedral."

"You can, when you marry Leo." My knee bounced. *Why weren't these people standing?*

"We're just friends." Dahlia scrolled through her messages.

"Uh huh."

Dahlia and Leo had danced around each other for the previous ten years but never officially dated. Though they denied it, I assumed they had sex since Leo was the only man in Dahlia's life besides her one-year-old son.

"Maggie said the guys are picking us up." Dahlia typed a text message, smiled, and sat back.

"Which guys?" I stood and pulled my carry-on from the overhead bin.

"Probably Gabe and Leo."

Standing hunched over, I waited for the people to start

moving. "Seriously, how long does it take to open a freaking door?"

Dahlia twisted her long dark hair into a messy bun. "Shanna, relax. They'll open it soon."

"They need to hurry the hell up, I'm claustrophobic." I drummed my fingers until the man in the seat in front of me glared.

"Since when?"

Since I'm halfway around the world, trapped on an island with Enzo Marchionni. The door opened and the passengers filled the aisle. "About time."

We picked up our luggage and exited the terminal building into paradise. A steady breeze blew from the Mediterranean, warming my face and lifting my spirits. That is, until masculine laughter filled the air, and someone pulled my carry-on from my shoulder.

I turned and locked gazes with the Ghoster.

"Here, let me help you." Enzo smiled, his teeth bright against his tanned face.

"Thanks, but I can manage." I tugged, but he held firm.

"I insist."

"For crying out loud, let the man help you." Dahlia handed her bag to Gabe. "She's been cranky since we left New Orleans."

"I'm not cranky. I'm exhausted. I don't know how Maggie made this flight four months pregnant." I left Enzo with my luggage. If he wanted to carry it, he could carry it all.

"In a private jet." Dahlia smirked.

"Hey, we offered to bring you two with us." Gabe swung the bags into the back of the SUV.

"Some of us had to work." I hustled into the front seat. Since Gabe had the keys, I assumed he'd drive. Dahlia and Enzo could share the back.

"Shanna, do you mind if I sit up front? I get car sick." Dahlia smiled a smile that told me she suffered from motion sickness about as often as I suffered claustrophobia.

Enzo chuckled. "Best to let her ride shotgun. Gabe's had enough vomit from Maggie to last two lifetimes."

"Is she okay? Will she be able to get through the wedding?" I relinquished my seat and climbed in the back.

"It's mostly in the morning now. She should be fine." Gabe pulled out of the parking lot.

The roads back home were bad, but they had nothing on the bumpy, narrow streets of Comiso. I rested my head against the seat as the shadowed scenery passed outside the window.

"Where's Leo?" Dahlia might have tried for casual, but I detected a hint of worry in her voice.

"He had some business in Palermo. He's coming in later tonight." Gabe tightened his grip on the wheel.

She sighed. "What's the plan for the rest of the evening?"

"Ma's making dinner at the villa. We figured you two would be hungry and ready for bed." Gabe turned onto a winding gravel road.

"Sounds good to me." I caught his eye in the rearview mirror and smiled. "Nervous about the wedding?"

"Hell, no."

Enzo leaned closer than was necessary. "If he had his way, they'd already be married."

My pulse raced, but I ignored it, and him—or tried to,

anyway. Pretending I couldn't smell his spicy cologne, or feel the warmth of his leg pressed against mine, proved impossible. However, I would not, and could not, allow myself to be the kind of woman who put up with a guy ghosting her because he happened to be sexy as homemade sin.

The car bounced hard enough to break an axel, and Enzo took the opportunity to slip his arm around my shoulder.

We hit another bump, and I jabbed my elbow into his ribs.

Dahlia laughed. "How many people are staying at your parents' house?"

"Just the wedding party. Everyone else is in hotels." Gabe stopped before an iron gate and entered a code into the keypad.

Lights illuminated the white-washed walls of Villa Dei Fiori, otherwise known as the Marchionni compound. Even in the dark, I understood how the house got its name—*villa of flowers*. Bougainvillea covered the walls, and plumbago filled large beds along the drive. A handful of palms glowed in the exterior lighting, giving the home a tropical feel.

Two Italian men stepped out of the front doors. I'd met all the brothers back in New Orleans, but couldn't remember which was Marco and which was Dante.

Unfortunately, the Marchionni I wanted to forget cornered me beside the trunk.

Enzo leaned close enough his soft curls brushed my cheek. "Shanna, we need to talk."

Oh boy, here comes the sorry-I-didn't-call speech. I

yanked my suitcase out and set it on the ground. "Sure, but we're fine. I mean, we're adults. There's nothing—"

"Enzo!" The willowy Italian goddess from the restaurant rushed to him and planted a kiss on his mouth. "You were gone for so long."

Just when I thought things couldn't be more awkward.

Highball and Chain is available on Amazon and Kindle Unlimited.

About the Author

Kathryn M. Hearst is a southern girl who seasons her romances with sprinkles of humor, mystery, and suspense. Her second book, The Spirit Tree, won the Kindle Scout competition, and her work has been featured in Chicken Soup for the Soul. She has been a storyteller her entire life. As a child, she took people watching to new heights by creating back stories of complete strangers. Besides writing, she has a passion for shoes, vintage clothing, antique British cars, and music. Kate lives in eastern North Carolina with her three dogs, Jolene, Roxanne, and Jagger—whose names were chosen based on popular tunes—because everyone needs a theme song.

Never miss a new release! Sign up for Kate's Reader's Club or visit her website www.kathrynmhearst.com

Stalk Kate here: BookBub, Amazon, Facebook, Twitter, Pinterest, and Goodreads

Made in the USA
Columbia, SC
25 June 2022